Gwasanaeth Llyfrgelloedd Powys Library Service
www.powys.gov.uk/libraries

D0305932

A Cruel Necessity

Also by L. C. Tyler

Herring on the Nile
The Herring in the Library
Ten Little Herrings
The Herring Seller's Apprentice
A Very Persistent Illusion

A Cruel Necessity

L. C. Tyler

Constable • London

CONSTABLE

First published in Great Britain in 2014 by Constable

Copyright © L. C. Tyler, 2014

The moral right of the author has been asserted.

*All characters and events in this publication, other than
those clearly in the public domain, are fictitious
and any resemblance to real persons,
living or dead, is purely coincidental.*

All rights reserved.
No part of this publication may be reproduced, stored in a retrieval
system, or transmitted, in any form, or by any means, without the
prior permission in writing of the publisher, nor be otherwise
circulated in any form of binding or cover other than
that in which it is published and without a similar
condition including this condition being imposed
on the subsequent purchaser.

A CIP catalogue record for this book
is available from the British Library.

ISBN: 978-1-47211-503-4 (hardback)
ISBN: 978-1-47211-505-8 (ebook)

Typeset by SX Composing DTP, Rayleigh, Essex
Printed and bound by CPI Group (UK) Ltd, Croydon, CR0 4YY

Constable
is an imprint of
Constable & Robinson Ltd
100 Victoria Embankment
London EC4Y 0DY

An Hachette UK Company
www.hachette.co.uk

www.constablerobinson.com

To D. H. H.

LLYFRGELLOEDD
POWYS
LIBRARIES

Night, June 1657

*I*t *was the small things that kept you alive in this curious world of espionage. Spotting the shadow ahead of you in the alleyway. Noticing that a once-closed door was now open just a crack. Noticing that the wine was slightly cloudy when it should be clear. You developed an instinct for it. That's how he knew something was very wrong tonight.*

The woman who had brought him here had been pleasant enough and well spoken. It was just that — how could he put it? — she had seemed in her careless chatter to be playing a part that she had rehearsed. In the same way there was, at first sight, nothing wrong with the place. It was ideally suited, one might say, to a clandestine meeting of a Royalist agent with some good-hearted gentlemen still loyal to a long-exiled king. But was it a little more private than it needed to be? Wouldn't a chamber at the inn have been safe enough?

He listened carefully for approaching footsteps, but as yet there was no sound. The fact that he had been asked to arrive first and await the others was not necessarily to his detriment. Arriving first meant that he could look around, see how the land lay, work out which way he would need to go if he had to leave in a hurry. He had the advantage that he would be able to watch them come and observe the clumsily concealed weapons beneath an unneeded cloak. He himself was armed only with his gully knife, but his preference was to kill with no weapon at all where possible. Or to bluster and threaten his way out. That was good too.

There were, of course, days when he wondered whether it was all so much wasted skulking and duplicity. Ten years had passed since the old king had been executed and six since his son had even dared to set his foot on English soil. Lord Protector Cromwell's grasp on power was as firm as ever. Soon the English Republic would peacefully enter its second decade. Espionage as a trade was dying on its feet. No doubt about that. Perhaps it was time to slip away and quietly become somebody else.

He eased a small gold signet ring from his finger and dropped it into his breeches pocket, where it rested snugly. For a moment he massaged his hand, as if to obliterate any faint mark it might have left. So, then, what was this obvious thing that he had missed?

He held up the lantern that the woman had left him. The single candle cast a dim light from behind the horn panes, reflecting dully on the rough wooden walls and the straw-covered floor. He could see clearly enough from here to the only doorway. Still nothing stirred. Well, let them come whenever they wished. Friend or foe, he was ready for them.

It was only when a strong arm seized him from behind that he realised that he had not, after all, been the first to arrive. He felt something lightly brush his throat, then a warm dampness spread quickly over the front of his shirt.

'So sharp, I almost didn't feel it,' he thought.

It was his last thought before the darkness closed in. It was, in fact, the last thought he ever had.

A Little Earlier

I raise my wide arms to the stars. They are my friends.

I am here, at the crossroads of the village. I am here because I am no longer at the inn. And I am no longer at the inn because, because . . .

Have patience, and very soon I shall explain to you why I am no longer at the inn. In the meantime, let us both breathe in the cool night air, which speaks to us of everything that is in this village to which I have just returned – the sweet white roses over the door of that beshitten cottage, the damp-leaf smell of the green orchard beyond and the rich, many-coloured stink of the cowshed. And above all – because you too are my friend – let me share with you this wonderful silence. Cambridge was never completely quiet, even at this strange hour, though the inns were friendlier.

But I am no longer at the inn. Why? I frown, not because I don't like you but because frowning may help me remember.

The stars above me turn slowly, drifting across the black sky. I hear the sound of a horseman approaching. As the stars complete another circuit, he comes into view. Perhaps he too is my friend.

'You, boy – are you drunk? Or is your strange posture some new Anabaptist form of prayer?'

I lower my arms to my sides. I consider this question carefully from all points of view. Have I inadvertently become an Anabaptist? Or *am I drunk*? At the inn I argued that I was not – argued most forcefully and persuasively that I was not. Argued long and manfully that I was not.

'It is not some new form of prayer,' I say.

'Then stop turning round and round like a heathen dervish and answer a question for me. 'Od's teeth, boy! Are you *completely* drunk?'

I lower my arms again and consider this question carefully from all points of view. If I had been permitted to stay at the inn, I would have quaffed another tankard of ale. Then I would have been drunker than I am now. Therefore, I am not as drunk as I might have been. Therefore, I cannot now be completely drunk. I feel that my tutor would have been impressed with this logic if only he were here now rather than snoring in noisy, friendly Cambridge. But it is some time since I said anything, and the horseman is growing impatient for a reply.

'I am not *completely* drunk,' I say. I speak slowly and carefully as evidence of this, though saying 'completely' is, I find, not as easy as I thought it would be.

'Then, my partly drunk friend, can you tell me if Ben Bowman still keeps the inn?' He pats his horse, which seems to think we have all been kept here too long. The animal shakes its head, rattling bit and bradoon.

I look at the rider curiously. He is tall as well as impatient, and he is dressed in dark clothing, though in the moonlight, black, grey and dark blue are all as one. His boots are new and glossy. His horse is grey and muddied from a long journey. His broad-brimmed hat is pulled low over his face. His voice is muffled, *and I know why*. I think all of these things, but wisely I do not say any of them.

'Christ's bones, boy! It's not that difficult a question. Does he or doesn't he still keep the inn? You must recall who was serving you.'

'Ben Bowman was certainly serving *other* people,' I say.

The rider laughs. I fancy I may have said something clever.

'Then my thanks, and please take this . . . friend . . . for your trouble!'

His right hand holds the bridle, and, with his left hand, he tosses something that makes a graceful silver arc in the moonlight. A star perhaps? Or a dream? I reach for it, fumbling with both left and right, but it falls on the ground. Its light goes out.

The rider seems minded to go on his way; then he pauses. 'What's your name, boy?'

'John Grey,' I say.

'John Grey?' asks the rider, which is odd because I have just said precisely that. Perhaps he is hard of hearing. I repeat it. It has, in my view, a pleasant ring to it.

He too is silent for a moment. Then he says softly: 'Go home, John. Go home to your mother.' He looks me up and down. He seems sad. Then he kicks the tired horse into a walk. I listen to the slow, uneven sound of the horse's hooves. The horse is lame. I should have noticed that before. The clop of hooves on road grows quieter. Then it stops.

Silence.

I breathe in the cool night air, which speaks to me of everything that is in this village to which I have just returned – the sweet honeysuckle in the hedgerow; the bright stars overhead; the fine aroma of horse that has lingered in the rider's wake. And the silence.

So, what would you have me do? Shall I return in this fragile, starlit silence to my mother's house – the thing that both Ben Bowman *and* the rider have proposed that I should do? I would not wish to awaken my mother, as I fear I might if I tried, for example, to open the front door or walk up the stairs – both activities that cannot be accomplished, as you well know, without a great deal of falling, stamping and swearing. Opening the front door might be better done in the clear light of day, though preferably while my mother and Martha are still asleep – if Martha ever does sleep. But Martha is my friend and will not tell tales.

Very well then. Since you propose no other course of action, I shall rest here against the cottage wall, safe and dry under the overhanging thatch, where the logs would be if it were not June, and enjoy the sweet scent of the white roses. But before I do so, I raise my wide arms once more to the stars. They are my friends.

Dawn

'There is,' says Ifnot Davies, 'no justice in this world.'

'Seemingly not,' I say cheerfully.

'Thy head should ache like God's wrath on Judgement Day, considering the ale thou didst consume last night.'

I wince, not because my head resembles God's wrath in any way, but because I have been thou'd twice in one sentence – and that before the day has properly begun.

'God is merciful,' I say. I wink and am not immediately struck down by a divine thunderbolt for my levity.

'God is merciful to the young, John Grey,' says Ifnot. His gaze, though compassionate, suggests that he knows the state of my conscience and the secrets of my soul. I do hope he doesn't. 'Try that in ten years' time,' Ifnot adds, 'and see what God's views on strong drink are then. Try it in twenty years' time, and see what God's views are on catching rheumatics if you sleep out of doors. Thou hast

9

spent the night there, under the eaves of Harry Hardy's cottage?'

'Thou' again. But, now I look around me, I am indeed under the eaves of Harry Hardy's modest home. When did that happen?

I stand up and dust off my hat, on which my head has rested for the night. I try punching it back into shape, but it has lost the will to be anything other than a pillow. Ah well, who needs a hat on a morning like this one? The sun is but a hand's breadth above the horizon. The whole green world's bedazzled now with dew. And the voice of the cuckoo is heard in the land. Five o'clock, as near as any man might judge, on a fine summer's morning. It already promises fair for a hot day, but Ifnot is dressed in a thick leather jerkin. If your normal place is beside a blacksmith's furnace, the rest of the world must feel cold.

'You're up betimes yourself, Ifnot,' I say, giving the brim of my pillow another tweak. 'Or didn't you go to bed either?'

'I need more charcoal for the forge, John Grey,' he says vaguely. 'There are half a dozen horses to shoe this morning. Apparently.'

His smile has faded a little, probably because he doesn't like being called Ifnot. It's what we all call him though. He gets his revenge, in a way, by addressing everybody as 'thou'. He's a Quaker obviously.

'The stranger's horse seemed a bit lame,' I say as we stroll back to the crossroads. 'Maybe he's one of your customers.'

'Stranger? What stranger?'

'A rider – last night. I saw him here, just where we're standing now. He asked for directions to the inn. You must have still been there when he arrived.'

'I didn't see no stranger,' says Ifnot. 'But maybe I left soon after thou didst.'

'Maybe thou … you didst … did. Well, you'll see him later, like as not,' I say. 'He'd had a long journey, I think, and may sleep away some of the morning.'

Ifnot is about to reply but then bends suddenly and picks something up. 'A shilling,' he says as if he has never seen one before. In this village shillings stay safe in purses; they rarely lie long in the road. 'And one with the head of our late and unlamented King Charles upon it.'

'That must be what the stranger threw me last night,' I say.

'Then, 'tis thine, John Grey,' says Ifnot, holding out the coin in his left hand. That's Quakers for you – they may have strange ideas about personal pronouns, but they're honest. It's what comes of having God watching you the whole time. In Cambridge we got God's attention half an hour a day at the most.

'Keep it,' I say. 'I did nothing that I can recall to merit payment.'

He places the small silver coin firmly in my hand and his vast blacksmith's paw closes over it. I couldn't open my hand again if I wanted to.

'I render unto Caesar that which is Caesar's,' he says, giving my fist another agonising squeeze. The sharp edges of the shilling dig into my palm. 'And unto God that which is God's. As I hope thou doest. Welcome home, by the way, and please give my respects to thy good mother.'

I agree that I shall do this, and in return he consents to let go of my hand. He continues on his way, taking the road south, while I prepare to go north, towards the family home and my hopefully slumbering family.

Others are slumbering too. Behind the shuttered windows of the decaying lime-washed cottages, under each untidy mass of grey thatch, they and their fleas sleep soundly – four or five human souls to a bed. Soon the village will be scratching itself, sniffing its armpits and pulling on its breeches. But for now the road lies empty, the air is sweet and, in the fields hard by the village, birds peck unhurriedly where the ripening corn casts long shadows.

From here I can see almost the entire village. Four dusty tracks approximate to the four points of the compass, taking their respective and equally leisurely paths to Royston, Cambridge, Saffron Walden and – more distantly – London. The road to London has always seemed, to my eyes, a little wider and a little grander than the other three, but each thoroughfare is lined with rows of timbered cottages in various states of disrepair, some pressing into the roadway, others set back behind vegetable gardens. Facing me, the high walls of the park belonging to the Big House present their blank brick visage for half a mile or more, running out into the country-side way beyond the last cottage. The wall is well maintained. (When it comes to keeping people out of things, you can't be too careful.) Ancient elms and oaks rise green above the soft red brickwork, hinting at a lost paradise that lies beyond. Which, in a sense, it does. But I have admired the view for longer than four streets of one very ordinary village deserve. I am bound for my mother's modest dwelling, currently just out of sight on the Cambridge road.

At the stream I stop briefly to splash its water, clear and cold after the cloudless summer night, over my face and hair. Then I press on apace, skipping lightly over the stepping stones, in the sure knowledge that my mother was ever the early riser – though I am still torn between claiming that I have been asleep in my bed since midnight and, arguing in the alternative, that I met Dickon Grice and spent the night at his house. Neither is creditable in the sense that I had undertaken to be home by ten of the clock, but both are probably better than admitting that I was thrown out of the inn and proved too drunk to walk very slowly from one side of the village to the other. Of course, my mother may get to hear the truth very soon anyway, because I fear there is no longer enough silver in my purse to buy the silence of everyone who witnessed last night's events.

But there are always those who are less fortunate than you. As I pass the village dung heap, I see a pair of feet sticking out from behind it. I at least had the good sense to find the shelter of a cottage wall. I wonder which of my drinking companions could have come to this pass. He is lying facedown, and I do not recognise his back or the soles of his shoes, which are all he has chosen to present to me. He cannot be comfortable in that position – kinder, then, to wake him before he gets a stiff neck. I kneel down and give him a friendly pat on his dew-covered shoulder.

Then I see what I should have seen long before. He will certainly never have the misfortune to awake with a stiff neck. His throat has been cut clear across from side to bloody side. I lift him slightly, and he grins at me through a gaping, wine-coloured gash.

Perhaps you secretly hope, as Ifnot probably would, that God is finally about to punish me for a hard night's drinking and that I will now spew my guts over the dung heap. But I have seen death before in its many colourful forms. And indeed, this was a good death – a kind and considerate one.

Whoever this is – and he is a stranger to me – died quickly, his blood spilling out and the darkness closing in almost before he would have known what was happening to him.

I crouch beside the body, any thoughts of my mother's reproaches deferred, and examine the wound more closely. A clean cut with a very sharp knife – probably made with a single, skilful movement of the arm. The killer would have approached him from behind, seized him, pulling his head back, and cut quickly from right to left. The cut is deeper on the right, where the knife entered the flesh. I re-enact the deed in my mind and frown. He would have been held firmly by a strong man, unless . . . I check the dead man's wrists. No, there is no sign of chafing from a rope. So he would have died suddenly and probably much to his wonder. But he died in another place, not here. I look around to see if I can tell where he died, but I cannot, which is passing strange. Passing strange indeed, my masters. He has travelled some way since he breathed his last.

I place my hand under one shoulder and lift him a little to peer at the ground beneath him. The man's head twists slightly as I do so, as if he is reluctant to look me in the eye. He guards his secrets still. But I know one more thing about him – the ground is wet underneath the body, so he must have arrived here after dewfall.

While I am pondering all this, Ben Bowman appears from the direction of the inn on some early-morning errand of his own. He smiles as if to chide me for enriching him last night. Then he sees the corpse, and he stops and shakes his head.

'So, the silly fool got his throat cut, did he? Well, that's not much of a surprise, is it now?'

I Am Introduced to Death – 1646 or Thereabouts

I had seen death before in its many colourful forms.

I blame my mother, of course, for this and much else. It was she who introduced me to the dead, though she in turn might have justifiably blamed my father. For this and much else.

My father, Matthew Grey, was, during the late wars between the King and Parliament, a surgeon in the Royalist army. Being more inclined to wield a knife than a pen, he sent letters to his family occasionally at best, and any rumour of troops on the march would have us packing bags and saddling horses to ride and enquire whether my father was living or no. There must have been less arduous ways of answering the same question, but my mother preferred to travel. Perhaps it was the thought of finding my father dead on some bloody field that kept her so cheerful through that long civil war.

Thus I saw the aftermath of many fights, but we were rarely the only ones picking our way amongst the debris. The dead – or at least those who meet a violent end in conflicts – have many friends. Those friends who arrive first relieve the dead of their burdensome purses and rings. A little afterwards others come for their slightly less portable but still very desirable swords, pistols, muskets, helmets and breastplates. Later still come those who would like a pair of boots or a good buff coat as a memento. Often the dead were reluctant to give up these last few trifles, willingly though they had surrendered their gold. Removing a pair of breeches from a five-day-old corpse is not as easy as you might think.

In crossing and recrossing the battlefield, my mother tended to avoid the more obvious freebooters, since they were sometimes careless as to whether they took the purses of the living or the deceased, and by midday they were usually well armed. She proceeded discreetly and without drawing much attention to herself. I, marvelling at the novelty of it all, escaped her apron strings as often as I could and found much to amuse me.

Perhaps it was because my father was a surgeon, and I was used to the sight of blood and the many gleaming instruments that can be employed to produce it, that I accepted whatever I found on the battlefield with no more horror than if I had been visiting the butcher's shop at home. Thus it was that in the year 1646 (or thereabouts) in the sunny Oxfordshire countryside you might have seen a small boy giving a wounded soldier water from his flask while politely questioning him on how he came by the wound and how many hours it was since his companion, now stiff and cold, breathed his last. You could say that I learned a great deal in a short time, and I might have become a surgeon myself had my mother not taken an aversion to that or anything else connected with my father and decided that a strong stomach would assist me every bit as much in the practice of Law.

After the war, the men started to return to the village, but not my father. Ifnot Davies returned from fighting for Parliament with a permanent limp but with his blacksmith's strength otherwise unimpaired. And at least he had been on the winning side. Sir Felix Clifford, who had joined the King's army on the first day of the war, returned to discover that he was ruined and that his wife had packed her bags and left. He had, it is true, been doing his best to bankrupt himself for some years before the Civil War and might well have completed the task unaided. But the voluntary loans that he had been obliged to pay to the King and the fines that he had later had to pay Parliament for 'malignancy' – that is to say for not minding being owed money by the King – had speeded the process more than a little. The Cliffords' days as lords of the manor were numbered. What remained of their estate was sold to a London banker to pay the last of the fines, and the banker sold it on at a speedy but substantial profit – the market for large houses proving better than Sir Felix had been given to believe – to one Joshua Payne, formerly Colonel of Infantry in the Parliamentary army, who took up residence in what had always been known in the village simply as the Big House.

Thus, in the space of less than a paragraph, the Cliffords learned the useful lesson that they should have placed their trust in neither kings nor bankers. Colonel Payne agreed to let the previous owner live in the Steward's cottage on the edge of the Park – for which Sir Felix was charged, but never actually paid, a nominal sum on each quarter day. Sir Felix's daughter, Aminta, also returned to live with him, but his son, Marius, like my father, remained absent and unaccounted for. As did Lady Clifford.

Any question of my father's return passed imperceptibly into the realms of vague conjecture. My mother dismissed all of our servants except Martha and Nathaniel, who was too old to go anywhere and hadn't seen a penny in wages from her since Lady Day 1647, and settled down at the New House to a life of genteel poverty, neighbourly slander and preserving fruit. I, in due course, was entered for Magdalene College at the University of Cambridge, with the intention that I should study there for my BA before completing my legal education at Lincoln's Inn in London.

It was during my first Long Vacation that I said to my mother: 'I often wonder at which battle my father died.'

'Battle?' she spat back at me. 'He went off with Bess Clifford.'

'Sir Felix's wife?'

'Of course it was Sir Felix's wife. Lord! How many Bess Cliffords are there in this village?'

'None at all,' I said.

Morning, June 1657

I stand up and brush the pale dust off my hands and then, with more or less clean palms, from the knees of my new green velvet breeches. Sadly, they look a little less new than before, and I have not yet paid for them.

'You know him then?' I say to Ben.

'I saw him at the inn,' says Ben. He clearly expects better of his customers than that they should fall victim to footpads. 'Flashing his money about. Doesn't do. Not that folk are dishonest in these parts – but it still doesn't do to show your purse too openly. In these troubled times, John Grey, wise men hide their money in their boot when they are on the road.'

'If everyone hid their money in their boot,' I say, 'the stratagem would deceive nobody.'

Ben has no reply, as is not uncommon with him. He tries a dismissive look, but his smooth, pink face isn't quite up to the mark.

'We'll need to report this to the Magistrate,' I say. 'Then he'll have to inform the Coroner. No point in telling the Constable – he won't be up for an hour or two yet.'

It's a quiet village. There's not much work for the Magistrate to do. Or the Constable. (The inn's busy, though, and so is the midwife.) The Magistrate is Colonel Payne – that's something that comes with owning the Big House. Will Cobley is the currently slumbering Constable. He'll be cross he's missed a murder.

Ben and I look at the stranger again. He is not a tall man, and our angle of view foreshortens him further. Whoever he is, he is not the impatient rider I saw last night. One further detail immediately strikes me: he has an old scar on his chin. Maybe it's not the first time he's come off worst in a scrap. He is, I should add, a little plump and more than a little bald. No hat of any sort.

'I suppose he didn't tell you his name when he was at the inn.'

'Not that I can recall,' says Ben. He scratches his head as if to encourage thought. There's a first time for everything.

'There could be papers on him that would identify him,' I say.

'I'd leave that to the Colonel,' says Ben, pulling a face. 'Best not touch, eh?'

'No, I'll check now,' I say.

I kneel down again. I hope that it will be worth recoating my knees with dust. The dead man is dressed in black breeches secured with greenish, frayed ribbon, and an old-fashioned black doublet tailored from good-quality woollen cloth, now sadly worn and shiny. The buttons are silver and are all in place, except where a loose thread bears witness to the loss of one.

I pat the clothing politely, working from his shoulders downwards. There is no jingle of coins or rustle of papers until I reach his breeches pockets. I put my hand carefully into the right pocket and withdraw a worn leather purse. On examination it contains twenty-two shillings and a few pennies.

'He was not murdered for his money then,' I say.

Ben shakes his head sadly. This has not been done well. He really ought to have been murdered for his money.

'So, why *was* he killed?' I say.

'He also had a ring,' says Ben as if with sudden inspiration. 'A gold one.' Perhaps the thieves will have failed in their duty here too, but Ben need not have feared. I check his fingers. I feel again inside both pockets; there is no ring. Ben nods approvingly. That's better.

'You see, he was flashing the ring about too,' says Ben. I think I have heard Ben on this subject before. If I let him, he will probably conclude by saying that the ring should have been hidden in his boot.

Of course, a well-made boot with a broad, flapping top to it *is* a handy place for keeping things. The inside of a hat is good too, but our man has none. Boots it is then. I slide my hand as far as I can down the side of each in turn. Ben watches anxiously; he doesn't think I should be doing this. Perhaps he's right. Again, I am quickly rewarded for my efforts, but not quite as I foresaw. I draw out not a ring but a sheet of thin paper, folded several times into a compact though rather grubby little wad.

'What's that then?' asks Ben. The unexpected always worries him. You'd think he'd never seen paper before in his life.

I open out the document carefully, because it seems much

used and it is not only grey but rather thin at the edges. I frown at the contents.

'It's some sort of cipher,' I say, showing the page to Ben. There are three rows of letters and matching numbers. I notice that A is represented by 7 and by 14 and 15. E is represented by 1 and 9 and 16 and 23 and 49. All of the other letters, in fact, seem to have at least two numbers assigned to them. There are also numbers for whole words. General Monck – who is he exactly? – is allocated 101, and General Harrison is 999. This is no simple substitution cipher; a word like 'the' or 'and' could be coded in a completely different way every time it was used in a message.

'A man with secrets, it would seem,' says Ben. He is less impressed than I am at the sophistication of the system. But at least he now knows that the paper won't bite him.

'Had he been flashing this around too?' I ask.

Ben looks at me sideways, unsure whether I am making fun of him. If he is really in doubt, then I'll need to make my sarcasm a touch less subtle in future. He settles on slightly wounded dignity for his reply. 'No, just the purse . . . and the ring, like I say. And the idiots clearly took the ring.'

I nod. The silver could have been spent in any inn on the road, but the ring will be difficult to dispose of at anything like its true value. Our man has had the misfortune to be killed by stupid people.

'Footpads,' says Ben, shaking his head. 'Suffolk men like as not. Nobody from the village would do a thing like this. Whoever it was will be long gone, I'm thinking.'

I'm thinking that too, but it strikes me that I might just have seen the murderer – indeed, I may have his shilling in my purse. 'What about the stranger on horseback?' I ask.

'Stranger?' asks Ben.

'The one in the dark clothing and cloak. Big, broad hat. He was riding a lame grey. Arrived from the direction of London a bit after midnight. Went to your inn.' That should narrow things down for him.

Ben shakes his head. 'Nobody like that came anywhere near the inn.'

'Yes, he did. I saw him. He asked me the way.'

Ben's look says it all.

'I was *not* drunk, Ben,' I say. 'Well, not completely. Anyway, when I saw him, he had only a few yards to ride. He can't possibly have got lost. Why would he say he was going to the inn if he wasn't?'

'Not having had a chance to discuss it with him, I couldn't rightly say,' says Ben.

'But here's his shilling,' I say, taking it out of my purse. 'He gave it to me.'

Ben looks at it. I can see that it is not in itself conclusive of anything.

'Now then, Master John,' says Ben, 'what are we to do with a dead man on a fine summer morning?'

I frown at Ben, but he seems to have said all he is going to say about my horseman. Of course, what we do with the gentleman in front of us is a pressing matter.

My first thought is to leave the body where it is and to fetch the Colonel, but two of the village dogs are already showing an unfortunate interest, albeit from a distance at present. They imply they'd like a taste when we've finished with him. 'We should take the body across the fields to the church, where it may rest with some dignity. Then I shall go and inform Colonel Payne.' I am pleased with my tone of authority. Perhaps there was some point in studying Law after all.

'I'll get Harry Hardy to give us a hand,' says Ben. 'There's a wisp of bright new smoke from his chimney, so he'll be up and doing.'

We carry the stranger on one of Harry's newer hurdles over the fields to St Peter's. Once or twice Harry tries to ask us questions, but each time Ben hushes him and says we must maintain a respectful silence. In this regard he shows an unusual delicacy of feeling, and I do not protest. For a while the only sound is the tramp of three pairs of feet and the swish of the long grass against our legs. Indeed, not another word passes our lips until we have reached the Rector's house, hard by the church. Ben and Harry feel that explaining away a bloody corpse on a hurdle is rightly lawyer's work, so I tell the Rector what little I know and leave the others to proceed in a decorous manner to the crypt, where the body is to be laid for the time being. Harry is also to let my mother know that I will be a little later than planned. It may be that a small part of her wrath will descend on his broad shoulders and not on mine.

Thus it is that I take the road alone eastwards to the Big House with the purse and the strange paper securely about my person, and with a story to tell that I expect will surprise the Colonel a great deal.

'You did right to report this to me first, John,' says Colonel Payne. He's a brisk, neat little man. His hair is short even for a Roundhead and is, I notice, now almost entirely grey. He strokes his closely shaven chin, newly scraped this hour, and his piercing blue eyes look out of the window into his Park. In the distance, beyond the trees, is the Steward's Lodge, where Sir Felix lives cheaply. 'I can contact the Coroner later, after I have viewed the body myself. The poor fellow is still lying where he fell?'

'We put him in the crypt at St Peter's,' I say. 'The chill there will stop him stinking. And the dogs were looking for a free meal. Ben Bowman and Harry Hardy helped me carry him thither on a hurdle.'

'I should perhaps give them some money for their trouble?' For Colonel Payne, being Lord of the Manor remains a burden and a puzzlement. Sir Felix would have known the right thing to do, what was customary, how much they might expect. The new Lord of the Manor looks at me quizzically in case I also know the right thing to do, what is customary, how much to expect. He hopes I will tell him.

'If you wish,' I say.

'I'll consider the matter later,' he says with a sigh. He runs a small hand over his grey head. There's no spare flesh on those fingers or anywhere else on the Colonel. The skin is taut and pale over his cheekbones and lined above from much frowning. He is frowning now. Anyone who spent five minutes with the Colonel would realise that he is a man of military briskness and determination. But another five minutes in his company would reveal the doubt that so often follows each of his decisions, and the gentle drift back to where he started or to some other comfortable place. There was a time when Colonel Payne had seemed destined for greatness – a respected soldier and a close friend of both Cromwell and my Lord Fairfax – but he lacked the guile to be any more than that. Peace has undone him every bit as much as the war undid Sir Felix.

It's a while since I was last at the Big House. I'd forgotten that time seems to run more slowly in these echoing oak-panelled rooms, or how the light slants in through the tall leaded windows. I watch the gleaming motes of dust hanging in the still air.

'You think the dead man was a spy then?' the Colonel says eventually, sinking onto a hard wooden chair. He seems tired. He thought that he had bought a pleasant country house in which he could live at his ease. Nobody warned him about the possibility of dead Royalist agents.

'Surely the cipher he was carrying proves it?' I say.

'That would be jumping to conclusions on the basis of very little evidence,' says the Colonel. 'What do people like us know of ciphers anyway?'

I do in fact know quite a lot about ciphers but wonder if it would be polite to correct the Lord of the Manor so abruptly.

'He has special codes for General Harrison and another general,' I say.

'Monck,' says the Colonel.

'I've heard of Harrison. He was cashiered and imprisoned, was he not? Who is Monck?'

'Commander in chief in Scotland,' says the Colonel. As a soldier he knows that. He's probably served with or fought against anyone in England who can call themselves a general. 'Monck was a Royalist once, but not any more. One of Lord Protector Cromwell's best and most trusted commanders. Unlike that dangerous fanatic Harrison.'

Well, at least I know who Monck is now. An important man it would seem. Harrison was important also once, but Cromwell is ruthless with those who cross him. Harrison is now almost as forgotten at Westminster as Colonel Payne must be.

I try to explain to the Colonel about the dead man's wound and the lack of blood on the ground close by. 'And he was killed some time after midnight,' I add. 'Or at least the body was most certainly dumped at the dung heap after midnight. There was dew on the ground beneath it.'

I expect the Colonel to nod sagely and compliment me on my observation, but he seems to be preoccupied with his fallow deer, which are grazing just beneath us, outside in the Park. When he turns again, he just says: 'You say you saw Ifnot Davies out this morning?'

'He needed more fuel. I imagine he was on his way to the charcoal burners' huts in the wood to bespeak another load.'

'Why is he called Ifnot? Is it a Welsh name?'

'Not as far as I know. He's a Quaker, but his parents were Puritans. He was baptised If Jesus Had Not Died For Thee, Thou Hadst Been Damned. So we call him Ifnot. Hadn't anyone told you that?'

'No,' he says. 'Nobody ever tells me anything about the village. They think I won't be here long enough to need to know. Did you see anyone else abroad other than Ben and Ifnot?'

'Not this morning. There was a stranger who rode into the village last night and went to the inn.'

The Colonel rubs his eyes. Perhaps he did not sleep well last night. It was a hot one, unless you chose to sleep out of doors.

'Another stranger?' he asks. 'I mean, could this rider not have been the same person that you found killed?'

'No, the dead man is quite short. The rider was much taller. Dressed in dark clothing. Mounted on a grey horse.'

Surely I must recall more than that. I am beginning to

wonder if Ben wasn't right that I had drunk slightly more than I should.

The Colonel does, however, take the most charitable view that he could.

'I suppose there was no light to see him clearly?' he says.

I think back to the muffled voice.

'No, there was a moon, but he held his cloak across his face. That was odd on a warm summer night, don't you think?'

If the Colonel does find this strange, he does not say so. 'You say the man just asked for the inn?' he says.

'Yes,' I say. There was also, as I recall, some discussion of Anabaptists, but I decide not to trouble the Colonel with this.

'So, Ben must have seen him?'

'Ben says not.'

'Then he didn't go to the inn,' says the Colonel.

'But he must have stopped here in the village – for a while anyway. Perhaps at some other house . . . The horse couldn't have gone further. Might he not have been the killer? Or have seen something at least?'

'Your rider went off in the direction of the inn – that is to say, the Saffron Walden road? Not along the Cambridge road, where the body was found?'

'Yes,' I say.

'And he didn't come from the direction of Cambridge?'

'No, I'm certain he came along the London road.'

The Colonel takes a deep breath. 'Then he never went anywhere near where the body was found. Wherever he went, I don't think that he need concern us. You saw nobody else abroad last night?'

'Not on the road. There were plenty at the inn. Ben Bowman obviously. And Nell Bowman. Roger Pole. Dickon Grice and his brothers – Nathan and young Jacob. William Warwick. William Cobley. Ifnot was there too but says he left the inn shortly after I did.' Then I feel obliged to add: 'Roger Pole left before me.' Pole is the Colonel's secretary and the man for whom the words 'prating coxcomb' were specifically invented. I am sorry to have to mention him at all.

'That's right,' says the Colonel approvingly. 'He returned here, to the manor house, around nine o'clock, I think. Not that I could have suspected Roger of any involvement in this business.'

Would it be tactless for me to say that I think Pole would cut anyone's throat if he found it mildly amusing and the blood didn't splash on his lace cuffs? But Roger Pole has an impeccable witness to say that he retired at a spinster-like hour to his own bed. That is a pity, but it cannot be helped.

'And where was the village Constable?' Colonel Payne suddenly demands. 'By the sound of it, he was tippling while a murderer was running loose in the village. He might at least have reported the discovery of the body.'

'I suspect Will Cobley is still abed,' I say. 'I'm sure he'll report to you once he is up and people have told him about it.'

'Asleep now and drunk when the murder occurred?' the Colonel demands. He apparently feels that the Constable could have performed his duties better.

'So it would seem,' I say. 'But I doubt that Cobley sober could have prevented a murder any more than Cobley drunk.'

'Isn't the suppression of drunkenness also one of his duties?' asks the Colonel.

The post of Constable has many cares and is, like that of watchman, entirely unpaid. It isn't something that most people are anxious to do, especially at harvest time or sowing time or haymaking time or shearing time or when they might be doing anything more useful than poking into other villagers' business. Those eligible for election often spend the whole year thinking of reasons why it is somebody else's turn. Cobley has obligingly undertaken the role for a while now. Of course, it has one or two useful benefits.

'Yes, he has to suppress drunkenness,' I say. 'That's why Ben lets him drink free of charge.'

'I shall speak to Cobley severely for failing to set a watch,' says the Colonel. 'I may have to fine him a pound for his negligence ...'

'I doubt if Will Cobley has ever seen twenty shillings all together in one place. He says in any case that since he was elected in 1649, his term of office was up long ago. He says he's only doing it because nobody has appointed a successor.'

'Really? Who is responsible for making the appointment?'

'You,' I say. 'As for levying fines, we may be fined ourselves if we don't quickly inform the neighbouring magistrates that a murder has been committed – and that a stranger passed through the village the same night.'

The Colonel clearly does not need to be reminded of his obligations, at least not by a half-trained lawyer. 'Cobley should be aware of his duties and the penalties.'

I would seem to have made Will Cobley's normally happy existence slightly more onerous. But perhaps I can still rescue him. 'I doubt that Sir Felix would have fined him,' I say, 'in the days when he was magistrate here. Sir Felix was loyal to anyone who sincerely believed they were trying to serve him, however incompetently. As for any drunkenness ... Cobley did not drink thus before the death of his son.'

The Colonel scowls, but I can see that my arrow has struck home. When he speaks again, it is not to talk of fines, and his tone is almost placatory. 'We may at least be sure that the killer has fled. Back to wherever he came from probably. Nobody who lives in this village would commit murder, John. You know that and I know that, don't we?'

'Yes,' I say, mentally excluding Roger Pole from this general amnesty.

'And if it wasn't one of *us*,' continues the Colonel, ignoring the fact that few of the villagers think of him as anything but an upstart outsider, 'then it must have been a stranger. Do you see my argument?'

'Yes,' I say. It's not a difficult argument to see. If it wasn't one of us, then it was one of them. Throats don't cut themselves.

'Footpads like as not,' says the Colonel. I wonder whether, like Ben, he will add that they must be from Suffolk, but the Colonel has not lived here long enough to have learned that honesty and decency are considered to stop short at the county boundary. The Rector referred to 'Suffolk and Gomorrah' in a sermon recently and nobody even thought to correct him.

'So, you will send to the other magistrates? It may be that it was footpads as you say, but we should at least tell them to watch for the horseman.'

'Your description of him, if I may say so, John, is hardly clear. And all we know about him is that he was asking for the inn at which the dead man was staying. What am I to say to the other magistrates? Please arrest a man on a grey horse? They'll laugh in my face!'

I think that my description was slightly better than that, and I doubt that the magistrates in Saffron Walden will find a killing as amusing as the Colonel suggests. Humour and murder are strange bedfellows. But that is not the point I wish to raise with him.

'*Was* the murdered man staying at the inn?' I ask.

I have caused the Colonel to look bemused. 'So I understood ... wasn't that what Ben told you?'

'He said the murdered man had been to the inn, not that he was staying there. He said he didn't know the man's name.'

For a moment the Colonel does not seem certain how to reply, then he pats me on the shoulder in a fatherly manner. 'Very well, John. I'll send out a description of your rider, if that is what you would like. In the meantime we'll have the other poor fellow buried at St Peter's. I'll pay naturally.'

'Once the inquest has taken place,' I say. 'The Rector won't be happy to bury a stranger without some sort of inquiry, surely?'

'Abraham Reading? Oh, he'll not cause us any trouble,' says the Colonel. And for the first time he actually smiles.

Late Morning

'The hair of the dog that bit you, young Master John,' says Ben Bowman, pushing a grey, dented tankard across the counter. Having come from the Colonel's lofty drawing room, I am aware how low the ceiling is in this smoke-blackened parlour, with its massive, gnarled beams, its great stone fireplace and the light creeping in cautiously through the tiny leaded panes of greenish glass. If I were to raise my hand, I could touch with ease the sooty timbers that support the floor above.

But it is my purse that I reach for. I am pleasantly surprised, in view of the amount I allegedly drank last night, how full it still is. Indeed, with the shilling I acquired this morning, I would appear to have sixpence more than I left Cambridge with. Hardly a night of debauchery then.

'No, put your money away,' says Ben with previously unrecorded generosity. 'Accept this as small apology for politely asking you to leave last night.'

Actually, I don't remember him being polite. Agitated possibly. Insistent definitely. But not polite. Nor did I have much support from my fellow drinkers when I raised reasonable objections. Still, I may as well let bygones be bygones.

'Both apology and ale accepted,' I say, taking a deep draught. It is cool, golden, nutty and aromatic, straight from Ben's excellent cellar. Bowman rubs his hands together while he waits for me to say how good it is. Unlike Ifnot and Sir Felix, he did not fight in the war. Had he fought for Parliament, he says, he would have lost his Royalist customers, and had he fought for the King, he would have lost his Roundhead customers. When men shot each other at Marston Moor, Ben was brewing ale. When young Mark Cobley was breathing his last at Naseby, Ben's plump red hands were soapily washing tankards.

'As good as ever you brewed,' I say, setting the mug down.

Ben nods as if at a self-evident truth. 'Been home yet?' he asks.

'I sent a message by Harry Hardy to say that I had to go and see the Colonel up at the Big House.' I wonder if my mother threw anything breakable at Harry while he was delivering the message. Probably. I'll check later.

'So, what did the Colonel have to say?' Ben has started to polish a tankard that is already as bright as it is ever going to be. The exertion threatens to make him breathless. He is perhaps a little too fond of his own ale and of Nell's food.

'Not much,' I reply. Indeed, I am troubled now by how little the Colonel said. I am not sure what I had expected of him, but more perhaps than the dismissive conclusion that the killers must have been footpads and that an inquest was optional under English Law. There is no sign of the Colonel arriving to make further enquiries in the village, so I may as well ask Ben a few questions myself.

'Ben,' I say, 'you said you didn't know the name of the man we found.'

Ben shrugs and starts rearranging his tankards on their shelf – misshapen pewter objects of all possible sizes, each allegedly capable of containing an honest pint.

'But he was staying here at the inn, wasn't he?' I say to the back of Ben's shirt. I am slightly put out that I have had to discover this for myself, when we had carried the heavy hurdle between us from the dung heap to the church. I was content to comply with Ben's injunction that there should be a respectful silence as we carried him, but I might at least have been given that snippet of gossip as we struggled across the field.

'Didn't I say so?'

'You just said that he'd been to the inn.'

'Been at. Staying at. It's all the same, isn't it?'

'No,' I say. 'It's not all the same.'

'Maybe I'm just not good with words like you lawyers. You won't hold that against a simple innkeeper, young Master John. Stop treating me like a witness in one of your courts. You've been studying Law too long for your own good, it would seem. Anyway, where else is a traveller supposed to stay?'

'He would have had little choice,' I say more grudgingly than I really intended. 'But if my rider was the murderer, it would explain why he was asking for the inn.'

Ben pivots round suddenly. 'I keep a respectable house here. He certainly wasn't murdered at my inn.'

I'm not sure that's quite what I meant, but my reassurances on this point do little to repair the damage. Ben isn't happy to have his inn even tenuously linked to a killing, which largely explains his earlier silence on the matter. Nobody's going to want to sleep in a room where a murder has taken place – or even where a murdered man was lately staying. Ghosts are amongst the more rational superstitions of people round here. Most of them have seen a hobgoblin clear as day. Don't even ask them about witches.

'Anyway,' I add, 'if our dead friend was staying here, you ought to have his name.'

'Maybe,' says Ben. The good thing about Ben is that you can see from a couple of miles off when he thinks he is being cunning. I'm quite a lot closer than that.

'*Maybe?*' I say.

'I think he said he was called Smith,' says Ben.

'Your memory's clearly improved,' I say.

'Nell reminded me,' says Ben. 'I asked her when I got home. She's the one with book-learning. She's the one who remembers things. "Murdered man?" she says to me. "That would be our Mr Smith." "So it was," I says. "Mr Smith."'

There is scarcely a word in this last utterance that you would trust to give you the right change of a florin. Ben has no idea that it is possible to lie and still speak in your normal voice.

'Smith? Just that? No Christian name? No travel pass signed by a justice of the peace for you to demand and then tut over?' I ask.

'I wouldn't trouble a *gentleman* for a pass. Mr Smith clearly wasn't a vagrant or a troublemaker.'

This is an unusually generous act on Ben's part. His natural distrust of strangers normally contends awkwardly but on an equal footing with his chosen vocation as an innkeeper.

'When he arrived,' Ben continues, 'he just said he was Mr Smith. From London Town.'

'Then we might be able to discover his family there,' I say. 'In London Town. We ought to try anyway.'

Ben's expression tells me that London is a big place and I can try if I wish, but he's not coming with me.

'I still don't understand, though, why the rider never came here,' I say.

'Changed his mind,' says Ben. 'Went to Saffron Walden.'

'No. His horse was lame, and he definitely asked . . .' What had he asked? I try to remember. He hadn't just enquired whether there was an inn close by – he wanted this one. Normally, Ben would have no difficulty in believing that of all the inns in Essex, his would be the one that a traveller would seek out. Yet he is now trying to persuade me that somebody with a crippled horse would willingly press on into the dark night, forgoing his legendary hospitality.

'Never saw him,' says Ben.

'Then maybe he went to some other house in the village . . .' I say. Because he might have ridden on to Ifnot's cottage and forge, or even to the Big House itself. But why, then, not ask for either one of those? He asked for the *inn*. How did he just vanish on that short stretch of road?

'Are you sure I can't get you some more ale, Master John? On the house of course.'

Well, that makes two more offers of free ale than I have ever had from Ben.

'Thanks,' I say, 'but I'd best be getting home.'

To do this, I have to pass last night's resting place. Harry Hardy is working in his garden in front of the cottage. He is picking beans in a leisurely way but slowly straightens his back when he sees me and nods a greeting. He's old enough to remember my great-grandfather lived in the Big House.

'How did things go with the old Colonel?' he asks.

'Well enough,' I say. Then I add, because I am sure the Colonel would wish me to say it: 'Colonel Payne asked me to thank you for helping to carry Mr Smith to the church.'

'Them thanks don't come with any money, I takes it?'

Ah yes – money. I realise that, in trying to be fair to the Colonel, I have deprived Harry of payment. I reach into my purse and, though I can ill afford it, take out the King's shilling. There's no reason why Harry should suffer for my negligence.

'That's kind of the Colonel,' says Harry, pocketing my silver. 'Or better than usual anyhow. He were called Smith then – that fellow we took to St Peter's?'

'So Ben says.'

'Friend of your'n?'

'Not that I know of.'

'Did you owe him some money then?'

'Not unless he's a Cambridge tailor.'

Harry pauses. He's not sure whether to tell me something, but my shilling tips the balance. 'You know he were axing a'ter you?'

'When?'

'Heard him at the inn, yesterday a'ternoon, axing Ben Bowman. Wanted to know if a John Grey lived in the village.'

'What did Ben say?'

'Not much. Just looked a bit mazed, like he'd never heard of you.'

'Maybe Ben misheard.'

'I heard clear enough, and I'm twice Ben's age.'

'Why should a Royalist spy ask after me anyway?'

Harry pauses again. 'Couldn't rightly say for why. But I just thought you should know. I'm not planning to tell anyone else of course. Not unless you want me to.'

'No,' I say. 'I don't want you to.'

I wish him good morning and continue on my way, but a little more slowly than before.

Midday

'As long as you are safe,' says my mother, patting my arm affectionately.

'Yes,' I say.

I would be happier in some ways if my mother were scolding me for my drunken habits in which I so resemble my father as to make me scarcely fit to be a part of humankind, let alone to be a gentleman, as her father was and her grandfather before him. But in most ways I am happy that she is not. Perhaps she has indeed already expended her wrath on the messenger. Or perhaps, now my studies at Cambridge are complete and there is a distant prospect of my earning money as a lawyer, her view of me is a little more tolerant than before.

As it is, not a word of reproach has passed her lips since my return. Even the state of my hat has prompted only a passing remark, and that mild enough. She herself is bedizened in a new velvet gown, a sort of mustard colour and laced all over, with a fine lawn collar that is big enough to resemble a small white cape. Glittering in her hair is an emerald set in a circle of pearls – the sight of which must have made Martha wonder why it is inconvenient for my mother to pay wages.

In short, all seems well. And yet I worry, because I cannot help feeling that some flood is being dammed back that will burst forth sooner or later when I least want it.

'Martha has prepared a chine of beef for dinner,' she says. 'And four fat pullets. Sir Felix has kindly consented to join us.'

Thus all is revealed and made open to me. In return for scandalising the village with my behaviour, I am condemned to spend two or three hours with that debauched and useless cavalier and watch him stuff our beef and chicken into and around his blubbery lips. *Four* pullets! And in return for my mother's not complaining about my expenditure on ale – which, unless I have a magic purse, was very, very little – I am not to object to her feeding this penniless and prating parasite until his threadbare doublet is fit to burst.

'Sir Felix does us too much honour,' I say.

'And his daughter, Aminta,' says my mother quickly.

I say nothing, but my face is clearly a sufficient protest.

'She has grown into a lovely girl,' says my mother, ignoring the fact that she is the runaway Bess Clifford's daughter. 'She has truly blossomed since you were home last Christmas.'

Did I see her last Christmas? Precocious little Aminta Clifford? The Cliffords are not people I seek out, and we live at opposite ends of the village. I doubt I did more than catch a glimpse of her in church.

'You hid up the apple tree to avoid her,' continues my mother.

As with so many things my mother says, I have to think

hard to make sense of it. 'Mother,' I say, 'I was ten, and Aminta was about six. That is not recent history.'

'It is scarce a dozen years ago,' says my mother. 'And there is no point in making a face like that. The invitations are already issued.'

To avoid having to dine with Sir Felix, I would be willing to make any sort of face at all. But, instead, I retire to brush the worst of the dust off my new suit. I can at least eat dinner without a hat.

Sir Felix wipes his mouth with the back of his hand and almost succeeds in suppressing a belch. He has already stuffed himself full but shows no sign of ceasing to eat up my meagre inheritance.

'They say, John, that you have returned from Cambridge more than half a Puritan. The University was not thus when I was there twenty or more years ago.'

'I assure you, Sir Felix . . .' I begin, but Aminta has already launched a new attack from across the table. She looks at me coquettishly over a chicken leg, which she holds neatly between her ladylike fingers.

'It would appear that you Cambridge Puritans waste a great deal of time in alehouses,' says Aminta. 'That's what Roger Pole tells me at least. He can be quite amusing about you, cousin John. I do hope you encountered no loose Puritan women in Cambridge.'

I am not, by any manipulation of our respective genealogies, her cousin. Nor am I, however notionally, a Puritan. And I refuse to acknowledge Pole's insult in any way whatsoever, though he shall be made to pay in some manner that is not yet clear to me.

'Loose women? There were none in Cambridge in my day,'

says Sir Felix, and he gives my mother a lewd wink that turns my very stomach. He strokes his black moustache, which is caked in grease from the pullets.

'*À d'autres*, Father,' says Aminta, putting the bone down on her plate and searching the table with her eyes for some other dainty morsel. She helps herself to cucumber slices dressed in oil.

My mother smiles vaguely, as though she really has the first idea what Aminta is talking about. Sir Felix guffaws. 'You sound just like your brother,' he says to Aminta.

'You speak almost as if Marius were still alive,' I say. 'Is there some fresh news of him?'

Sir Felix stops himself in mid chuckle, and his face is serious again. 'No,' he says with a sigh. 'No. If he escaped after the Battle of Worcester, which we doubt, he almost certainly died somewhere of his wounds. We have sought news of him in France and the Low Countries but to no avail. I wish that I could give you better tidings, since he was your friend as well as my son. We resigned ourselves long ago to his sad loss, much as Will Cobley has resigned himself to the loss of his own son in the wars.'

'My father means,' says Aminta, leaning across the table, 'that Marius and I, having shared a tutor for so long, acquired many of the same turns of phrase – do you not, my dear father? Just as cousin John, having studied in the alehouses of Cambridge, must have learned to swear and curse like a Puritan fishwife.'

'Of course he must,' says Sir Felix tolerantly. 'Whereas I attended upon my tutor at all hours and stayed away from tobacco, women and foul language. Ha! As if I'd swive some poxy Cambridge whore!'

My mother, who is cutting thick slices of meat with a practised hand, pauses for a moment and then says: 'You met your wife, Bess, at Cambridge, surely, Sir Felix?'

And the three of them burst out laughing in such a silly way that they risk choking on Martha's excellent chine of beef.

'Martha is an excellent cook,' says Aminta. 'Your mother is fortunate.'

We are walking in the garden, whither my mother has sent us. We have inspected the damson tree by the house, which looks likely to produce a good harvest this year. Aminta has observed that the Cliffords' own damson tree is similarly fecund. Our cucumbers compare well with those at the Steward's cottage, though are not as advanced as Ben Bowman's in his vegetable patch behind the inn. I do not ask after Ben Bowman's damsons, because I wish to stay awake, and no answer Aminta could possibly give would fail to induce slumber. We are now proceeding along the avenue of over-grown pleached limes, which Nathaniel planted and trained many years ago but which nobody has tended properly since my father departed. Their outline is ragged and unpleasing, but at least you can't eat them, as far as I know. Aminta holds my arm lightly but firmly as we walk – a precaution, she says, against stumbling on the uneven path. I feel the warmth of her little hand through my sleeve, and I have to confess that it is not unpleasant.

I steal a glance at her. When did she metamorphose from a gawky little girl into the young woman beside me? She is dressed for this visit to our house very simply in a gown of soft grey wool, the skirt fashionably open in front and bunched back to display a light-coloured petticoat embroidered in silver. Her collar is plain and, unlike my mother's ridiculous mantle, of a modest size. Her lace cuffs are neat and gleaming white. Some might perhaps call her pretty with her small stuck-up nose and her bright blue eyes. But my ideal woman would have greatness of soul rather than a cute nose – and a meek and obedient disposition. Aminta's disposition is far from meek or obedient. She is sadly her father's daughter in too many ways.

'Martha? Yes, my mother is lucky to have her,' I say. 'We can afford to pay her very little. We are quite *poor*.'

I stress this last word because the thought has occurred to me that Sir Felix's interest in my mother may be founded on some notion that she has money. I want to ensure there is no mistake on that score.

'Like us then,' says Aminta cheerfully. She gives my arm a conspiratorial squeeze. I try not to enjoy the sensation.

'Perhaps not quite as poor as that,' I say, wishing to be wholly accurate. Though in fact, as I have said, my mother pays Martha absolutely nothing. Generations of Martha's family have worked for generations of my mother's family. Being paid nothing is an improvement on the contractual terms that many of Martha's distant ancestors enjoyed.

Aminta nods at this and smiles sweetly. I have seen that smile before. She wants something from me. Flight is point-less; she has possession of my arm and, in any case, she knows where the apple tree is now. 'So, tell me about this body that you found,' she says.

I had thought that I had covered that subject adequately over dinner – at least so far as I could with two ladies present.

'As I say, I was out early this morning . . . on some trifling errand . . . when I came across the poor fellow with his throat cut. That's more or less all there is to it.'

Aminta screws up her small, cute nose. She does not entirely trust my account.

'Roger Pole says it was slashed from side to side in a hideous crimson gash. He also says that you had been out all night because you were too drunk to find your way home.'

'Does he?' I say. Then I add: 'I'm not sure how he is in a position to know that.'

'The Colonel told him,' says Aminta. 'He tells Roger most things.'

I resist the temptation to say 'Does he?' because I have already said it. I hope that my silence will convey my contempt, though at the same time I fear it may not.

'I don't think the Colonel quite understood the significance of the dew under the body,' says Aminta. 'I also think he made too little of the cipher that you found.'

Of course, it is pleasing that somebody agrees with me that the cipher is of significance, even if that person is Aminta. And her informant was Pole.

'So, you saw Roger Pole this morning?' I say conversationally. Not that I care much.

'He too was up early,' says Aminta. 'Though unlike you, he had gone to bed beforehand. Now, tell me again about the wound the poor man suffered. Roger's account was merely second-hand and, I felt, lacked colour.'

I sigh and describe the wound as best I can: the size, the depth, the very clean edges. Somebody clearly possessed a sharp knife and was skilled in its use. Aminta nods. She seems sorry not to have seen it. 'And you told the Colonel all this?'

'Yes,' I say. 'Perhaps the Coroner will take more interest in such matters. The Colonel paid little attention; he is convinced that it was footpads on the highroad to Cambridge.'

'Meaning the man was killed close to where he was found. You told us over dinner that Ben was mortally offended when he thought you were suggesting the man was murdered at the inn – but that is not impossible, is it?'

Ben's outrage was, I thought, one of the more amusing details of my account – at least, the way I told it. I can still see Ben's face reddening at the idea that a reputable establishment such as his would host a murder. There is, however, a more solid reason than reputation why it simply cannot be.

'But think, Aminta – the killer would have had to take the body from the inn, past the crossroads, where I was . . . standing . . . then up the Cambridge road in the moonlight. The risk of being caught was too great.'

'Have you also considered the path across the meadow, behind the inn, my dear cousin? It is a convenient shortcut, and whoever was *standing* at the crossroads would not have seen anyone passing that way.'

'That is always boggy and often impassable.' And I am not her cousin.

'It is usually dry enough in summer,' says Aminta. 'The path leads almost directly from the dung heap to Ben's stables.'

'But you wouldn't use it at night, you know. The ground is too rough.'

'There was a moon, as you say. And people do have lanterns, dim though their light may be.'

'Yes, but you would also have to wade across the stream. There are no stepping stones as there are on the Cambridge road.' This is, I think, an irrefutable argument.

'A murderer might be prepared to get his breeches wet,' says Aminta, 'if the alternative was being hanged. Do watch that branch, cousin! I fear your mind is elsewhere at the moment.'

I duck and say nothing. I have no intention of conceding how right Aminta is. Aminta is insufferable even when she is completely wrong.

'Well, if anyone did go that way,' I point out, once we are clear of the limes, 'I doubt there will still be much to show now for their night-time journey.'

'It would still be worth looking. Not as worthwhile as it would have been first thing this morning, but quite worthwhile nonetheless, don't you think?'

It might, though more likely I'll just spoil an almost new pair of boots in the mud. Aminta is good at giving instructions but less good at considering the consequences. Like when, many years ago, she dared me to drink a whole bottle of her father's Rhenish that she had stolen from the cellar. I didn't touch another drop of wine until I was almost twelve.

'And did the Colonel say if he was planning to search the inn?' she continues. 'The inn would be a good place for him to begin his investigations, don't you think?'

More instructions. For the Colonel this time.

'Colonel Payne says he will question those who were at the inn last night,' I say. Then I add: 'I suppose Roger Pole also told you about the rider I saw.'

'No,' says Aminta. 'Who did you see?'

This is a surprise. I would have thought that Pole would have enjoyed recounting that part of the story. So I tell Aminta, stressing that I was less drunk than some may have claimed.

'And I suppose *you* don't believe me about the horseman either?' I add on completion.

Aminta, who has been listening to me with a frown of concentration, suddenly gives a little laugh. '*Of course* I believe you, cousin John.'

She doesn't then. Why, in view of the general credulity and idiocy of the village, is a straightforward man on a horse so difficult to believe in? Harry Hardy claimed to have seen the devil riding a goat round the village pond one Halloween, and nobody doubted him for a moment.

'He threw me a shilling,' I say.

'Then, cousin, you are certainly richer than us,' says Aminta, taking my arm again. She pulls me closer to her as we continue our walk. For a moment I am aware only of Aminta and the scent of lavender and clean linen. Her skirt brushes against my leg.

I do not deny what she has said. I have given the shilling away, but I do have others.

'Everyone in the village is richer than us,' Aminta continues, 'for we really have nothing at all. You must find it amusing that the wheel has come full circle for the Cliffords, do you not, cousin John?'

'In what way?' I ask.

'Why, because Colonel Payne has dispossessed us in the same way that we dispossessed you. You don't mean that you never think of that? It must please you at least a little to see us humbled.' She releases my arm and stands back to look at me, a strange specimen that she needs to study properly.

'No,' I say. Because, to be honest, I haven't thought of it and, having thought of it now, I am neither pleased nor displeased by it.

'You never recall that your family owned the manor before us?'

'My *mother's* family,' I say. 'Yes, of course I do. Sometimes. But that was in Queen Bess's day – almost sixty years ago.'

'And you don't want the manor back?'

'Not especially.'

'Surely your mother does?'

'She hasn't mentioned it lately. And she scarcely stops talking about one thing or another. She finds the New House very convenient. The Big House is . . . well, big. Too big for us. And the park costs money to maintain and brings in little revenue. No, I don't think she regrets the loss of the manor.'

'Well, we do. We'll sit outside the park for the next two hundred years if we have to and wait for the last of the Paynes to die. Then we'll sneak back in.'

'That would not necessarily give you lawful title,' I point out.

'Just the sort of response I would expect from a Puritan lawyer,' says Aminta.

'I'm *not* a Puritan,' I protest. 'I am merely a loyal citizen of the Republic, as you should be.'

'Cambridge has changed you,' she says.

'Yes, it has made me a lawyer, and I have just given you good legal advice.'

'It will come to pass,' she says with more confidence than seems immediately justified. 'When the King is restored, we'll be back too. In the meantime we'll put a curse on the Colonel's chickens so they won't lay.'

'And his deer,' I suggest helpfully.

'They are *our* deer,' says Aminta indignantly. 'I'm not cursing them. I want to be sure there will be venison from the park when we are back at the manor.'

'Legally,' I say 'it is very unlikely that—'

Then Aminta hits me. Hard. Just like she used to. And for what exactly? I may have changed, but Aminta is exactly as she was aged six.

*

For the journey back to the house, Aminta decides she no longer needs my arm. The path has grown smoother in the past half-hour. We walk mainly in silence, but as we enter through the garden door, Aminta says in an unnecessarily loud voice (it seems to me), 'So, we are back now, John. Well, I did enjoy our walk.'

I cross the flagstoned hallway and open the low door into the parlour. My mother is seated on the oak settle, smoothing her velvet skirts and looking slightly flustered. Sir Felix is standing a little way off, examining his grease-encrusted nails. I try to catch Aminta's eye to confirm that she is as shocked as she should be at the behaviour of our respective parents, but she is looking the other way and humming to herself.

'You are back before we expected you,' says my mother brightly.

'Indeed,' says Sir Felix. 'We had thought you would be longer. I am surprised that my daughter wishes to relinquish the attentions of this handsome young man so soon. Of course, if you wished to take another turn . . .'

'Aminta has seen the garden many times before,' I point out. 'Those limes really do need pruning, Mother.'

'I'll send my gardener over to do it,' says Sir Felix.

'You still retain a gardener?' I ask.

'Strictly speaking, he's the Colonel's gardener now, but he helps me out when I need him,' says Sir Felix. 'That fool Payne hasn't the faintest idea what his people are doing most of the time.'

'Which is most fortunate for his butler,' says Aminta primly.

I wonder what she means and whether it has anything to do with the four bottles of sack that Sir Felix sent over earlier today, two of which we drank at dinner.

'It will all be yours again one day,' says my mother dreamily. 'When the King returns.'

'Mother!' I exclaim. It is one thing for Aminta to whisper treasons of this sort to me in the garden, but another entirely for my own mother to do so in public.

Sir Felix laughs. 'Your son is afraid you will lose your pretty head, Mistress Grey. It would be a terrible waste if you did.'

'Being beheaded is a family tradition,' says my mother with just a hint of pride.

Not a tradition I would wish to see continued, however. 'What if the servants heard?' I ask indignantly.

'*À d'autres!*' she says, and gives Sir Felix a wink.

'You do well to warn us, John,' says Sir Felix in an avuncular manner that he has no right to. 'Good folk are hauled off to the county gaol or the pillory every day for saying less. But even you must miss the merry times when we had a king amongst us. For all that we are loyal citizens of the Republic or Commonwealth or Protectorate or whatever we are supposed to call it now.'

'We'll be able to call it a kingdom again soon,' says Aminta. She watches my face with amusement and then adds: 'That is to say, when His Highness The Lord Protector has himself crowned.'

I shake my head. 'Oliver was offered the crown and immediately declined it with contempt.'

'It took him six weeks to decide to immediately decline it,' says Aminta. 'There are still those urging him to accept. And he wants his eldest son to succeed him. One way or another, we'll have a king by the end of next year – a Stuart or a Cromwell.'

'To answer your question, Sir Felix,' I say, desirous that a small part of our conversation should not be treasonable, 'I miss nothing. Nothing at all.'

'But what about the maypoles?' asks Aminta.

'Pagan relics for silly girls to dance round,' I say pointedly. 'Parliament did well to order their destruction.'

'And Christmas?' asks Sir Felix. 'Surely, we should be able to celebrate the birth of Our Saviour?'

'There is no evidence that Christ's nativity took place on 25 December,' I say. 'It is merely some heathenish midwinter debauch disguised as a holy day.'

My mother opens her mouth to speak in defence of debauchery, but this time a look from me silences her. I do not remind her, in front of our guests, that she shamefully smuggled holly and mistletoe into the house last December.

'What about plays then?' asks Sir Felix, leaning back in his chair and picking his teeth. 'How does the closure of a few theatres make us safe from the return of the Stuarts, against which the Good Lord defend us? And what about poor Nell Bowman? Once the theatres closed and she was out of a job, she had no choice but to marry our village innkeeper. Surely, that at least was too cruel? Admit it, young John. The world has grown drab in the last ten years.'

Just out of sight of her father, Aminta is pointing a finger at me and mouthing the word 'Puritan'.

'We live,' I say, 'in dangerous times. Parliament may have executed the Tyrant himself, but his son is lurking in the Spanish Netherlands, debauching himself by night and ever hopeful that plots by renegade Royalists will bring him to the throne.'

I pause, realising that Sir Felix might think that I was

including him in this class of clandestine plotters, but he smiles at me amiably.

'I think you will find he debauches himself by day as well,' he says. 'But you are right that there are some misguided people working towards his return. After all, the dead man that you and Ben Bowman found this morning was carrying a ring with the royal coat of arms, was he not?'

The royal coat of arms?

'Where did you hear that?' I ask. 'Ben Bowman only mentioned a gold ring that was stolen; he said nothing about a coat of arms.'

'That is the rumour in the village,' says Sir Felix. 'I cannot say that I saw it myself.'

Of course, it made sense. A man might not have his throat cut for a simple gold ring – though throats have been cut for much less – but for carrying a ring with the detested Stuart coat of arms . . . And it explained why the killer might take the ring but disdain the silver in his purse.

'I must report this to Colonel Payne,' I say. 'He seemed to doubt that Smith was a Royalist spy, but with this additional piece of evidence . . .'

'Rumour could have been wrong,' says Sir Felix. 'It often is. But if Smith was indeed a Royalist agent, then we can scarcely expect the Colonel to waste much effort on bringing the killers of such a villain to justice. The sooner that traitor is quietly buried in an unhallowed grave, the better, eh? As a loyal citizen of the Republic, John, I am sure you will agree.'

I pause. In a sense this is very true. It would certainly explain why the Colonel is inclined to do so little. And yet, though I have said nothing even to my mother about this, Harry Hardy's words still run through my head. Smith was asking for *me*. And Ben was reluctant to tell him anything. The death of this Royalist spy touches me personally, albeit in some manner I cannot yet give a name to. I shall need to tread carefully.

'You are right, Sir Felix,' I say. 'I am sure the Colonel understands his duties.'

Sir Felix smiles at me tolerantly, as if at a wayward puppy who has just pissed on somebody else's leg. 'You think that common upstart Payne understands the duties of a lord of the manor? *À d'autres*,' he says.

Afternoon

The sun warms my face, and the pale dust rises from the road as I tramp along, coating the lowest leaves of the hawthorn hedges with a creamy powder. The Cliffords have departed to their Lodge, happily stuffed with our chicken and beef, all washed down with wine shamelessly stolen from the Colonel's cellar. I am free to attend to business. I must go and talk to the Colonel again, because I cannot see how I can resolve this puzzle without his help; but first I shall exchange a few hard words with Ben Bowman and let him know I am not quite the fool he takes me for.

The inn is cool, gloomy and welcoming, and there is the scent of sawdust freshly sprinkled on the floor. I bang on the counter with a clenched fist and call Ben up from the cellar. He appears suddenly through the trap door in the floor, like the Devil in one of the plays now so wisely banned by Parliament. He is dressed in a clean apron – Nell keeps him tidy – and his shirtsleeves are rolled up to the elbows.

'Master John! You must have a thirst on you today that you are with us again so soon. A pint of my best ale, is it?'

'I'll have a pint of truth from you this time, Ben Bowman,' I say.

He is at once on his guard, suggesting that there might have been better ways to begin this conversation than by scoring a cheap point with a trite metaphor. But no matter.

'There's something odd going on, Ben,' I say. 'First, the murdered man was staying here and you didn't tell me.'

'Didn't I?' asks Ben.

'No,' I remind him. 'You didn't. Then you seem to have forgotten to mention that there was a Stuart coat of arms on this ring that he was flashing about.'

'Was there?'

'So it would seem.'

'Who says?'

'Everyone, apparently.'

'Do they?'

Ben has the ability to delay answering a question almost indefinitely by turning anything you say into a question of his own. It is amusing only if you are easily amused.

'Ben,' I say firmly, 'was there or was there not a Stuart coat of arms on the ring?'

Ben's look shows that he is aware that none of the three possible answers to that question will guarantee his safety. Nor can he remain silent forever, much though he would like to.

'Look, can I get you a pint of ale, young Master John? No charge.'

'And Smith was apparently asking after me, here at the inn.'

'Was he?'

'Ben, what is going on?' I ask.

'Nothing.'

'I don't think so. Let me ask you again: Ben, what is going on?'

Even the most amiable of hounds, when backed against the wall, will bare its teeth eventually. I watch Ben's expression harden.

'It's for the Magistrate to investigate murders, Master John. Not me. Not you either. So you'd better ask the Colonel, hadn't you?'

I pick up my hat and clap it on my head. I fear that it sits there a little awkwardly.

'That's exactly what I'm going to do,' I say. 'After which, you can be sure that I'll be back here – and not for a pint of ale.'

'Seems like I'd better get a cask of Truth up from the cellar then,' he says. 'If that's what you lawyers drink these days.'

I look at Ben, and he looks back at me. Whatever he knows, he has no plans to tell it.

I step out of the pleasant gloom of the inn into a hot, dusty June afternoon, and I slam the heavy iron-studded door behind me. I stop and listen for a moment. From the inn there is no sound at all. And outside even the birdsong has ceased.

I find Colonel Payne in the oak-panelled chamber again, but this time he is not alone. He looks at me blankly as if his mind were elsewhere and I were a complete stranger.

'John,' he says as if recalling my name with difficulty. Then more briskly: 'I had not been expecting you. Let me introduce Mr Thomas Clarges, a good friend of mine. Thomas, this is

John Grey, who lives at the New House, just outside the village on the Cambridge road. I was saying to Mr Clarges that the Greys once held this manor, did they not, John?'

'The Greys? Not a bit of it,' I say. 'It was my mother's family – the Wests. They owned it until my great-grandfather was executed for treason after the Earl of Essex's rebellion. The estate was confiscated by the Crown and later given to the Cliffords by King James.'

'So this was once your family's house?' asks Mr Clarges.

'Not even that. The Cliffords demolished the old house and built this one about thirty years ago. But I visited it as a child. Marius Clifford was older than I, but I often played with him. He taught me to fence and to shoot arrows and to sharpen a knife. He died in the late wars but, had he lived, he too, I fear, would have faced ruin.'

'Thus it is with many cavaliers,' says Mr Clarges. 'They can leave nothing to their children except their name and their loyalties. But I doubt you have come here to discuss family history, Mr Grey. It is a warm day, Colonel Payne; I shall take a stroll under the shade of your trees, if you give me leave, and return when you have determined your business with this young man.'

Now I have finished speaking my piece, I am aware that I have perhaps spoken for longer and more forcefully than I should. The Colonel rubs his eyes. He too would rather be walking in his park than shut up with me in the still air of a hot room. For a moment I think that he is not going to give me any reply at all, then he smiles.

'Thank you for telling me about the ring. I agree that it does strengthen the case for Mr Smith being a spy, though many former Royalists secretly carry mementos of the late Tyrant. I think, however, that your judgement of Ben is a little uncharitable if I may say so, John. I am sure that he meant to keep nothing from you – but perhaps did not express himself well.' He pauses, then gives a little chuckle. 'Anyway, I doubt that Ben would recognise the royal coat of arms if he saw it. You have to understand that most folk in this village couldn't tell a lion rampant from a pickled herring.'

Well, up to a point. I do not join him in laughing about Ben or my village.

'But you and I shall not be able to plead such charming bucolic ignorance,' I point out. 'We do know some heraldry and, more importantly, we know that a Royalist spy has been killed here. We must report it.'

'Indeed,' says the Colonel with some emphasis. 'We *must* report it. But to whom? That is the question. A spy has been killed. But whom or what was he seeking here? Are other recalcitrant Royalists lurking in the village?'

He looks at me. Does he know Smith mentioned my name? No, I think not. For the moment that is my secret. Roger Pole is an undoubted Royalist, but there is no point in trying to persuade the Colonel of that. The Colonel will hear no criticism of his secretary. Of course, there are others who have no love of Parliament.

'The Cliffords perhaps,' I say. 'But I scarcely suspect them of plotting against the State.'

'Of course not,' says the Colonel. 'But still, these are deep waters. We must proceed with caution, John. This is not a matter for Will Cobley or even for me. I shall write to the Lord Protector's head of intelligence, Mr Secretary Thurloe, and inform him. *That* is what must be done. My name must still carry some weight in Westminster; Thurloe can scarcely fail to take notice. In the meantime, however, the fewer people who know about this, the better. This is a confidential matter, John. I trust that I can rely on you?'

'Of course,' I say. 'But if you cannot now inform the neighbouring magistrates, will you at least mention the horseman in your report to Mr Thurloe?'

'Ah yes, your horseman . . . the man that you cannot describe. Has anyone else told you that they saw him?'

'No,' I say.

'The Saffron Walden magistrates might be lenient with us, but I would fear for my head if I sent Mr Thurloe chasing after phantoms on horseback.'

'He was no phantom. I saw him,' I say.

'You *think* you saw him,' says the Colonel.

'Well, yes, of course,' I say. I can't deny that's what I think.

'That's settled then,' says the Colonel, who clearly does not wish to inconvenience me by discussing this further.

Perhaps he is anxious to resume his conversation with Mr Clarges. He looks towards the door as if expecting me to use it quite soon.

I bow. 'Your servant, Colonel Payne,' I say.

He nods. I have finally said something he can agree with.

I am quitting the house when I meet Roger Pole, who is returning from some unimportant errand for the Colonel. He is dressed in the sort of finery that I despise. He wears a pale blue silk jackanapes coat with silver buttons, wide beribboned petticoat breeches of the same hue, Spanish leather boots and a beaver hat with two vast feathers in it and a hatband of indented lace. Clouds of white shirt billow out between the bottom of the ridiculously short coat and the top of the ridiculously spacious nether garments. White shirt-cuffs cascade from the too-short sleeves of his coat down almost to his fingertips. Everything about him is a question of carefully calculated excess. It gives me great pleasure that I have no idea what his Brussels lace collar must have cost, nor ever will have. His face is sharp and unpleasant like . . . like . . . some sharp and unpleasant thing.

'I give you good day, Mr Pole,' I say, trying to recall what things are both sharp and unpleasant. No matter. His hat is ridiculous anyway.

'Good day, Mr Grey,' he says. He looks pointedly at my own modest headgear.

'Is there something about my hat that displeases you?' I ask. I fear that, for all Martha's steaming and ironing, there remains something of the pillow about it.

'Amongst those who have been taught good manners, it is customary to remove it when greeting your betters,' says Pole.

'Thus I shall keep mine on,' I say.

'I do so beg your pardon, Mr Grey,' he says. With his right hand poised on his hip, he sweeps his own hat off, brushing my cheek with its feathers as he does so. 'I had not realised that you men of Law had grown so grand. The world has truly been turned upside down.' He smirks as if that were an excellent joke. Though my hat is still on my head and his is not, I feel that I have in some way been outwitted – that he would indeed have placed me at a disadvantage whether I had doffed my headgear or retained it. Of course, he has a point of sorts. The Poles are descended in some way from King Edward III, which is rare enough but requires little effort. They have never needed to work for money or anything else. I certainly doubt that this Pole would find work congenial. I cannot see him lifting bales of hay with those arms. But he still feels he can sneer at me. He probably lumps lawyers together with bakers and rat-catchers as mere tradesmen.

'I had not realised that secretaries had grown so grand,' I say. But I am aware that I am merely parroting his own jibe. There is a pause in the conversation as I try to think of something clever to say. The pause becomes quite a long one.

'I met with Aminta and her father returning from your mother's cottage,' Pole says, admiring one of the pale-blue silk bows on his sleeve.

'House,' I say. 'My mother's *house*.'

Pole ignores this correction. 'Sir Felix greeted me very cordially. As ever. And Aminta is charming of course. She has really blossomed of late.'

He speaks of the Cliffords with great familiarity. Perhaps during my absence at university they have grown closer. The Cliffords and the Poles are, after all, both cavalier families who lost much through their support of the Stuarts. And it is a small village. It is not unnatural that they should meet from time to time. And yet I cannot help feel that there is more to what Pole has just said than immediately meets the eye. Obviously, it does not follow that Aminta in any way reciprocates Pole's feelings – I do not think Pole has blossomed in any way at all.

'Aminta has no dowry,' I say, though why I wish to tell Pole this is a mystery to me. But still I blunder on: 'The Cliffords are penniless. The war ruined them.'

'I think you'll find everyone in the village knows that,' says Pole. 'That's why they lost the manor. But thank you none-theless. I am sure Aminta would appreciate your explaining this to me. Still, you must agree that she has many other virtues. She is rather pretty in fact. But . . .' Pole pauses, also perhaps wondering why I have clumsily raised the issue of dowries for ladies in whom I have no interest. 'But possibly there is already some understanding between the two of you?' He puts the tips of his slender fingers to his delicate little mouth in mock concern.

'Aminta and I? Not a bit of it,' I say.

'How wise you are to set your sights lower,' says Pole, preening one of the feathers in his hat. 'A farmer's daughter perhaps, who could dispense with a lady's maid and many of the other servants that you would not be able to afford. Somebody who would be happy to take you for your good looks and not regret too much your lack of any inheritance. Am I right in thinking that your mother has only two servants and pays neither?'

'Good day to you, Mr Pole,' I say.

'Your ever-obedient servant, Mr Grey,' says Pole with a very low bow.

I put my hand up to my hat and then quickly take it away again. As I close the door, I hear Pole give a prim little snigger – though whether for my benefit or his own, I could not rightly say.

As I go back along the path, I think, *Thorns!* Thorns are sharp and unpleasant. I'll remember that for next time.

But now I have urgent business. Murder cannot be swept behind the door, as some clearly wish it should be. Especially the murder of one who was seeking me out. I must consult the only person in the village I can wholly trust.

For the avoidance of doubt, as we lawyers say, that's Dickon Grice.

Late Afternoon

I am riding our only remaining horse over the hill to the Grices' farm. If we were to canter, we would make the hard earth ring beneath her hooves – but we do not canter. For ten years nobody has given the horse any cause to believe that our family's business could be urgent. She plods along, happy as far as I can tell. I do not clap my spurs to her side, impatient though I am. She is our only horse and may prove to be the last we ever own, unless I can earn the money for another. In the meantime I would do well to return her to the stable in much the same condition that she left it. I think she too knows this.

High above me, in some sort of crude allegory of summer, an invisible lark is singing. A sticky breeze blows off the fields, bringing me the scent of hay and sweet camomile. It will be a hot evening and a hot night to follow. I am beginning to realise that my resting place last night was not as comfortable as I imagined at the time – my body aches for a feather bed and linen sheets. But first I need to talk to Dickon.

'Have you grown old, or is it just your mare?' asks Dickon as I clatter across the stones in the courtyard. 'I've been watching you descend that hill for near half an hour. I remember when you'd have taken it at a gallop and then jumped the hedge you picked your way round so daintily.'

'Have you grown fat, or is it just that you're wearing your little brother's coat?' I respond. 'The buttons look about to burst off it.'

'True enough,' he says, good-naturedly patting his stomach. 'I need a new coat. You, on the other hand, are starting to acquire a thin and pinched appearance well suited to a rascally lawyer.'

'I am not.'

'You are. Another term at Cambridge and you would resemble a withered pippin stuck on a rake handle. We were once much the same build. In a fair fight you could throw me maybe one time in ten.'

'Nine in ten,' I say.

But perhaps Dickon is right. I have spent too long poring over dusty lawbooks. It might be better not to compare my own face too closely with his sunburnt cheeks and short blond hair.

Now I am descended from the saddle, Dickon's hand thumps my shoulder – a little too heartily. He has in my absence become by several degrees more of a farmer, while I have left this flat countryside behind me. We have grown in opposite directions since I was last home. But I still have no better friend in the village or anywhere else.

I enquire after his parents, and, as if she might have overheard, Dickon's mother appears in the doorway. Though Dickon's father comes from a long line of farmers, his mother grew up in one of the nearby towns, the daughter of a merchant – of what type I am unsure, since it is not the sort of thing Dickon would think to tell me or, for that matter, I would think to ask. Like Nell Bowman, Dickon's mother seems slightly exotic in this remote clay-country village. But whereas Nell continues to sparkle like a gem in a muddy puddle, Mistress Grice has reluctantly taken on the drab hues of rural Essex. She might, to look at her, be any Essex farmer's wife with her weather-beaten face and powerful arms. She wears a greenish-brown dress, and her hair is concealed under a scarf that may once have been white. The dress is partly protected by an apron of coarse grey linen, much washed and mended. Out here there's no point in wearing anything that might get spoiled by mud. There's never any shortage of mud in Essex.

She wipes her hands carefully on the apron before speaking. 'Your mother is well?' she asks. She talks with the accent of another place and perhaps another time that she now only dimly remembers. But Essex is nibbling at the edges of her speech, and she is aware of this.

I tell her my mother is well enough and that she sends her best wishes. I am not sure whether she expects me to have news of my father. That few people in the village mention him to me suggests that most know he was not a casualty of the war. Nobody mentions Bess Clifford to me either, though I am sure many whisper behind my back. It's a village after all. It's what we do. Dickon's mother asks after 'the family', meaning the gentrified Wests rather than the obscure Greys. That they once lived in the Big House raises them – and me – in her eyes, even though the Grices' comfortable, rambling, timber-framed farm is much bigger than the New House. The Grices have farmed here or hereabouts for as long as the village has existed. Lords of the manor have come and gone, while they have quietly added to their holding a field or a strip at a time. And no field or strip, once in their grasp, is ever given up.

Dickon's mother seems happy with the little I have to say and disappears back into her kitchen to resume the never-ending round of sweeping, dusting, polishing, washing, fire-tending, brewing, baking, roasting, boiling, skinning, salting, cheese-making, child-bearing and pickling that is her lot in life. I am hoping that she has not neglected the brewing.

We are both on our second tankard before I broach the main reason for my visit.

'Dickon,' I say, 'what do you know about this dead man Ben and I found this morning?'

Dickon's tankard pauses briefly on its next journey to his mouth. Nobody in his family usually says anything without considering it for a day or two. 'Smith? Arrived the afternoon before you came back from Cambridge. I only spoke to him the one time. A small, dark man he was. Solidly built. Scar on his chin, I think. He was sitting in Ben Bowman's front parlour with his ale in front of him and his pipe in his mouth, minding his own business. I did no more than wish him good day. Strange to think of him dying scarce half a mile away while we were all carousing in Ben's parlour.'

'Why was he staying at the inn anyway?' I ask.

'I heard he was on his way to Norwich or somewhere.'

'And not in a hurry to get there?'

'Seemingly.'

'Did he arrive on horseback?'

Dickon looks at me quizzically. 'What difference does that make?'

'London to Norwich is a long way on foot. If the horse was still in the stables, Ben would be torn between complaining that nobody was paying for its oats and selling the beast quietly to the next traveller. He's certainly not complained about the cost of oats.'

We both take a long, contemplative swig of ale. It's good stuff. Powerful.

'Smith apparently had a ring with the Stuart coat of arms,' I say.

'You've heard that? Yes, Ben mentioned it to me too. He's got sharp eyes. Risky to carry an item like that around with you. Even riskier to show it to half the village, as he must have done.'

I note the source of his information. I think Ben knows his pickled herrings, for all the Colonel doubts it.

'Smith clearly thought he was amongst friends then,' I say.

'His mistake,' says Dickon. 'There are few Royalist sympathisers round here. Except Ma maybe. Says things were better before the war.'

'Christmas?' I ask sympathetically.

'Maypoles,' says Dickon. 'It's as well we men don't waste our time on such frivolity. Somebody has to get the work done.'

I nod, and we both turn our attentions to our tankards for a bit.

'Dickon,' I say, 'I think I may have spoken to the killer. There was a stranger who arrived on a lame horse a little after midnight. He asked for the inn. Maybe you saw him there.'

I hope Dickon will say he remembers the rider well, for I am beginning to doubt my own memory on the subject. My heart sinks a little as Dickon shakes his head. 'There were no strangers at the inn last night. If I'd seen anyone suspicious, don't you think I'd have already reported it to the Colonel?'

'What time did you leave the inn?'

'I stayed drinking with Ben almost until cockcrow. Then I went off to milk the cows with a clear head and a steady hand. And Pa wanted me to slaughter a pig of ours – steady hand for that work too.'

'I *saw* him,' I say. 'He couldn't have ridden on to Saffron Walden – not on that horse. How does a man and a horse vanish into thin air between the crossroads and the inn? And why does nobody believe I saw him?'

Dickon pats me on the shoulder. 'Because, John, everyone has heard how drunk you were,' he says. 'Why don't you ask Ma? She believes in Robin Goodfellow and fairies and sprites and all sorts.'

Even a couple of years back, a condescending remark of that sort would have been the cue for me to throw a punch at Dickon and for the pair of us to tussle for a couple of minutes until one of us was thrown down or we got bored and decided to do something else. But we are older now, and one of us is almost a lawyer.

'I wasn't drunk,' I say. 'Well, not very. And I can't have bought much ale, because when I checked my purse I had spent very little.'

'Others may have paid,' says Dickon. 'It was your first night back after all.'

'Did *you* buy me any ale?' I ask.

Dickon looks at me to see what I might be prepared to believe. He puts me down for four tankards. 'You'll repay me soon, I don't doubt,' he adds.

My raised eyebrow causes this estimate to be reduced to one tankard, with repayment deferred indefinitely.

'Anyway,' I say, 'I've been thinking.'

Dickon does not find this reassuring, but I am allowed to continue.

'The fact that none of you saw him doesn't mean that he didn't go to the inn,' I say.

'How do you make that out?'

'Let's start with Smith. I don't think he ever left the inn alive.'

'And you have some reason for thinking that?'

'There was something odd about the way he was dressed – no hat. What man goes out without a hat?'

'Go on,' says Dickon, but he's not convinced. Dickon must know somebody who once went out bareheaded. 'So, you say Smith was killed at the inn. How does the horseman make himself invisible and get past all of us?'

'Because, quite simply, he doesn't go to the front parlour, where the rest of you are. What if he creeps in through the back door and up the stairs to Mr Smith's chamber, where he cuts his throat? Then he drags the body out of the inn and over to the dung hill, where he leaves him.'

Dickon does not consider my proposition for long. 'Not a chance,' he says. 'We'd have heard if there was a fight in one of the chambers above our heads. And your horseman would have had to drag the body down the stairs, thump, thump, thump, thump . . .'

'Yes, I understand what you are saying,' I say.

'Still got five stairs to go,' says Dickon. 'Thump, thump, thump, thump, thump.'

'This isn't a joke, Dickon,' I say.

'Then he has to get the body out of the back door and round to the front of the inn and all the way along the road. He would have been seen.'

'What about the route across the meadow?' I ask.

'Carrying the body on his own?'

'Ben could have helped him,' I say. 'There's something weighty on Ben's conscience. He's been lying to me ever since we found the body.'

'Ben's got no stomach for a murder. In any case, he was serving us all evening. We'd have noticed if he'd been off dragging a dead body across the meadows and wading the stream. Unless you think he sprouted wings and flew. And where's the rider's lame horse while all this is going on?'

Dickon's arguments are sound, though I would have appreciated a little less use of heavy irony. If he's so clever, perhaps he has a theory of his own.

'Well, if Smith was a Royalist spy, then don't you think that he might have been killed by one of Mr Thurloe's agents?' says Dickon. 'In which case, it would be best not to enquire too closely into who or where or why, or even what happened to his hat.'

'You mean the rider was a government agent?'

Dickon nods meaningfully. 'Why not? These are dangerous times, John. A wise man sometimes looks the other way. Maybe you should too. It's none of your business.'

I wish this were true.

'Look, Dickon, I haven't told anyone else, but Smith was apparently asking after me. Harry Hardy overheard him talking to Ben. And Ben's not said a word about it – to me or anyone else, I think.'

'Then Harry probably misheard.'

'No, I think Smith somehow knew me, and the rider somehow knew me. I'm right in the middle of this, and I don't understand why.'

'Or Harry's getting deaf and you're plain wrong about everything else. Maybe the horse wasn't that lame after all, and your man just rode on innocently through the village and knows no more about the murder than we do.'

'Well, somebody killed Smith.'

'That's undeniable.'

'And Smith was staying at the inn,' I say. 'I should at least like to get a look at his room.'

'There'll be nothing there.'

'How do you know?'

Dickon sighs the sigh of a defeated man. 'I suppose I'll have to watch your back as usual.'

I try to remember when Dickon has ever successfully watched my back for me. Not in the days when we used to steal apples from the Cliffords' orchard certainly. Still, as I may have observed before, there's a first time for everything.

Early Evening

'You gave my good wishes to Dickon's mother?' says my mother as she darns some shapeless woollen object that may be one of my stockings.

'Yes,' I say. I did that.

'And the jar of preserved cherries? You didn't forget to take them?'

'Of course not,' I say. 'I remembered to take them.' I must now remove the jar from my saddlebag, where it has rested warmly for most of the afternoon and evening, and see if I can smuggle it over to Mistress Grice before she and my mother next meet and discuss fruit. I'll get Dickon to do it. That shouldn't be too difficult.

'Do you not think that Aminta has grown into a charming young woman?'

No, I don't; but we have at least moved away from the potentially hazardous subject of jam. 'She is quite pretty,' I say.

'But frivolous.' I don't add that she hits me, but it does seem a relevant consideration.

'Roger Pole will steal her from under your nose unless you take care. I don't know how you let things get into such a state.'

The last remark appears to relate to the shapeless woollen object in her hands. At least, I think it does.

'Legally,' I say, 'it could be accounted theft only if Aminta were my property. Which she is not. If Roger Pole steals her, I shall summon the parish Constable and raise the hue and cry. But he will not have stolen her from me. Why should Pole want to marry her anyway? I would have thought that a rich heiress would be more in his line.'

'He would, of course, be wise to seek out some rich heiress, preferably not too hideous in appearance and still of child-bearing age if at all possible. But young men are not always sensible in these matters. And Aminta is pretty enough to turn most heads – with the possible exception of your own.'

'I shall take that as a compliment.'

'She has always been very fond of you.'

'Fond? I think not, Mother,' I say. 'Not in any way that the term is normally understood.'

'*Very* fond of you,' my mother repeats in the belief that constant repetition eventually makes things true. 'Even if you don't credit it, Roger Pole does.'

'He told you that?'

'No, Aminta told me that. I think that she may have been making Roger Pole a little jealous. She can be quite mischievous.'

Well, that at least explains why Roger Pole, who had previously been obnoxiously, snottily civil, now seems to be my implacable enemy.

'Then I shall tell him that he has nothing to worry about, at least as far as I am concerned,' I say. But perhaps I shall not tell him today. If it pleases him, then let him imagine by all means that he has a rival. Not that I care one way or the other.

'Aminta has lots of admirers – your friend Dickon, for example,' says my mother. 'There! That's darned now. Please do take more care of them in future.'

'Lord, I'd rather she married Dickon than Roger Pole,' I say, taking the object from her. Yes, it's a stocking.

'Do you really see her as a farmer's wife?' asks my mother. 'She would end up like poor Mistress Grice. Such a shame for everyone. But as the wife of a prosperous lawyer, on the other hand . . . You really are most well suited.'

'In the sense that we are both vain and shallow and enjoy viewing our own faces in the looking glass?' I suggest. 'In the sense that we both have silly little stuck-up noses? In the sense that . . .'

'Tush,' says my mother. 'Nobody marries their twin sister. At least, not in this part of the county. In any case, neither of you has a silly stuck-up little nose. I simply mean that you are both good-looking young people.'

'Dickon says that I shall soon resemble a withered pippin stuck on a rake handle.'

'Dickon will soon resemble one of his own oxen. You are a little thinner than you were, but I have never seen my son so handsome.'

I laugh at this last piece of flattery. 'Like my father no doubt,' I say.

'Yes,' says my mother in all seriousness. 'He had few good qualities, but that was one of them.'

'It is the least important of qualities,' I say.

'So it is fortunate that Aminta has many others, even though you don't see them.'

'Then let Roger Pole appreciate them,' I say.

'The Poles are a very old family,' says my mother. 'I have it on good authority that they are descended from King Edward III. And until the war they were very rich. Their lands were confiscated by Parliament. Like Sir Felix.'

'No, not like Sir Felix,' I say. 'Sir Felix had to sell up to pay his debts and his fines. But the late Viscount, Roger's father, was, as I understand it, attainted by Act of Parliament, and his lands were forfeit to the State. It is a very different legal process.'

'The same result,' says my mother.

'But totally different,' I say.

My mother sniffs. She has her own view on the matter. You'd think she was the Lord Chancellor.

'So, Sir Felix would not regain the manor if the King were to return?' she says, burrowing into her bag for something else to mend. 'But Roger's father's lands and the title may yet revert to his heirs?'

'In theory. I mean, Parliament could reverse the attainder.'

'Is that likely?'

'Only if Pole ingratiates himself with those in power. Even then I doubt that Cromwell would wish to see him a viscount again, less still to have the expense of restoring his estate.'

'Then perhaps when the King returns . . .' She produces a shirt and examines it to see whether it is worth her attention or no.

'Mother!' I say. 'The King is not going to return. England will remain a republic for ever.'

'If you say so, dear. Just bear in mind that Roger, as a viscount, would be a very eligible young man, even with his pockmarked face. Do you want this old shirt repaired, or shall I cut it up for cleaning cloths?'

'You mean Aminta might wish to be a viscountess?'

'Her father might wish it for her and advise her accordingly. Some children listen to their parents. In my view, she simply needs a nice young man with good prospects in a respected profession. Such as Law, if you decide to complete your training. Perhaps I shall repair this after all. The holes are not so large.'

I pause because of my mother's unexpected 'if'. There is indeed some doubt in my mind as to whether I shall go to Lincoln's Inn, but I have mentioned this to nobody. My mother certainly can have no way of knowing.

'Mother, has it ever occurred to you that Sir Felix may be planning to restore his own fortunes by marrying you?'

'Marry me? Lord, Sir Felix knows how little we have.'

'You have this cottage . . . *house* . . . and you have an annuity.'

'Your dear father is, for all we know, still alive,' she sighs. She clearly wishes it were otherwise.

'You have had a letter from him?' I ask.

'Not since he left,' she says.

'You have had news of him from somebody else?'

'No,' she says, threading a needle.

It is not a convincing 'no'.

'Mother,' I say, 'have you heard from my father?'

'Do you suppose that I would keep such important news from you?'

'Of course not,' I say.

This talk of my father is, then, nothing more than a

ploy to persuade me that she would not listen to Sir Felix's blandishments.

'Promise me,' I say, 'you will not marry again without consulting me first.'

'If I receive another proposal,' she says, 'I shall let you know.'

'*Another* proposal?' I ask.

'Your father obviously proposed to me, a long time ago,' she says, but she is a little too pleased with herself for this to be the honest answer it purports to be. Sir Felix's designs, in any case, are all too clear.

'It would be a dangerous thing,' I say, 'to be allied to the Cliffords.'

My mother looks ready to say 'tush' again. She shakes her head. 'Why is it,' she says, 'that children can never imagine that their parents were young once? Why is it that they can never see that their parents are not completely in their dotage? Even at my age, I am not wholly averse to the thought of pleasure.'

'Is that true?' I ask, meaning, do children really think that?

'Oh yes,' she says – but so fervently I am no longer sure which question she is answering.

Dickon has undertaken to keep Ben Bowman talking – not a difficult task, even for Dickon. Nell is busy in the kitchen. The inn is unusually empty. Normally, this hour of the evening would provide much shouting, yelling and drunken singing to cover my footsteps. I shall need to be quiet. I am therefore creeping cautiously up the stairs of the inn to the three chambers that Ben optimistically reserves for paying guests.

I put my thumb gently on the latch and slowly open the door of the first chamber. The hinges squeak, but not, I hope, too much. I pause, listening for any change to the distant rise and fall of speech in the room below. I hear Dickon laugh a little too appreciatively at some remark of Ben's. I count to twenty under my breath; there are still no footsteps behind me on the stairs. I slip into the room.

It is simple and clean. The walls are newly lime-washed. There is a low bed large enough for two guests who do not mind sleeping in close proximity to each other. There is a small oak table with a candle upon it. Three large nails have been banged into the wall in case guests have anything they wish to hang on a large nail. That's it.

I tip the straw mattress almost onto its side and peer into the wedge of shadows and floating dust that I have created. There is no gold ring between the mattress and the boards on which it rests. I look under the bed. Nothing. Not even dust. Just a damp scent of newly washed wood. I look into the cracks in the floorboards, of which there are many. No ring. No blood. I tiptoe out of the chamber and onto the landing. Downstairs, I think I hear Ben ask 'What's that?' and Dickon mutter a reply. Even though I cannot make out a single word, I do not believe him. I doubt Ben does either.

Deciding that it is no worse to be caught in one place than another, I carefully open the door of the chamber opposite. This is even smaller. Two purplish smoked hams, propped up against the wall, suggest that Ben regards this as a storeroom. It would be a rare night indeed when all three chambers are full, and they must earn their keep in other ways. Apart from the ham, there is a small bed, a mattress, some creamy woollen blankets piled neatly on top. Nothing to suggest that a man might recently have died here, a rough hand over his mouth, his blood spilling out in scarlet streams. Nothing to suggest where he might have hidden a ring that he would have been better off not revealing to anyone in the first place.

On tiptoe but aware of the slightest sound, I cross the passage again to the remaining guest chamber. Gentle pressure on the latch produces no results. I put my shoulder against wood in case it is merely sticking in the summer heat. The door does not budge. It is clearly locked. Now *that* is more promising. I am wondering how strong the lock might be when I hear steps behind me. Dickon's conversational skills are clearly not as good as he claimed. A voice says: 'A rat indeed!' I turn.

'Can I assist you in some way, Mr Lawyer?' asks Ben. I get the impression he wishes to convey the message that this is his inn. Not mine. 'You seem to want to break down one of my doors. I can't help wondering why you should wish to do that, or why you are prowling amongst my chambers like a common thief – a common thief with large feet.'

'I simply wondered which of them Mr Smith had occupied,' I say.

'Had you asked me,' says Ben, very restrained, 'had you asked me civil-like, I could have told you that he occupied that one at the back.' He indicates the first that I inspected, with its three nails and no dust. 'Which may or may not be any business of yours, Mr Cambridge Lawyer, but now you do know.'

'And what's in this one?' I ask, indicating the locked door.

'Is there any reason why I should tell you?' asks Ben. Could that be a rhetorical question? Neither of us tries to answer it anyway.

'Smith didn't die where he was found,' I say, watching Ben's face closely.

Ben has previously been indignant or evasive. My transgression now apparently gives him the right to be angry and sarcastic.

'Does the back chamber look as though somebody died in it?'

'It's very clean,' I say. 'Recently scrubbed and polished. It does you credit. But what's in the other room, Ben? The locked one? I can get the Colonel to make you open it.'

'Why don't you, then, Mr Grey?' Like a bad smell that you can't at first identify, Roger Pole has oozed silently up the stairs. 'Creeping about like a common thief, are we?' He voices much the same opinion as Ben but places more emphasis on the word 'common'. He is not wearing his hat for once, though more because the staircase is narrower than his ridiculous plume than because he wishes to show respect for anyone or anything.

'I have the Colonel's authority to search the room,' I say, in the sense that I am sure he would have given me such authority had I asked.

'Oh, I doubt that,' says Pole. 'I think I would know if the Colonel had authorised you to do anything of the sort. I am, after all, his secretary, whereas you are . . . I'm not sure you are anything really, are you? A lawyer with no clients? You don't have to open that door, Ben. Not for Mister No Clients.'

Pole doesn't know any more than my mother knows that I am not planning to become a lawyer. Of course, he is still right that I have no clients.

Ben looks relieved at Pole's intervention and says: 'I had no intention of opening the door for Mister No Clients. I keep all sorts of valuable things in there. The door is locked for a reason.'

'Get along, Ben,' says Pole. 'I'll deal with this.'

'Yes, Mr Pole,' says Ben respectfully. And he's gone.

'I don't know what you're covering up,' I say.

Pole smiles.

'Or what influence you have over the Colonel,' I say.

Pole smiles.

'But I'm going to get to the bottom of it,' I say.

Pole smiles.

I stamp off down the stairs. Pole has dealt with it, and without the aid of his hat this time.

'I did my best,' says Dickon, as close to contrite as needs be. 'But you were banging away so much above our heads that I could hardly hear myself speak. Ben asked me a couple of times what the noise was, and I kept saying "rats" – but he would go and check.'

'He clearly didn't want rats chewing away at his hams,' I say. 'You more or less told him to go and find me.'

'Didn't think of that,' says Dickon. 'Next time I'll say "ghosts". They don't eat much, do they?'

'Not as much as rats,' I say. 'I'd have been better off with nobody down here than you.'

Having deeply offended Ben, I have now deeply offended Dickon. 'Well, next time you can have nobody for all I care.'

'Sorry, Dickon,' I say. 'I'm sure you did your best.'

We are drinking ale in an obscure corner of the inn. We could sit anywhere, but we decide we like the obscure corner. It's a quiet evening – just the two of us and Ben Bowman now that Pole has snatched up his fine hat and gone away to report back to the Colonel whatever lies he is choosing to report. Ben occasionally glances in our direction, half contemptuous, half wary. The contempt is reserved mainly for me. I'd drink elsewhere, but this is the only inn in the village.

After a while, Nell comes over to us to ask us if we wish to order anything else. Her manner is reserved, but she does not imply she thinks we're complete idiots. That's kind of her. Strangely, she seems more distant to Dickon than she does to me. Maybe her expectations of him were higher.

Nell's pretty, with her dark curls and ringlets. Her clear, almost bell-like tones are as unlike the slurred local accent as you could hope to find. She's not from round here, as I say, but nobody minds in her case. When we choose to be, we are quite tolerant of strangers. I sometimes wonder if Ben realises what an asset she is to the house or why his sales increased after he married her. Probably not.

'So, it's another pint of ale for you young gentlemen?' she enquires.

'If it's as good as the last,' I say, hoping a little ingratiation may speed my forgiveness.

'If it is delivered by your own fair hands,' says Dickon, succeeding perhaps a little better than I.

I expect Nell to smile, feeble though the compliment is, but she simply says, 'It would be difficult to deliver it with any other part of my body.'

She turns on her heel and departs with a swish of petticoats and the tap of her shoes on the boards. A few minutes later Nell delivers the ale with her own fair hands, precisely as requested, and is gone almost without our noticing. It's a trick she seems to have.

'We have to get into that room,' I say when I am sure she is gone. 'Two chambers unlocked, one locked. I'll lay you any odds you like that there's something interesting in there.'

'Smuggled brandy probably. Ben only takes risks if there is a clear profit to be made. And he never takes sides. Look, John, you seem to have got it into your head that your horseman came here and killed Smith. But *nobody* saw him, and there's nothing upstairs to suggest that was what happened. How long have we known each other?'

'Why, all our lives, pretty well.'

'Then take some advice from your oldest friend. I've helped you with your investigations and you've got nowhere at all. You've just made Ben annoyed with both of us. Nell too, though she shows it less. Just go back to your lawbooks and stop worrying about things that don't concern you.'

'It *does* concern me,' I say. 'Smith and the rider both knew me. Whatever they were here for, I'm already tied up in it somehow.'

'You're not so tied up that you can't walk away. And you still ought to recognise danger when you see it. One man's already dead, in case you hadn't noticed. I'd rather not find you with your throat cut one fine summer morning.'

'I'll think about it,' I say.

Westminster

*T*he pearly light of a summer evening is scarcely strong enough to penetrate the grimy panes of glass, but it is enough to examine papers by. Some activities are in any case better suited to a world of shadows. The room is small, low and panelled with dark wood. A map of Europe hangs on one wall, but that is the only ornamentation considered necessary. It is, however, well provided for by way of tables, and each is heaped with papers, some flat, some rolled, some folded, some sealed, some tied with red or pink ribbon. Just the desk at the centre of the room is neat, clear, uncluttered.

The man seated at the desk holds a piece of paper in his hand. His pale, oval face gives away only what he wishes it to give away – or perhaps not even that. His flowing hair would be the envy of many an ageing cavalier. His large square linen collar and his spotless black velvet suit would be considered appropriate by many a fashionable Puritan. His chin is delicate, his nose slightly fleshy. His gaze is untroubled, but his fingers fidget with his cuff. You could meet him in the street and not realise that he is one of the most powerful men in the country. You could talk to him for half an hour and still not realise it. There is, in a sense, both more to him and less to him than meets the eye.

He rubs his temples with a careful circular motion and squints again at what he has been reading. He has read a great deal and still has a great deal more to read. Since 1652 his formal title has been Secretary of State. He is also Clerk of the Committee of Foreign Affairs and head of the Post Office. This last is of great assistance in the role for which he will be remembered by history – Cromwell's spymaster. His name is John Thurloe.

There is a knock at his door – polite but insistent. Thurloe says nothing. The door opens anyway. His secretary, Samuel Morland, shuffles in with a diffidence that is too mannered, too all-encompassing to be quite genuine. Morland smiles, because he always does. His is the mask of comedy to complement Thurloe's mask of tragedy.

'You wanted to see me, my lord?' says Morland.

Thurloe pauses. Did he? Something about the idleness and corruption of the officials at the port of Dover perhaps. Or the idiocy of their agent in Cologne. He has been engrossed in the letter he holds, and whatever he had wanted to discuss with Morland is no longer as important as it had seemed. He glances again at the letter. Well, while Morland is here, he may as well get his views on that.

'An interesting piece of correspondence, Sam. We intercepted it a couple of days ago. The original was enciphered. I have had it written out in clear to save us both a few minutes. Judging by the charming simplicity of the code, this comes from the Sealed Knot. What a sad waste of half an hour it was for them to encode it and us to decode it . . . It is addressed to the Benedictine convent at

Ghent, for onward transmission to Sir Edward Hyde at Charles Stuart's court in Bruges – the usual route, in other words.'

Morland gives the letter a resentful sideways glance. 'I could have dealt with this for you, my lord. It really is not worthy of your time.'

'It isn't the first I've seen from this source,' says Thurloe. 'An agent with the code name 472. Have you come across any like this, Sam?'

'I have seen similar letters,' says Morland. He is trying to hide his displeasure, though Thurloe is unlikely to notice it even if he doesn't. He clears his throat. 'I was unaware that Your Excellency had also seen them. You should have told me. As you said, they are scarcely worth the effort of decoding . . .'

'Did I really say that?' asks Thurloe, running his finger down the page. 'They are interesting, and honest too. The writer says that they have many willing volunteers to rise against the Lord Protector, but that they possess just six muskets, and those old and of little use. The muskets are hidden safely, however, where none shall ever find them. As you know, that means the stables of the local inn. Then this signature 472. Would you like to hazard a guess as to where these letters are from?'

Morland has exchanged the mask of Comedy for the mask of Polite Regret. 'The West Country . . .' he suggests.

'Essex,' says Thurloe. 'The same village we had suspicions about the year before last. There were references to Saffron Walden and Royston and to a church dedicated to St Peter – it didn't take too much effort to pinpoint the place.'

'You have the advantage of me, coming as you do from that part of the country,' says Morland. 'But I congratulate you, my lord, on your deductions.'

'You know that part of the country well enough, Sam.'

Morland purses his lips. 'The visit you sent me on was short,'
he says.

'And unproductive,' says Thurloe. 'Still, I would have expected
you to remember . . .'

Morland turns from the contemplation of his own manifold
inadequacies and back to the letter.

'You wish me to return and investigate the matter?'

'No, Sam. I have things in hand.'

'Colonel Payne is the magistrate there, I think,' says Morland. 'I
assume you have written to him.'

'I won't trouble him for the moment,' says Thurloe. 'I'm not at
all convinced of Payne's loyalty to the Lord Protector.'

'Payne and the Lord Protector were once the best of friends – at
least, that is what Payne told me.'

'They were once. I've sent somebody else to investigate anyway.'

'When?'

'Three days ago.'

'Has he reported back?'

'It's still a little early. Don't worry. I chose somebody who can
take care of himself. His instructions were to be in and out as
quickly as he could.'

Morland pouts and says nothing.

'Perhaps you could also take a look at the original encoded
version,' says Thurloe. His manner is almost placatory. Morland
decides he may as well be placated.

'I'm not sure it tells us much more,' says Morland, quickly
scanning the sheet of paper.

'A lady's hand?' Thurloe suggests.

'An effeminate hand,' says Morland. 'Perhaps disguised.'

Thurloe considers this for a moment, as if unable to believe that
the enemies of the State would stoop so low. 'The lines are even

and consistent,' he says. 'I doubt this is feigned. Reseal the original, Sam, and send it on to Ghent. Keep the translation.'

'I'm not sure it is worth sending . . .'

'You'd have them know we intercepted it? It's part of a numbered sequence, Sam. Get a clerk to dispatch it to the Abbess today. Watch out for the reply when it comes. Have there been replies to those that you saw earlier?'

Morland frowns as though remembering a minor matter with some difficulty.

'None as yet. But they may be sent by a different route. I shall look out for them, as I say.'

'Odd thing that,' says Thurloe. 'They have another route but choose to send this coded message by the regular post. Especially when it is common knowledge that we take a personal interest in all letters that pass through the postal service.'

'Perhaps, my lord, they do not appreciate the zeal with which we carry out our duties.'

Morland smiles at his own joke, but Thurloe merely nods as if at an undisputed fact and returns to his paperwork.

Another Dawn

I am here, at the crossroads of the village. I am here because I am no longer in bed. I am no longer in bed because, because . . .

It is, I tell myself, because it was another warm night, and I could not sleep, though I threw to the floor first my red wool blanket and then my linen sheet. As the edge of the world finally began to turn from blue-black to rose pink, I stood at my small, square window, breathing in air that was at last cool and faintly damp. I dressed as quietly as I could and crept down the polished stairs in my stockinged feet. I pulled on my boots, unlatched the door and stepped out into a young morning full of promise.

And yet I have slept before on hotter nights than this, and slept well. So perhaps I am here for some other reason.

I retrace my steps to the dung heap. I look carefully at the ground. Others have been here during the last day and night, but they would not have effaced the blood that should have soaked into the ground had Mr Smith died where he was found. So where did you come from, Mr Smith? I circle the dung heap, then again a little further out, then again further still. I walk northwards along the grassy edge of the highway, watching out for any traces of blood. There are none. I cross the rutted road, the dust powdering my boots afresh as I do so with a fine, buff film, and retrace my steps, eyes glued to the ground. Thus it is that I fail to see Aminta, basket in hand, until I almost run into her.

'Lawyers rise from their feather beds earlier than I thought,' she says. 'Or have you spent a second night guarding our village crossroads? That would have been very brave of you.'

Something in her tone tells me that she does not really regard lying in a drunken stupor as brave.

'You are right,' I say. 'We lawyers never sleep. But what brings you out so early? Are you gathering the morning dew for your complexion?'

'That's done on May Day,' says Aminta, 'as you well know. And my basket is better suited to mushrooms. So, what *are* you doing, cousin John? I watched you tramp up the road and then back down again, staring at the ground all the while. If you were not yourself looking for dew to gather, then what can you have had in mind?'

'I was looking for bloodstains,' I say.

'Better late than never,' says Aminta. 'I think, however, that bloodstains so close to the highway would already have been noticed by somebody.'

We both look eastwards. Here begins the path across the meadows to the inn – the shortcut that Aminta proposed as being convenient for murderers, and Dickon as inconvenient for lame horses.

'We're going that way,' she says, hitching up her skirt and petticoats. 'Look lively! Half the village will come tramping across the meadow soon, with or without dead bodies.'

The land here is ever moist, even without a dew, and the morning grass quickly wets my boots and the trailing hem of Aminta's dress; but by the first stile we make an interesting discovery. On the ground, half hidden in the sward, is a small silver button. I pick it up and hand it dutifully to Aminta. She raises her eyebrows.

'One of Smith's buttons was missing,' I say.

'And his buttons were like this?'

'Very like this.'

She examines it dubiously. 'Well, it might be worth sixpence, so our time has not been entirely lost.'

Her tone is dismissive, but I can tell she is pleased. She has been proved right, after a fashion. I take the button back. There is a small piece of black thread attached to it. I know that Aminta will tell me that black thread is also much in use in Essex this year, but I think I . . . we . . . have found something significant.

Halfway across the meadow is a fence and second stile. I examine the top bar and am rewarded by the sight of a brown stain on the wood.

'What about that?' I ask.

Aminta's view is that it could be almost anything that is brown. I rub a wet finger on the stain, then sniff it. Not too bad. I lick my finger cautiously. Blood? Or something else? Perhaps better not to know. But we do have a button. So, Mr Smith, were you brought this way and dragged over two stiles, leaving behind a silver button and perhaps a brown stain?

I am aware that we should have been doing this yesterday, as Aminta suggested, not now, when any blood would have dried, and the grass has sprung back to its old shape. We press on to the stream, where we come up against a problem – I can, of course, take off my boots and wade, but it is rather deep for skirts and petticoats.

'Well, what are you waiting for?' asks Aminta. 'Or are you suggesting I have grown too heavy for you to carry me?'

I remove my boots and stockings and, lifting Aminta in my arms, I wade into the stream. The water is colder than I expected and, with Aminta's additional weight, I feel my feet sink into the soft and clinging mud of the riverbed. Waterweed wraps itself around each leg. I stumble once or twice, but we get across with Aminta's skirt no more than a little moistened. I deposit her on the far bank.

'So,' says Aminta, 'what can we learn from that?'

My immediate thought is: 'If you're going to take a girl any-where, go by the main road,' but Aminta's thought is different.

'Smith was probably heavier than I am,' she says, 'and it was night-time. If you struggled with me – and I fear you did – then the killer would have struggled even more to get Smith over the stream.'

I thought I'd done rather well actually. 'So?' I say.

'If the killer came this way, either he was very strong, or he had a friend to help him with Smith's body.'

'Maybe he just dragged the body across.'

'Were the clothes soaking wet and covered with weed?'

'No.'

But I think I knew that already: my cloaked rider with his arms under Smith's shoulders, while Ben stumbles across the stream clutching the legs. Then up the other bank, with Smith still in the state you would expect if he'd gone by the main road.

'True,' I say. 'Easier returning, of course, though the water is icy and the mud unpleasant.'

'What a shame you will have to go back in it then,' says Aminta, 'for I see that your boots and stockings are still on the far side.'

I sit on the stump of an old willow – what we call the 'arse end' in this part of the world – while Aminta dries my freezing feet with the hem of her skirt. This too she finds amusing, though I cannot say why.

In the winter this meadow is usually flooded many inches deep, but now rose-pink ragged robin and blue bugle grow amidst the grass, with patches of dark green sedge and rush in the hollows. Across the flat fields we can see the backs of the cottages, their thatched roofs golden in the early-morning sun, and the steep, tiled mansard of the inn.

This is certainly the quietest way from the inn to the dung heap. Though it is, as Dickon said, rarely used by those on horseback, two men with a manageable burden – two men who knew the lie of the land – well might tread lightly through the sedge and across the cold stream, and might go back just as peacefully. On their return, they would skirt the stables, as we are about to do, and find themselves in the yard at the back of the inn.

What they would not necessarily have discovered, as we do, is Dickon.

'Good morning, Dickon,' says Aminta.

'Good morning, Mistress Aminta,' says Dickon.

It all seems a little cool and formal. They've known each

other as long as they've known me, though Dickon never got invited back to the Big House as I did, which may still rankle, assuming my mother is even half correct that Dickon once admired Aminta. The smaller the village, the longer people's memories – and this is a very small village.

Well, I'm pleased to see Dickon anyway. I slap him on the back as hard as I can, though he scarcely seems to notice. 'So, what brings you here?' I ask.

'Nathan said that Ben needed some cucumbers,' says Dickon, looking out across the meadow the way Aminta and I have just come. Viewed from here, the dewy ground sparkles, and the path of the stream is a snaking band of mist.

'I thought Ben grew his own,' I say.

'Does he? Just like Nathan to get these things wrong. I might equally ask what brings you – the two of you – here.'

'John had a fancy to gather morning dew,' says Aminta.

'This has nothing to do with Smith's death, I hope,' says Dickon, rightly ignoring any suggestions that I might be worried about my complexion.

I tell him about possible blood on the stile and the undoubted silver button, though I can see Aminta would prefer that I mentioned neither. 'I thought I might search the stables,' I add, 'before Ben's up and about.'

The three of us look up at the blank windows of the inn. No member of the Bowman family yet stirs. So, I am less likely to be discovered this time. At least, that is what I hope.

'You actually *want* Ben to find you poking around again?' says Dickon. 'Where are you planning to drink in future then? Royston?'

'You'll be watching my back,' I say, 'so I'm not going to get caught.'

'He won't catch me, that's for sure,' says Dickon. 'And I'm not watching anything.'

'Come on, Dickon; we're in this together.'

'No, I'm not.'

'Well, I'll come with you,' says Aminta. 'Let me just hitch my skirt up if I'm going into those stables. Dickon – take this, please.'

She passes her basket to Dickon and makes some trivial adjustment to her costume, then gets him to pass it back again. She looks at me significantly, though what she has proved apart from the fact that she can get Dickon as well as me running around in her service, I'm not entirely sure.

Dickon is scowling at her. 'Fine,' he says to me. 'I'll watch your back, if that's what you want.'

I punch Dickon's shoulder to demonstrate my eternal gratitude. My fist meets firm, unyielding muscle.

I turn to Aminta, pleased that we now have Dickon's help as well, but she is tight-lipped and tapping her little foot. There is clearly something she was expecting me to do that I have not done, but, since she has not told me what it is, I have no idea how I am to do it. I doubt that she wishes me to punch her on the shoulder anyway.

'I'll go first,' I say.

The door creaks slightly as I open it no more than I have to. Three bodies slide into the twilight world of the early-morning stables, one gathering up her skirts as she does so. A little of the day creeps in after us in a long shaft, but the rest is tranquil gloom. Ben is playing host to one horse at present, but that is not what interests me.

Dickon stays close to the door, peering out into the yard.

The low sun lights his face. He is not happy. Aminta stays close to Dickon. She is not happy either. I, meanwhile, examine the floor carefully, pushing back the dung-caked straw with my foot. My dusty, wet boots are now also covered with straw and horseshit, which one or other of the servants will have to remove when I return home. I begin to suspect that I am wasting my time – that I have been drawn here on the silken thread of Aminta's folly. But I am wrong. Underneath the straw in one corner is a large area of earth that is stained red brown. I don't need to lick my finger and taste that. And I was clearly looking in the completely wrong place last night. It was obvious really – part of the inn but far enough from the parlour not to be overheard. The only questions are: was Smith lured down here, and if so, by whom? I straighten up, wondering what else the stable may tell me. I do not expect to learn it by way of a disembodied voice.

'What are you doing there?'

The sound is not ghostly, but I have a preference for voices with bodies attached to them. I spin round twice, though completely sober, and still see nobody.

'You better get out of here, mister!'

If I can find no good explanation for the voice, then I may take its advice, and right speedily. Dickon and Aminta have already left, which I find cowardly.

'Clear off, you poxy horse thief!'

Finally, I look up and see a pale face peering at me from out of the hayloft.

'Who are you?' I ask. I draw myself up to my full height and allow him to notice my well-cut coat and breeches, and the white lace at my cuffs and throat. I jingle the coins in my purse. He doesn't know how much I still owe my tailor, and the music of pennies is as pleasant as that of gold crowns.

'I'm Jem. I look after the horses. Sir.'

'Come down. I have some questions to ask you, Jem.' I take from my purse a silver coin and hold it up. Though this does not constitute a full contract, Jem has been shown the Heads of Terms. He descends via a ladder that I should have noticed before.

'So, Jem,' I say, 'you were sleeping up there?'

'I'm up and dressed now, as I should be.'

'Yes, but I mean, you normally sleep up there?'

He is immediately cautious, and his manner suggests that he has studied cunning at the same academy as Ben Bowman. Whatever he says next will be a lie.

'Maybe,' he says.

'You must know where you sleep,' I say.

He swallows hard, wondering how to deny this. Most people do, after all, know where they sleep.

'Were you up there the night before last?'

'I don't have to tell you anything. Master says.'

'Mr Bowman may be your master, but he can't exempt you from giving evidence concerning a felony. So, Jem, tell me: you wouldn't recall some men coming into the stables the night before last? You wouldn't be able to tell me if there was a fight, say?' The light from the half-open door glints briefly on the half-crown. I get the impression that, for Jem, the coin represents considerable wealth.

'Men coming into the stables? I don't mind anything like that. Not the night afore last. Sir.'

'What's that bloodstain doing on the floor over there?'

'A horse knocked himself on the stall and bled. Bled shocking.'

'It's a lot of blood.'

'There was a big old nail sticking out. Went in a long way.'

'Really? Big old nail? That's careless in a stable, isn't it? Other people will come and ask you these questions again, Jem. Wouldn't you rather tell me about it now? Maybe the version without fictitious nails. If you tell me, I'll make sure nobody punishes you. But if you try to hide what happened, then you could be hanged with the others.'

'What others?'

Well, if you're going to be hanged, it's helpful to know what company you'll be in.

'The men who killed Mr Smith,' I tell him. 'So, what do you say, Jem?'

'A horse knocked himself on the stall and bled.'

No nails this time. He's taken some of my advice to heart then.

'Don't you trust me, Jem?'

'No.'

Jem's looking over my shoulder rather than into my eye as an honest man might. I believe him though.

'If you'd like to talk about anything, I'm at the New House,' I say.

Jem's nod in reply commits him to nothing. He doesn't do a lot of talking and certainly wouldn't go as far as the New House to do it.

'A horse knocked himself . . .' he begins. The phrase has ceased to sound practised and now strikes the ear as the mere repetition of words – a spell or a charm maybe, to ward off evil.

'Thank you, Jem,' I say. I hand him the coin. This worries him more than the threat of a mere hanging.

'What's that for? I didn't tell you nothing.'

'It's for *not* telling Ben Bowman I was here this morning. You haven't seen me here. And I haven't spoken to you.'

He nods and adds this proposition to the one about the horse. His lips move silently as he commits it to memory.

'Was it this horse that hurt itself, by the way?' I ask, pointing to the only one present.

'No,' he says, as if relieved not to have to lie. 'It wasn't that one.' He starts to climb the ladder again.

'Thanks, Jem,' I say. 'It was brave of you to tell me as much as you have.' That should worry him a bit. Maybe enough to get him to come and tell me the rest.

I take a glance at the horse as I leave though. It's a nice grey. In good condition. And it looks a bit familiar. Actually, I'd swear that the last time I saw it, it was carrying a cloaked rider and was limping a bit. I cautiously check his hooves. Three old, rather worn horseshoes and one gleaming new one. Right fore. The horse nuzzles my hand, which might mean he recognises me too, or might mean that he is hoping for a carrot. I short-change him with an affectionate pat and slip out through the door.

Dickon and Aminta are waiting outside.

'Well, you two weren't much help,' I say. 'It was only Jem, the stableboy.'

'So I gathered,' says Dickon. 'I thought we'd keep out of sight in case having all of us there just scared him off.'

Aminta nods, for once agreeing with Dickon.

'That was quick thinking,' I say.

'Still, we heard most of what he told you,' Dickon adds. 'Sounds as if he saw something then.'

'I'd say so,' I say. 'Maybe after he's thought a bit, he'll tell me.'

'You reckon?' says Dickon with a frown.

'Yes,' I say, 'I reckon. Why shouldn't he trust me?'

The sun is now well up and warming our backs, and we can hear noises from inside the inn. Rather than retrace our steps, I suggest that we take the narrow path that leads from here by the leafy ways to the forge. Dickon nods.

'Don't you need to see Ben about cucumbers?' asks Aminta.

'Sounds as if Nathan got the order wrong. Looking all ways for Sunday, that boy is.'

'Hadn't you better find out what Ben did want then?' she says.

'I suppose,' sighs Dickon. 'As if there's not enough work to do on the farm without this.'

Aminta takes my arm – the path, it seems, is stony – and we set off. Dickon stays, whistling tunelessly. I suspect it is in fact his mother who does most of the work on the farm. Still, I hope he doesn't have to wait long for Ben.

I like Ifnot's forge. I always have. It's a magic place where hard iron is made to yield and where broken things are made whole. Earth, water, fire and air all meet here. It's a place where sparks fly and steam rises and the great, blackened leather bellows create their own gale a thousand times a day. It's a place of chaos and order. And in the middle of it all, Ifnot's arm rising and falling, and the music of metal on metal. He can wield the hammer as well in his left hand as his right. He has the two strongest arms in the village.

Ifnot is already up and coaxing the fire into life. I greet him. I hope he won't want to clasp my hand. He waves, then strides towards me, his own giant paw outstretched. How can a man with a limp move so fast?

'God be with thee on such a fine morning, John Grey,' he

says. 'And with thee, Aminta Clifford.' His voice is deep. Solid. Well wrought. You would have to trust somebody with a voice like that.

I try not to wince as my fingers are lovingly crushed. Somebody must tell him one day that other people have normal bones and muscle.

'Another busy morning?' I ask. Perhaps on my way home I will stop and put my hand in the cold stream.

'Not as busy as yesterday,' he says.

'Did you shoe a grey horse yesterday?'

'I shod horses of almost every colour you can name. Yes, I shod a grey. He'd lost the shoe on his right fore. The other three were a bit worn, but Ben said they were good enough.'

'Did Ben say it was his horse?' asks Aminta.

'No. Ben said it was Smith's. Said he was taking care of the horse until somebody claimed it. He could end up giving it free board and lodging for some time, I think.'

'That would be kind of him,' says Aminta.

'Or maybe he's planning to sell it,' I say.

'Nice animal,' says Ifnot. 'It would fetch three pounds even if you couldn't tell the buyer exactly where you found it. Which Ben might not choose to.'

I nod. No further questions for the witness, my lord.

Aminta is clutching her still-empty mushroom basket when we part company under Ben's damson tree. Sir Felix may go hungry at dinnertime.

I look for Dickon, but there is no sign of him.

'What do you think your friend was doing at the inn so early in the morning?' asks Aminta.

'Delivering cucumbers?' I say.

'Maybe,' says Aminta. 'Or maybe something else. Do you think Jem will decide to tell us what he saw?'

'Give him time,' I say. 'We've plenty of that after all. Jem's not going anywhere.

Ben emerges from his front door and starts to open the shutters noisily, though the first customer is unlikely to arrive for another hour or so. It is still too early for many travellers to be abroad. Ben does not look happy. Perhaps he still feels my behaviour last night does not entitle me to more than a sour glance. Or perhaps he has weightier troubles. I ask him politely.

'It's that dratted boy,' he says. 'I went to the stables just now and he's gone.'

'For a walk?' I suggest.

'What would a stableboy want with a walk?' he asks. 'No, he's gone. He's taken his clothes, and in a moment I'm going to check what else he has taken. There's gratitude for you.'

'Could he have gone home?'

'Home? His father died at the Battle of Worcester, he says. His mother died last year. He has no home apart from this one. I took him in out of charity. Only been here a few weeks – scarcely knows anyone in the village even. What can have possessed the boy? You didn't see him on the road, did you?'

I shake my head. 'No, I didn't see him on the road.' The half-crown has sealed a double bargain in this respect.

Ben gives a sigh and opens the last of the shutters with a crash. He stomps off back inside the inn. He seems not to have even noticed Aminta is there. He has a lot on his mind.

Another Evening

The sun is still hovering uncertainly above the horizon. The honeyed air of a summer evening hangs heavy over the cornfields. Though this June day has been long enough for anyone, I have made no further progress. I have re-trodden the path behind the inn several times in the hope of discovering something fresh. But the meadow has yielded all it intends to yield. I have also been again to the Big House to tell the Colonel what Aminta and I had discovered. He showed polite interest in my silver button and noted the very small amount of black thread attached to it. He nodded dutifully at my report of the blood in the stables but felt that, on balance, it was possible that a horse really did knock itself on a stall. He thought, moreover, that a stableboy might run off if ill-treated or offered a better position, and that a horseshoe might need replacing. He regretted that estate business had taken up much of his own time today, but a letter would certainly be sent to Mr Secretary Thurloe in the morning. He did not wish to detain me long in a stuffy room when I might be out enjoying the last precious moments of the day.

Thus I am trudging home, kicking up the dust with the toes of my boots. I do not see Sir Felix in the shade of the willow until I am already at the stream. I think he may have been waiting there some time.

He rises stiffly from the fallen tree on which he has been sitting, rubbing his back as he does so. It does not look the most comfortable of seats or a place that one would stay without a purpose.

'John!' he says by way of a greeting. 'A happy chance indeed that we should meet again so soon.'

'Good evening, Sir Felix,' I say cautiously, because I feel that I have been waylaid, and I fear that he may be hoping to accompany me to the New House with a view to supper. I am afraid, moreover, that if I arrive with this uninvited guest my mother may not be as annoyed as I would wish her to be.

'You are on your way home,' he observes.

'Yes,' I say. 'A little past the dung heap, and then I am there, as you know.'

'The dung heap . . . It does not inconvenience you at the New House?'

'No,' I say truly. Then, thinking not to make my mother's house too attractive a prize for Sir Felix, I add: 'I mean that I myself do not object to the smell of dung. In the summer the stink of it might offend those of a sensitive nature.'

'It would not trouble me then,' says Sir Felix. Perhaps it wouldn't. I am wondering whether there are other lies I might usefully tell to the detriment of the New House, but Sir Felix's agile mind has already moved on. 'So, it was up yonder that you discovered the poor fellow ...'

'Smith,' I say, for Sir Felix seems to need prompting. 'Yes, right by the dung heap.'

'Thank you,' he says. '*Smith*. Of course. Have you discovered aught else about his death?'

'Nothing more than Aminta will have told you this morning,' I say.

'You have seen Aminta today?'

We both pause, each realising that we have revealed something we may have been unwise to reveal.

'I saw her when she was collecting mushrooms,' I say. 'Did she not mention that?'

'Yes, of course,' he says. 'Though she only said a little of your thinking on the matter ...'

He waits for me to say something, but I don't.

'Has Colonel Payne taken any further steps to apprehend the killers?' he asks.

'I believe not,' I say.

'I wonder why?' He has taken off his hat and is smoothing out the lace band.

'He is a very cautious man,' I say. 'I think he is being badly advised. The matter must be reported to the Coroner and to the neighbouring magistrates.'

'Badly advised by Roger Pole?'

'Yes,' I say.

'But you do not suspect Roger Pole of the murder.'

'The Colonel vouches for him. Though I have one good

reason for suspecting him, his plea of alibi is good. He could not have done it.'

Sir Felix smiles. 'And you have no plans to report the incident yourself to London or to the magistrates in Saffron Walden?'

'It is a matter for Colonel Payne,' I say.

'That is a very proper sentiment. But you have no suspicions of your own?'

He waits for me to say more, but I don't.

I expect him to offer to walk home with me, but he replaces his hat on his head and bids me a very polite good evening. I frown as he departs. Aminta has clearly told him nothing of our discoveries this morning. That, surely, is odd. But perhaps I shall not tell my mother that I met Sir Felix and did not invite him home to supper. There is often an innocent explanation for most things.

Letters

Letter Number 12
29 June 1657
*To Sir Edward Hyde, Lord Chancellor, c/o The Abbess,
Benedictine Convent, Ghent*

*A man named Henderson has arrived in the village, but his
throat was cut before we could ascertain his Purpose. I do not
need to tell you how inconvenient this is for all of us. P makes
no attempt to investigate the matter, which I assume is as you
would wish. P is in correspondence with Scotland. I therefore
hope to have further news of 444's intentions shortly, which I
shall convey to you.*

*For M – If you desire me to stir P into action, then please inform
me what sort of action you desire.*

The weather continues fine, and the damsons are ripening nicely.

Yours to command,
472

Letter Number 13
30 June 1657
To Sir Edward Hyde, Lord Chancellor, c/o The Abbess,
Benedictine Convent, Ghent

I write in some haste. It seems likely that Henderson's death was witnessed. I shall, of course, do everything in my power to keep the witness quiet. P continues to do little about this or any other thing. He has been visited by Thomas Clarges, whom you will know by repute. I shall ascertain as soon as I can what 444's views are.
For M – I await instructions.

Your ever-obedient
472

At the New House, and Afterwards

'All I am saying,' says my mother, 'is that it would have been better had it been done properly.'

'I thought that was what I was saying,' I said.

The difficulty is that our words are the same but our meanings very different. My mother's meaning is that she resents being denied the pleasure of a perfectly good burial. For her, funerals are now a form of entertainment – entertainment to which, as she points out, even Lord Protector Cromwell cannot possibly object. Moreover, each funeral is to be celebrated as being somebody else's and not her own. Each funeral is a small personal triumph over mortality. But Smith has been buried quietly, at night, without a passing bell, and now rests under the clay in St Peter's churchyard. My mother was not invited. That is her meaning.

My meaning is related more to the absence of any investigation by the Coroner prior to interment. I also fear that a letter may still not have been dispatched from our local magistrate to Mr Secretary Thurloe, setting out the circumstances around Smith's death. I am increasingly concerned about how little the Colonel has done. And I think I know who to blame.

'Pole is behind it,' I say.

'Mr Pole?' my mother asks. At least she does not call him Viscount Pole.

'Yes,' I say, 'I am sure that it is Pole who is urging the Colonel to do nothing.'

'I doubt that Mr Pole favours idleness. In fact, I have always thought he was a very vigorous young man,' says my mother.

She is wrong. Pole is not vigorous. He is an arrant coxcomb, bedecked in lace and ribbons. You cannot have bunches of ribbons to your breeches and be called vigorous.

'Something odd has certainly happened,' I say, bringing the conversation back to the merely relevant. 'Why should Jem vanish like that?'

'Ben had no idea where he might have gone?'

'No,' I say. 'It would seem that he has no friends – in this part of the country at least.'

'Then perhaps he will not be so hard to find,' my mother says. 'Let us hope so anyway. As for the horse you found in the stables, that is perhaps not so very remarkable. There are, after all, many grey horses. And I myself have always felt that one horse looked much like another.'

'It *is* the one I saw,' I say. 'Or else the county is full of greys with one new horseshoe.'

'Not full exactly,' says my mother, 'but surely not that uncommon either. Horseshoes need replacing all the time.

And grey horses are very common. Really, unless you were the horse's mother, I don't believe it is possible to tell them apart.'

So, unless I can show beyond reasonable doubt that I am the horse's mother, I am wasting my time arguing further. I shall return to the inn and enquire whether Jem has been found. It will give me something to do while I decide what I ought to be doing.

The walk gives me time to formulate some questions that I might still ask of Ben if I can but take him aside quietly. When I arrive at the inn, however, I find a traveller is already sitting at the table near the front door in the welcome shade of Ben's damson tree. He smiles and nods at me in a friendly way. I do neither. There is not the slightest thing about him suggesting I should trust him.

He is dressed in a suit of clothes that may have once been russet or may have once been crimson. A cloth is tied loosely round his neck. The cloth is none too clean but looks cleaner than his neck. As a small concession to fashion, one greasy lock of hair has been tied up in a bright red ribbon and rests easily on his shoulder. One stocking is rolled down, but he does not appear to have noticed. The clothes, like him, are large and comfortable. The coat is decorated with small holes, burned into the cloth by sparks from his pipe. This has not deterred him from smoking a pipe this morning. A glowing speck has just landed on his arm, where it burns brightly for a moment and then fades to a small black point. He sees the black spot and slaps at it. He misses by several inches but is content.

'You are John Grey,' he says to me eventually.

'I am, but you have the advantage of me, sir,' I reply.

'Have I? Then you may call me George Probert.'

'And how do you claim to know who I am?'

He draws again on his pipe, not because he needs time to think, but because he wishes to make me wait a little longer. 'I have been seated here for an hour and watched an assortment of yokels and hobbledehoys and bumpkins going about their normal business. None of them appeared to be John Grey *Artium Baccalaureus Universitatis Cantabrigiensis.*' He pauses and belches loudly. 'Come and sit with me, Mr Grey. I think we shall be friends, you and I.'

I take the seat opposite him, though I am no wiser than I was before about how he knows my identity. He slaps his hand on the board and bellows for the landlord. He gets the only one available: Ben's round, pink, worried face appears through the doorway.

'Two tankards of ale, Mr Bowman,' he says. 'I have not yet taken my morning draught, and this young man looks thirsty enough.'

'Certainly, Mr Probert,' Ben says, rubbing his hands together, but Ben's eye is very much on me. When he thinks Probert is looking elsewhere, he mouths something at me, but Ben's mouthing is just that. He opens his mouth and closes it like a fish out of water, leaving the spectator no wiser than before. It would seem, however, to be a fishy warning of some sort, and one that he does not want Mr Probert to see. This is still all I have to go on when the ale is delivered to us by Nell Bowman, who has appeared by our sides without either of us noticing her soft footfall. She's always there somewhere in the background, making things work while Ben huffs and puffs.

'A fine young woman,' says Probert appreciatively. 'I'd make Bowman a cuckold if I had but time enough.'

'I believe her to be virtuous,' I say.

'She has refused you then, Grey? I am surprised and sorry for it. But I think she would not refuse me. Or the young farmer who engaged her in conversation earlier. They had a most earnest discussion, though too softly for me to be able to overhear it. A pity. Your health, my dear sir,' he adds, raising his tankard. '*Nunc est bibendum.*'

I respond in kind but in my native tongue. I decline to correct him on the subject of Nell lest I encourage him further. The 'young farmer' must have been Dickon, but their discussion was probably about the price of onions. I note that Ben has given Probert one of the smallest pint tankards he possesses, a sure sign of his disapproval. Sadly, I have its twin. I think my impersonation of a rat is still not entirely forgiven.

'You are recently returned from Cambridge, I think?' asks Probert. 'I understand that you were an ornament of Magdalene College.'

'You seem to know a great deal about me, sir,' I say, 'though I still know nothing about you.'

We eye each other across two untouched almost-pints of Ben's ale.

'Yes,' he says. 'That is very true. You know nothing about me. Your tutor at Cambridge speaks well of you, however.'

'Dr Grahame?'

Probert takes another long puff on his pipe. That is his only response to my question. I wonder if he will belch again, a fitting rejoinder to Dr Grahame's name in my humble opinion, but he does not. 'Your tutor commends your ability and your sound principles.'

'Did he?' I say. 'I don't think he ever said as much to me.'

'But he said it to *me*,' says Probert. 'People tell me things that they would not tell others. It is a way that I have. Or perhaps I read it in a letter he wrote to somebody else. That is a way I have too.'

Probert draws on his pipe, sending a shower of sparks flying in all directions. I instinctively brush the front of my coat, which is much newer than Probert's, though not so ridiculously foppish and new-fashioned as Pole's.

'Indeed,' I say very coolly. 'What business brings you to our village, Mr Probert?' I am determined he shall not have the advantage over me for long.

Probert raises his eyebrows as if to say that he has even more interesting tales to tell about Dr Grahame but that he will change the subject simply to oblige me. 'I'm seeking a friend of mine. Mr Henderson. Would you have met him by any chance? He might not be calling himself Henderson of course. He might be calling himself Mr Freeman. Or maybe Mr Jennings.'

'Is any of those his real name?' I ask. 'Or has he forgotten the circumstances of his baptism?'

'His baptism would not have touched on his surname,' says Probert reprovingly. 'Of course, he would possess a Christian name of some sort, but he would have had very little need of it.'

'I have met nobody here named Henderson,' I say.

Probert looks disappointed. 'Small, black man. Big belly. Livid scar on his chin. Dead probably. Have you noticed anyone like that walking about here?'

Well, I've seen a dead Royalist spy answering very much to that description.

'Or maybe he was calling himself Smith?' I ask.

'Smith? Of course. He used that name. Why not? A man

named Smith might pass unnoticed anywhere. He would be almost invisible to mortal eye. Did this Smith you speak of bear a fine scar below his mouth?'

Well, Probert doesn't lack courage. He must know I shall report this conversation as soon as I have the opportunity to do so. Or does he imagine I too am a Royalist? Smith clearly thought so if he was asking after me. The influence of my tutor, foolish or malign, lies somewhere behind these delusions.

'Perhaps,' I say, 'you would like to tell me who you are and what right you have to demand answers of anyone here.'

'Very good. I commend your caution. I like caution in one with whom I shall be working closely.'

'You seem mightily convinced that I am of your party,' I say.

'I would scarcely be drinking with you if I thought you were of the other party. Dr Grahame vouches for your loyalty.'

'Everyone here is loyal,' I say. 'Loyal to His Highness the Lord Protector.'

Probert roars with laugher and reaches across the table and slaps me on the shoulder. I think he could arm-wrestle Ifnot. 'Everyone! Ha! That is rare wit, Grey. Dr Grahame did not tell me that you were so merry. He told me you were as dull as a dog's arse. But he was sorely mistaken. Everyone here loyal to the Lord Protector . . . Ha! Very good indeed!'

I wonder if Probert is aware how loud his voice is. It rises from a mere forte for the word 'ha!' to fortissimo for 'dog's arse'. His closing statement is clearly intended to reach the good people of Suffolk.

'If you wish to trap me into disparaging His Highness,' I say quietly and just for the two of us, 'you will need to try much harder than that.'

Probert looks at me, disappointed. 'Really? Perhaps Dr Grahame was not so mistaken after all,' he says eventually.

'Whether Dr Grahame is mistaken about me or no, I am not in the habit of mocking His Highness the Lord Protector. As for your friend Smith, alias Henderson . . .'

'Grey, let me give you some advice.' Probert leans across the table. 'For reasons that I do not entirely understand, you look as if you may be about to lie to me. If so, then let your lie be large! Let it be bold! Let your lie contain some small germ of truth, if you will, but small lies are sad things that wither and die at the first blast of an icy wind. *Credat Iudeas Apella, non ego*! Only big lies are truly robust, though sometimes they throw out branches strong enough to hang a man from.'

'Who are you?' I ask for what I hope is the last time.

'A friend, Grey. At least, I hope we shall be friends. If we prove to be less, then it may chance that I must cut your throat in the course of my business here. But in the meantime, and in proof of my amity, can I buy you more ale, my dear fellow? Your Essex pints seem smaller than our London ones.' He drains his tankard at a single draught and slaps it down on the table. 'More ale, Bowman!' he yells. 'And this time we'll have the full legal measure. Or I'll have both your ears cut off and fried in your own butter!'

'No more ale for me,' I say.

Ben appears quickly. He may have been lurking close by, listening. He needs those ears. And butter's not cheap.

'More ale for me, but none for the pathetic milksop lawyer,' says Probert. 'So, Grey, what can you tell me of Mr Henderson? I know that he planned to pass through this village. He had business here, you might say. He was to report to us on the outcome of his endeavours, but sadly he has not. So, what became of him? There is but one inn, and yet the landlord has no clear recollection of him. I have asked him several times, but he has *no clear recollection*. The big lie, you see, would be to say that he is certain that nobody of that description came here. The small, feeble lie is to say that he might have been here or might not have been here, but that he cannot rightly say. And yet Henderson is, in my view, the most memorable of men. Not handsome, I will grant you, but that scar on his chin is much admired. His body is compact, but there is more menace in him, more genuine malevolence, than in ten others of a more normal size. Nobody who has been threatened by Henderson forgets him, and he threatens almost everyone he meets. *Homo homini lupus*, as you will be only too aware. Those who have not seen a man cannot be made to remember him, do to them what you will. But those who are not certain may find that their memories can be stimulated in all manner of ways. So, what say you, Grey? How is your memory?' He leans across the table and grins a lopsided grin. For a moment he has the appearance of an old, arthritic mastiff, hoping for a bone.

I stand. 'I wish you all the success you deserve in finding your friend,' I say. 'But I do not believe I can assist you.'

'Merely the success I deserve?' says Probert in simulated dismay. 'Oh dear. Poor Henderson. But I shall find him. And you are going to help me, for all your belief to the contrary. Do you want to know why?'

I give the brim of my hat the merest touch, perfectly civil. As I walk away, I do not look back.

'Another Royalist spy?' asks the Colonel. 'Are you certain?'

'He says he is a friend of this man Smith – or Henderson

as he knows him, though he seems to have had plenty of other names. He claims acquaintance with my old tutor, Dr Grahame, but that is, I think, a trick. The things he claimed to have heard from him were ... unlikely. I also think Probert plans to stay until he finds the body, which he may before long. The first place I would look for a fresh grave is the churchyard. We need to get word to Mr Thurloe, but we cannot wait for his response before we act. You must arrest Probert and hold him until he can be taken to London for questioning.'

'What did he say *exactly*?' asks Pole, who unfortunately is also here. Whatever I reply, Pole will proceed to show us how much better he would have handled things.

'He said he was seeking Henderson. And he tried to cozen me into making treasonable remarks about the Lord Protector. Oh, and he also spoke Latin – quoting Horace mainly, I think. He pointed out to me that man is a wolf to man.' I look Pole in the eye and add for his education: '*Homo homini lupus.*'

'*Lupus est homo homini, non homo, quom qualis sit non novit,*' says Pole. (I'll wager he was the Latin master's simpering little favourite.) 'And that is Plautus, by the way, not Horace. I am surprised, Mr Grey, that a man with any education would make such a simple mistake.'

'I said that Probert quoted Horace *mainly*,' I say, 'not that Horace actually wrote *lupus est homo homini, non* ...' I pause, trying to recall the last bit.

'*Non homo, quom qualis sit non novit,*' Pole continues smugly, his condescension made doubly effective with my helpful assistance. 'It would seem, in any event, that you have been given a warning, Mr Grey. You are vermin to be hunted down without pity by your fellow wolves. I do hope that you can run fast. As for arresting Mr Probert – my counsel, Colonel, is that we should tread carefully.'

'But he is clearly a malignant Royalist and a spy!' I say. 'He will make a clean getaway unless we act swiftly.'

The Colonel looks from Pole to me and then back to Pole.

'What say you to that, Roger?'

'We do not know who Henderson was. We know even less who Probert is. But the choice is yours, sir. You should arrest him if you are certain that is the right course of action.'

The Colonel would rather the choice lay elsewhere. But however long he dithers, it will not become my decision or Will Cobley's. He gives a profound sigh. 'Roger is right. It would be misguided to act hastily in this matter. We must watch this Probert and see what he does. After all, what was Henderson's motive in coming to this village? We still have no idea. Let us see where Probert goes and to whom he speaks. He can do little harm with Henderson safely in the ground, and, if we watch him, we may learn something of importance.'

Pole smirks.

'Are you asking me to watch Probert then?' I say to the Colonel. 'Until we are in a position to report him?'

The Colonel again looks at Pole, as if for guidance, and then says: 'There would be no hurt in your doing so.'

'Do try not to let him catch you spying on him,' says Pole. 'It might, if you will accept my advice on the matter, be better not to stomp around too much.'

I scowl at him, but he is now examining one of the ribbons on his glove. Ribbons on a glove always look ridiculous.

*

'They are all lying to me,' I say to Dickon. 'Pole especially.'

We are closeted in one corner of a Grice field, away from any prying ears or eyes. I am sitting on the ground with my arms wrapped round my knees. Dickon is on his back, staring up at the sky, a leaf of grass between his teeth. The land dips away gently to a distant hedge. The sun is warm. The buzzing of the bees is almost deafening. Soon, Dickon will complain to me again about the hardships of being a farmer.

'Pole?' says Dickon. 'I wouldn't trust a word he says.'

'I don't. Pole's a Royalist and, whatever his reasons may be, he's covering up the death of a Royalist agent.'

Dickon considers. 'Pole claims to be a good Republican now. It's all "my Lord Protector this" and "His Highness the Lord Protector that". It would do Cromwell's heart good to hear it, but my own ears ache with the repetition.'

'Why? Pole's father died fighting for the King.'

'If he wants his lands and his titles back, he'll need to prove he's Cromwell's man in spite of it. So, he works for the Colonel and professes his loyalty to the Protectorate ten times a day. I hear he's petitioned Parliament to reverse the attainder, much good may it do him.'

'Has he indeed? Well, however he may dissemble, the leopard doesn't change his spots. When the Royalist snake sloughs one skin, he just reveals a shinier set of scales beneath. I don't understand precisely why Pole is dissuading the Colonel from taking action, but he's hiding something. So is Ben. Ben can have hardly missed a bloodstain like that in his own stable. And he must have noticed he has the stranger's horse as his guest.'

I hear Dickon give a long sigh. 'You are wearing me out

with this talk of a strange horseman. I was *at the inn*. Don't you think I would have seen him or heard him?'

'But you saw the horse this morning.'

'I saw a grey horse. Stables often have horses in them.'

'It's the rider's horse.'

'John, you were too drunk to get home that night, and you still claim you can recall the horse as clear as day. Ben, who was sober all evening, swears it is Henderson's.'

'Perhaps I should ask Nell,' I say. 'She notices more than Ben.'

'I wouldn't trouble Nell,' says Dickon chivalrously. 'I mean, she'd have told us if she saw anything.'

Well, if Dickon says so.

'Then what's going on, Dickon? Horseman or no horseman . . . first we find a dead spy, and nobody seems much concerned. Now we have another Royalist agent alive and amongst us, and that seems to trouble folk as little. If the Colonel won't arrest Probert as a spy, I shall ride into Saffron Walden or Royston and get the magistrate there to issue a warrant. Unless they are also in thrall to Roger Pole.'

'I'll come with you,' says Dickon. 'I haven't been to Saffron Walden for a while. I need to order a new suit of clothes. This one is, as you observed, a little snug about the waist. As long as you don't also ask for a warrant to arrest the first gentleman you see on a grey horse.'

'Jem will give us a better description of the killer,' I say. 'Once we find out where he is.'

'My guess is that Jem hasn't gone far,' says Dickon. 'He has no money.'

'Well, half a crown perhaps,' I say.

'I doubt he'll be able to flee to France on that. He'll be in the village somewhere. So, where would he hide? In somebody else's stables? In a barn?'

'Or the woods. With the charcoal burners perhaps. We need to think, Dickon. We've used almost all the local hiding places at one time or another. If we can't find him, nobody can.'

'Yes, we know most of them, I suppose,' says Dickon. 'Though I always knew a few you didn't.'

'Well, I'll search the woods anyway,' I say. 'If he isn't there, I'll search the barns and outhouses – with the owners' permissions obviously. But first I have to observe Mr Probert for the Colonel.'

'Let me know how you get on with Probert,' says Dickon. 'It sounds as though your back will need watching again. Or is that Aminta Clifford's job now?'

'She could hardly watch my back worse than you have.'

'Really? I wouldn't trust her any more than I'd trust her father,' says Dickon. 'She just happened to be out in the meadow collecting mushrooms, did she?'

'Yes,' I say. Rather – it occurs to me – as her father just happened to be sitting by the stream.

'You be careful what you tell either of them Cliffords. Now, they really *are* dyed-in-the-wool Royalists.'

'I'll bear that in mind,' I say.

Probert has not stayed obligingly at the inn, where I might have observed him in comfort. As I ride back to the New House, I see him in the distance under the shade of the trees, strolling along the road in a leisurely manner. I negotiate with my mare, talking her into a reluctant canter, and I quickly find myself alongside the Royalist agent.

'Good day, Mr Probert,' I say. I am pleased to be mounted and he, for the moment, on foot. I look down on him from my saddle and nod pretty haughtily. He doesn't know this is the slowest mare in Essex. He looks up at me, squinting into the sun.

'Good day, Grey. That's probably the oldest animal I've ever seen anyone ride. If she could talk, she'd probably tell us stories of King James's time.'

'She's sound in wind and limb,' I say. 'And she can scarce recall King Charles.'

'Then she has a poor memory in addition to her other faults.'

'I mean that she was merely a foal in King Charles's day.'

'Never believe what the female of any species tells you about her age. I certainly wouldn't buy her myself.'

'I'm not selling her,' I say.

Probert shakes his head and chuckles. 'You wouldn't sell? You are a wit, sir. A rare wit and not as your tutor described you . . . How was it? As dull as a cow's backside?'

'A dog's arse,' I say.

'So it was. A dog's arse. That was well remembered – or perhaps people often describe you thus?'

'Have you found your friend?' I ask.

'I feel I am getting very close. I might perhaps be closer with your help, but for the moment I do well enough alone.'

'I am pleased for you.'

'Are you? I am not sure that everyone in the village shares that view. Or they all have very poor memories, like your horse. Or they are lying, like your horse. But I shall quietly prevail. And nothing shall stand in my way.'

'Possibly,' I say.

'Now, Grey, a small question that even you cannot fail to answer for me: am I going the right way to find the Rector?'

'No,' I say. 'You must return to the crossroads and turn left. You will find the church and the rectory on your right.'

'Thank you, Grey. Then it would seem that yonder footpath amongst the trees must also take me there and save me some precious minutes. *Fugit irreparabile tempus.*'

'Better to return to the crossroads. You may lose your way in the woods.'

'Oh, I think not. I rarely lose my way, Grey. It's something else I am noted for.'

'Then be careful to take the right fork shortly after you enter the woods. The left fork only takes you to the charcoal burners' huts.'

I watch him vanish into the trees. I hope that he has taken the right fork. But I cannot see that far.

I tie my horse up in front of the inn. Ben emerges almost immediately. He looks flustered and ill at ease. Dickon was right about one thing: it is difficult to imagine Ben having the resolve for a killing.

'What did you say to Probert?' he demands breathlessly.

'He was seeking his friend Henderson,' I say. 'I am assuming you already know Henderson and Smith are one and the same.'

'I thought that might be,' he says. 'What did you tell him?'

'What would you expect me to tell a Royalist spy?' I ask.

'Nothing, I hope.'

I nod. 'Your hopes are fulfilled.'

'None of the others will say a word either,' says Ben. 'They don't like foreigners in these parts – doesn't signify whether they are from Suffolk or London or Tartary. Probert will go back to his master in Westminster empty-handed.'

'Bruges,' I say. 'Charles Stuart is in Bruges. That debauched renegade would scarcely dare to show his face in Westminster.'

'Bruges? Is that right?' says Ben. 'Well, whether Probert's from Westminster or Bruges is all the same. He'll get nothing out of folk here.'

I nod again and think of the Colonel. It's true: they don't like strangers in these parts. The Greys have been here only two generations, but my maternal ancestors have lived in the village for six hundred years – just about long enough.

'Perhaps so, but the Rector can hardly lie about having buried a stranger in the graveyard of St Peter's.'

'Rector won't say more than he has to,' says Ben with a confidence that seems far from justified.

'Is there any sign of Jem?' I ask.

'No,' he says. 'What concern is it of yours anyway?'

'I'd just like to know he's safe,' I say.

'He's run off. Why shouldn't he be safe? Have you been talking to him about the murder? I hope you haven't done anything stupid.'

I think of Probert heading off into the woods. Nothing will stand in his way. And Jem has just the information Probert needs.

'I have to go,' I say to Ben. 'There's something I need to check. Now.'

'So you did talk to Jem.'

'I might have done.'

'Lord help us,' says Ben. 'First her, then you. No wonder he left in a hurry.'

I scarcely register what he says as I urgently kick my horse into a very slow canter. Later, Ben's words come back to me and I wish that I had stopped long enough to ask who 'she' is.

But I don't stop. I have done something stupid, and time is no longer my friend.

At Home with the Charcoal Burners

These paths into the woods were not made for riders, and the going is slow. The family's mare steps carefully and resentfully over tree roots while I duck low branches. She knows this is foolishness, even if I do not. We should be home by now and she in her stall. Eventually, we both emerge from the winding green tunnel into an irregularly shaped clearing a hundred yards across. In the centre of the clearing is a mound some ten feet high covered in earth, from which wisps of smoke are rising. Stacked around the edge are neat piles of coppiced hazel and ash. Under a crude shelter of planks and branches, heaps of charcoal lie waiting. The smell of new sawdust and smoke hang together in the air in equal measure. But there is no sign of any human being.

'Hello!' I call. 'Is anyone here?'

'Who wants to know?' A tall man dressed in a leather jerkin and leather apron strides purposefully into the clearing. He wears no hat, and his locks flow cleanly over his shoulders. His beard is long but carefully tended. Both hair and beard show a little grey, but not much as yet. He bears, with no visible effort, a trussed-up bundle of hazel. He drops the load with the rest of the wood and pauses, as if to take in my appearance as fully as I have just taken in his. He seems not entirely happy with what he sees. It is at this point that I notice he is also carrying a large billhook tucked into the right-hand side of his belt. I have no reason to believe that it was not freshly sharpened this morning; indeed, it would seem likely that this is what charcoal burners do. Even if I had my sword with me, I am not sure that it would help me much against the tall man. Or against his two friends who have just thrown their own loads to the ground and who seem no friendlier. I wonder whether it is worth explaining that, unlike the Colonel and Roger Pole, I am part of this country and that my mother's grandfather once owned this wood and, indeed, probably owned many of their ancestors.

'I'm John Grey,' I say. 'I'm looking for Ben Bowman's stable lad. I fear he may be in danger for his life.'

'John Grey . . . I recognise you now,' he says. 'Your face is thinner and more pinched than when I last set eyes on you. At least you're not here to steal apples.'

'It was Dickon Grice,' I say instinctively. Well, he was supposed to be keeping lookout anyway. 'But where have we met . . . ?'

The man smiles, showing a good set of white teeth. 'You'll have seen me around in the village, like as not. You can call me Kit.'

'Can I? So, Kit, have you seen Jem?'

'Yes.'

'Is he here? Can I talk to him?'

'That's up to him.'

I explain why the matter is urgent and why Jem should preferably not fall into Probert's hands. None of this appears to be news to Kit.

'He'll be safe here,' he says.

'But I found him easily enough,' I say. 'For anyone who knows the village, this is an obvious place to hide.'

'But Probert's a stranger. As a boy, he stole apples in another place entirely. He probably has no idea this clearing exists.'

'Well . . .' I say. Should I admit that I have just handed Probert precisely this piece of information? No. Probably best to give these good people as few reasons as possible for knifing me.

'Where do you suggest I go then, mister?' I turn to see Jem emerging from concealment under a heap of firewood. It is cleverly contrived – a roomy sort of tunnel with hazel branches packed tightly around. He might have stayed there safely for some time.

I could ask him how he is and whether he passed a comfortable night in the woods, but it seems better to get straight down to business.

'Jem, if you saw who the killer was, you need to tell me,' I say. 'Then the Colonel will arrest him and you'll be safe.'

Jem looks at me doubtfully. My bluntness has simply convinced him that he is far from safe now.

'If you won't tell me, will you tell the Colonel himself? I can take you to him, and we can keep you safe in the Big

House until the murderer has been arrested and taken to the county gaol.'

Jem looks at Kit and Kit shrugs. Though he clearly knows something of my past, what he knows is not especially to my credit.

'I want to talk to Mr Kit,' says Jem, and together they go to the far side of the clearing, where they hold a whispered conversation just out of sight. The discussion stretches to ten minutes; then Kit returns alone. I can just hear Jem's tuneless whistle, proving to the rest of us that he has not a care in the world.

'Jem says he'll go to the Big House himself tonight.'

'But I can see him safely out of the wood,' I say.

'He says he's safer on his own. He knows the paths.'

'I know them better than he does,' I say. 'I played in these woods almost every day as a child.'

Kit nods. 'So you did, John Grey. And in other places you were meant not to be. But Jem is not of a mind to trust anyone at present – even you. He'll be at the Big House tonight – or tomorrow night at the latest. I promise he'll come and not sneak off somewhere else. In the meantime we'll watch over him. And you'll tell nobody he's here.'

'You have my word,' I say.

As I start to lead my mare back through the woods, Kit says to me: 'Fear not, John Grey. Jem will keep his promise. Oh, and it *was* you scrumping apples by the way, for all you tried to blame Dickon Grice.'

I have arranged to meet Dickon at the inn. But first I call in at the Steward's cottage. Dickon might not approve, but I am sure his mistrust of Aminta is ill-founded and she will be pleased to hear that Jem is safe.

'God be praised for that,' says Aminta. 'Our visit to the stables frightened him. I would not wish harm to come to him as a result.'

She wipes her hands on her white linen apron. I have caught her in the middle of some domestic task. A stray lock of hair peeps out from under her lace cap. There is a rather endearing smudge of flour on her nose, which I decide not to tell her about.

'But you were right,' I say, 'about the meadow. That was the route by which the body was taken. And the blood in Ben's stable . . . You as good as told me to go there. How did you know?'

'A lucky guess,' she says.

'You hadn't already been to the stables and talked to Jem?'

'Why would I do that?'

'I don't know. Ben said that a woman had been to the stables.'

She shakes her head. I wonder what it would be like to kiss her on the nose exactly where the smudge of flour is sitting.

'Don't tell anyone where Jem is hiding,' I say. 'I promised it would remain a secret.'

She nods. 'Of course. I'd be careful who *you* speak to as well. This business may be more dangerous than you think.'

Once again she is right. Speaking to the wrong person could be fatal. I just wish I knew who the wrong person was. I wonder whether to tell Aminta that Henderson had been looking for me. Perhaps she can make some sense of that puzzle. But, in the same way that I know I am not going to kiss her on the nose, some instinct – or is it Dickon's warning?

– makes me hold back from giving her this information. I wish her a polite good day, pick up my hat and depart for the inn.

Though I cannot tell Ben exactly where his boy is, my oath does not, I think, stop me letting him or Dickon know that Jem is safe.

The inn is crowded on this summer afternoon. The Colonel rarely visits it, having his own brewhouse and his own cook, but he is there, sitting at a table with Roger Pole. Dickon is already there too, talking to Nell. Nell nods and hurries off.

'Ordering ale, I hope,' I say.

'Ale? No, our last ham was not salted enough and has turned. I need to bring a new one.'

He acknowledges, however, the wisdom of buying me a drink and orders two tankards from Ben. When I think nobody is listening, I lower my voice and say to him: 'I've found Jem.'

Dickon knows, of course, that I went to see the charcoal burners today, so I am not entirely surprised that he just nods and does not ask where. I am grateful for this. 'But he is coming to the Big House tonight or tomorrow night,' I add, 'and will tell the Colonel what he saw.'

'I thought you didn't trust the Colonel.'

'I am hoping that Jem's evidence will release the Colonel from whatever enchantment Pole has placed him under,' I say. 'He may then finally take some action.'

'And nobody except you knows where Jem is now?'

'Only the people he is with,' I say.

Dickon nods thoughtfully.

'You didn't tell Aminta Clifford, for example?'

'Why do you ask?'

'I saw your old mare tied up outside her house when I was riding here.'

'I just called—' I say.

'Her and her father – malignant Royalists, the pair of them. Did she try to get any information out of you?'

'No,' I say. Because, to be quite honest, she didn't try to get anything – I just told her. Not much though. No need to mention it to Dickon.

I am looking round for Ben, because I wish to tell him the same, when Dickon grasps my shoulder.

'Jem!' he says. 'I'm sure I saw Jem through the window!'

I look out into the bright sunlight but see nobody.

'He's changed his mind then. Something must have happened.' I jump up from my seat. 'I'll go out and find him.'

I leave Dickon guarding our pots of ale on the low table and walk swiftly to the door and out into the dry heat of a June afternoon.

The road is deserted. I look both ways along the dusty highway, but nothing stirs on this sleepy summer day, except the topmost branches of the oaks in the Park. I stand for a moment, listening to their gentle hiss and swish high above me. If Jem was ever there outside the window, he has concealed himself well.

I stamp back into the inn to find that Dickon has not only misled me but has failed even to guard our ale. His chair is also empty, and both pewter pots stand unattended, though, I am pleased to see, still full.

Dickon re-enters from the door to the stable yard. 'I wondered whether he had sneaked round the back,' he says. 'But there is no sign of him. I'm sure it was Jem though. Perhaps he came to collect something from the stable.'

'He's eluded us if so. At least nobody has drunk our ale,' I say, lifting the tankard to my lips. Somebody has, however, slipped something under my drink. In the place where it sat until a moment ago is a folded sheet of paper. Where it has touched the tankard, it is slightly damp. I unfold it. It reads:

POLE HAZ THE RINGE IN HIZ HATTE

Well, doesn't that change everything?

Pole's Hat

It is fortunate that Pole is looking the other way, because at this precise moment my whole being is concentrating on his hat. It looks, you might say, much as any other hat would look. But it is possible that, concealed in the broad lace hatband or pinned somewhere inside the crown, there is a gold ring bearing the Stuart coat of arms. I could wait until he leaves the hat aside and secretly question it. But a ring found there covertly will not answer. It must be seen to be found in the hat by as many people as possible – including the Colonel. My fear, of course, is that the ring is nowhere of the sort. Perhaps I shall seize the hat from Pole's head and, after an increasingly fevered search, be obliged to return it to him with muttered apologies. Perhaps I shall then leave the parlour with the laughter of many people ringing in my ears. Perhaps Pole will never let me forget it. This must be considered.

'Well,' says Dickon, 'are you just going to sit there?'

'But who left the paper?'

'I don't know. We were both out of the room, weren't we?'

I leave Pole's hat unwatched for a moment and look round the parlour. Is it slightly less crowded than before? The Colonel still sits with Pole. Cobley and Warwick have taken a break from their labours, as has Harry Hardy, and the three are in a lively conversation with Nell Bowman. With the light from the window behind her, I notice what a fine profile Nell has. I wonder if she is happy here in this small village with nobody except Ben's customers for diversion. She keeps her own counsel on that and, I suspect, many other things.

'This is no gentleman's hand,' I say, looking again at the paper. 'The letters are large and ill-formed.'

'Looks good enough to me,' says Dickon, scrutinising it again. 'The hand of a plain, honest man, though perhaps not a scholar as you are.'

'I don't know,' I say. 'What if it's disguised . . . ?'

'When ifs and ands are pots and pans . . .' says Dickon contemptuously. 'We do the thing now, or we lose our quarry.' He grasps the paper in his hand and stands up.

'It was under my tankard,' I say. 'Whoever wrote it wants me to do it.'

'One tankard is much like another. The note doesn't have your name on it. It could have been intended just as well for me.'

'But, in the end, it was under mine.'

Dickon yields the paper reluctantly, and I walk slowly across the room to where Pole is sitting. I'm not sure why I haven't let Dickon do this. I'd have enjoyed watching him seize Pole's hat, and the risk to my own reputation would have been negligible. As it is, my heart is beating hard, and I am having difficulty controlling my breathing.

'Good day, Mr Pole,' I manage to say.

He looks up at me and nods.

'I think you should remove your hat,' I say.

'Have we not already discussed my hat, Mr Grey?' he asks. 'It interests me less than it interests you. And I am happy with it where it is.'

'Then I shall have to remove it for you,' I say.

He is not expecting me to whisk it off his head and so is mighty surprised to see it in my hand, the plumes bobbing up and down. He is too outraged even to protest. His face is a dangerous shade of scarlet.

'Thank you,' I say. 'This would appear to be a very expensive hat.'

He recovers enough to splutter: 'It most certainly is. Better than any hat you are likely to own, Grey. And I'd be much obliged if you would return it to me, unless you plan further buffoonery to amuse the people of this village. Remember, Grey, that you are a gentleman – almost – and try to behave in a fitting manner.' He stretches out an over-optimistic hand. As if in imitation of every school bully, I move it just beyond his reach.

There is a chuckle behind me. Whatever else I may have achieved, I certainly now have everyone's attention. I wonder what exactly I shall do next.

'Yes,' I continue, 'a very expensive hat, though perhaps not as valuable as what you keep in it.'

For a moment Pole seems to think that I mean his head or something of the sort, because he is almost on the point of agreeing with me. Then he sees that I am examining the inside of the crown.

'Grey – have you gone mad?' he asks.

He is slightly, but only slightly, ahead of me in this question. And the answer is probably 'yes', for the crown of the hat is empty. No ring is pinned inside. The hatband it is, then, as my worst nightmare becomes reality. My fingers probe the lace inch by inch all the way round the hat. It's just lace. I look inside the hat again. At this point I notice that most people in the inn are laughing. I don't think they are laughing at Pole.

Roger Pole's contemptuous sneer is good, even by his standards. 'My hat, if you please, *Mister* Grey.'

I pass the hat back to him, trying to come up with some form of words that is both a sincere apology and clever enough to win me back a little of the regard I have just lost. I don't have long to do it.

'Wait!' says Dickon behind me. 'I saw the ring.'

I have rarely been so pleased to hear his voice. The inn is suddenly silent.

'What ring?' asks Pole. But it is written on his face that he knows there is only one ring that can be of any interest to us. His eyes too now search the hatband in vain.

'It's there.' Dickon reaches out and takes the hat from Pole's limp grasp. Dickon's fingers tease away part of one of the feathers and there is the ring – not in the crown of the hat, not in the band, but sitting neatly round the downy base of one of the plumes. It is smaller than I was expecting – big enough only for the smallest finger of a small man's hand – but it bears the royal crest.

'. . .' says Pole.

'I suppose you are about to claim that you have never seen the ring in your life,' I say.

Pole wisely makes no such claim. He would, however, like to kill me at the first convenient opportunity.

'This is Henderson's ring,' I say.

'If you say so,' Pole snarls. No wonder he is so familiar with the habits of wolves. 'But you must have put it there yourself. You must have slipped it over the feather when . . .'

'That would be a clever trick indeed,' says Dickon. 'In front of all these people. He's a lawyer – well, almost – not a conjuror, Mr Pole.'

This is better. I hold up the note for all to see. 'Thus I was informed of the ring's whereabouts,' I say.

I look round the room, but there is no rush to acknowledge authorship of the document.

'Did anyone notice who left the note beneath my tankard?' I ask the silent room.

The Colonel now speaks. As ever, his is the voice of well-considered reasonable doubt. It is the sort of voice that makes you think twice about what you had taken for granted all your life. 'It is a gold ring certainly. But how do we know that it was the murdered man's? Is anyone here prepared to say that they saw it close enough to identify it now? Come, who will own to having seen Henderson with it?'

There is little enthusiasm too for confirming that this is Henderson's ring, though many must have seen it. Feet shuffle on the wooden floor. The Colonel seems to have won the day. Then a voice from the doorway says: 'I can identify it. I can most certainly identify it. That is Henderson's ring. That is my dear friend's ring.'

We turn. The vast bulk of Probert's body is blocking out

the light and warmth that has been flooding in through the door. His face is one of pure tragedy. He is a man about to die of grief. Then, having perhaps made his point, his expression relaxes and he smiles at us all.

I turn to look at the Colonel and see that he is as white as a sheet – whiter probably than those supplied in this inn.

'Well, Colonel Payne,' says Probert, 'I am delighted to meet you at last. *Salve, domine*! I might almost have thought you were avoiding my company. Will you not now arrest your secretary for Henderson's murder? I have rarely seen more convincing proof of a man's guilt, at least without resort to thumbscrews and the rack.'

The Colonel looks at Pole as if seeking advice on Pole's own arrest.

'You and the Constable must take Pole into custody,' Probert continues, 'until he can be lodged more securely at the county gaol. Who is Constable here?'

'Cobley,' says the Colonel with a sigh.

'Not I,' says Cobley. He begins an interesting analysis of the election and period of tenure of village officials, touching on the responsibility of magistrates to ensure that successors are appointed timeously and with due regard to their previous service.

'Enough!' bellows Probert. Cobley is immediately silent. 'You, Cobley, and you, Payne, take Mr Pole to the village lock-up.'

'You'll need to get Harry Hardy's pigs out first if you are planning to use it as a gaol,' says Cobley.

'It'll need a new lock,' says Hardy. 'Had to break the last'n to get the pigs in. Damnation nuisance it was.'

'No matter. He can be more securely housed at the manor,' says the Colonel.

'You mean the Big House?' says Cobley. 'Folk round here call it the Big House.'

'I mean the Big House,' says the Colonel. 'It is built on the foundations of the old castle. The cellars are deep and very strong. They date back to the time of Henry the Second.'

'Henry the First,' I say. 'Your cellars date back to the time of Henry the First. And it wasn't a castle exactly. It was more of a . . .'

'Thank you, Mr Grey. Their precise date, give or take a Henry, does not affect the strength of my walls – unless you wish to correct me on that too? And Mr Pole will in any case give his word as a gentleman that he will not attempt to escape.'

'Some enemy of mine put the ring there,' splutters Pole, still very much the wolf at bay. 'Grey . . . if this is your doing I . . .' He is close to being speechless with anger, which proves neither innocence nor guilt, though the feeling of the company is tending towards the latter. He's not from round here of course. For my part, I decide I prefer a speechless Pole to any of the other Poles we might have.

'That is all as it may be,' says the Colonel. 'But on my word of honour to these people, Roger, you will be housed securely at the manor until the evidence can be properly assessed and your innocence established. And I further give my word that you will not even try to escape.'

'If you do try to escape,' says Probert, 'it may chance that you don't get very far.' He chuckles. But the joke is a private one, and he is not inviting any of us to share it with him. Even me.

*

'I am sure that Roger Pole cannot be the murderer,' says my mother.

Long experience of my mother tells me that her view of his innocence is based imprimis on Pole's being the heir to a nonexistent viscountcy, supplemented by his ability to pay oily compliments to one and all and to my mother in particular. It takes no account, as far as I can tell, of the indignities that I have suffered at his hands. Or of the known facts.

'He had the ring, Mother,' I say. 'And the ring has been missing since Henderson died. He must have been involved.'

'But he claims he knew nothing of the ring until you produced it from his hatband. I do like lace on a hat, don't you?'

'It was not in his hatband,' I say, skating swiftly over that part of my investigation. 'It was secured round the shaft of one of his ridiculous plumes.'

'And you were informed by this badly penned and unsigned letter?'

'Unsigned but wholly accurate letter,' I say.

'No gentleman would form his letters so ill. And no gentleman would denounce another clandestinely. Why did the person who wrote the letter not just accuse Roger himself? Why get you to do it?'

'Because . . .' I say. But this has worried me too. Somebody has ensured that Pole is accused without having to accuse him. 'That is true. *Condicio dulcis sine pulvere palmae*, as Mr Probert would doubtless say.'

'I have no idea what you are talking about,' says my mother.

'To win the palm without the dust of racing,' I say.

'I am very little the wiser,' says my mother. 'You should

tell a story in decent plain English or not at all. People who pepper their discourse with Latin phrases are merely showing off. Did anyone else accuse Roger?'

'No,' I say. The crowd has enjoyed the possibility of his guilt, but nobody had felt able to offer evidence against him.

My mother nods as if proved right. 'Who is this Mr Probert anyway?'

'Another Royalist spy, like Henderson.'

'Ah yes, I had heard he was called Henderson,' says my mother.

In some respects, we are a village without secrets of any kind. Though not in others.

'Jem at least is safe,' I say.

'Ben's boy?'

'That's right. He is in hiding in the woods, but I have persuaded him to tell the Colonel what he knows.'

'I hope that's wise,' says my mother.

'Don't worry,' I say. 'Probert will never find him where he is.'

My mother looks doubtful, but we are interrupted by a visitor. A female visitor. She asks to speak to me alone. She is angry. She is very angry. It may be because I have had Roger Pole arrested. In a few minutes I shall find out.

Pole's Promises

I let Aminta call me various things. It is, I know from long experience, the shortest way. Occasionally, the thought occurs to me that she is rather pretty when she is angry. But most of the time I am ready to dodge when she hits me. It's something I've been practising since Aminta was three years old.

'I had no choice,' I say when I am allowed to say anything.

'No choice?' For the storm has not yet blown itself out. 'No choice? Even if you chose to doubt my word in the matter, could you not have approached Roger privately, somewhere other than the inn, and asked if it was true?'

'You mean that he would give me his undertaking as a gentleman that it was untrue?' I say.

'Yes,' she hisses. 'You should have heard of such things, even if you have no personal experience of them.'

She's been talking to my mother then.

Still, *ira furor brevis est*, or hopefully anyway. I must concede that, with hindsight, my believing an anonymous and badly written note rather than her own assurances might seem disrespectful to her, but in a moment Aminta will have to calm herself. She too has no choice. She hasn't hit me yet. So, she still needs me reasonably undamaged for some plan of her own.

'In any case,' I say, 'what is Roger Pole to you? You may feel his arrest is an injustice, but it strikes neither at you nor at your father.'

'Yesterday,' she says in very measured tones, 'Roger Pole asked for my hand in marriage.'

I remember my mother warning me that I might lose Aminta to Pole. And I remember Pole saying that Aminta was quite pretty. But surely he said that only to annoy me.

'And you, of course, refused him,' I say. 'And therefore feel a sense of guilt, which has manifested itself . . .'

'I told him that I would marry him,' she says.

'Why?' I say. It seems an odd thing to do. Even for Aminta.

'Let's see, shall we? I have no money. My father has no money. We live in the cottage that our own steward once occupied. We cannot pay the rent even on that. When my father dies . . . No, I cannot begin to contemplate what my position will be then, without a friend in the world. If I do not marry, what else am I supposed to do? Shall I beg in the street? Shall I take in washing? Should I sell my body on market day in Saffron Walden?'

'Of course not,' I say. It would be entirely the wrong place to sell her body. Even on market day.

'And if I do not marry Roger Pole, who else am I to marry? I have long given up any hope that you will ask me.'

'But . . .' I say. 'You mean . . . ?'

'I've always liked you, ever since I was a little girl, even if you did try to hide from me in a tree.'

'You knew?'

'Of course I knew. I was six. I wasn't entirely stupid. I saw you the moment I came out into the garden. But you were having such fun up there that I pretended to blunder about as if you were too clever for me. I just wanted you to be happy up there for as long as possible.'

'Did you?'

'You were so sweet then. So confident of yourself, but at the same time so easy to deceive. Just like a puppy. I'll wager it took you days to realise that I'd tricked you.'

'About twelve years,' I say.

'You are still sweet now of course. And still touchingly easy to deceive. I missed you so much when you went away to university. When you came home last Christmas, with your studies at Cambridge almost finished, I hoped you would come and visit us and maybe . . . Well, in the end we didn't see you at all. And Roger came to visit us often. That was when I realised that we would just remain friends, you and I. We are still friends, aren't we?'

'Yes,' I say. 'We are friends.'

I reflect that just occasionally we realise that we have got something very wrong and it may not be possible to put it right again. Ever. All is not lost of course. Pole may yet be executed for murder. Because I know he is guilty.

'John,' says Aminta, 'you *know* Roger is innocent. You have to help me prove it.'

She touches me lightly on the arm. Something inside of me melts. Even my resolve to see Pole's head on a spike on

London Bridge fades away like the morning mist when the sun breaks through. I try to recapture the happy image, but it is gone.

'Pole had the ring,' I point out. 'In his hat.' But I don't find myself at all convincing. Why would anyone hide an incriminating ring round a feather in their own hat? And Pole's surprise seemed genuine enough.

'An enemy placed the ring there and then left the note for you.'

Aminta's theory, you will have observed, is not so different from my mother's theory. That may or may not be an inexplicable coincidence.

'Pole has nothing to fear in any case,' I say. 'The Colonel says he was at the Big House all night and will, I am sure, vouch for him. I saw him leave the inn. So did lots of others.'

Aminta shakes her head. 'Roger left the inn, as you say, but there will be those who will argue that he could easily have returned. After all, the Colonel has to sleep, does he not? And the Big House is close to the inn and to its stables. The point is, John, that those who stayed at the inn have each other to confirm their plea of alibi, should it be needed. It is not that Roger's story can be vouched for and that the others are under suspicion – quite the reverse in fact.'

'But Jem will give evidence to the Colonel. He will say who killed Henderson.' Which is, it suddenly strikes me, a powerful argument for Pole's innocence. 'Jem would scarcely insist on telling it to the Colonel if he had seen Roger Pole killing Henderson. He must know Pole is the Colonel's secretary. Why would he then trust the Colonel rather than me?'

'A lot rests on Jem returning safely to the village,' says

Aminta. 'He's just a boy. How do you know that he won't run off somewhere where we cannot find him?'

'He will return,' I say. 'One of the colliers – Kit – gave his word.'

I realise that this too is less substantial than it might be, but it seems to be enough for Aminta.

'If he is with Kit, he will be safe enough.' Aminta stands on tiptoe and kisses me on the cheek. 'Thank you, John. I knew that I could depend on you.' She raises her hand to the same cheek and strokes it gently with the back of her hand. She smiles at me. It is the most beautiful smile I have ever seen. Then she is gone.

An hour later my mother knocks cautiously at the door.

'You are sitting in the dark,' she says to me. 'Do you not want a candle, John?'

'No,' I say.

'Would you like some supper. Martha has prepared . . .'

'No,' I say.

'So, you just want to sit there in the dark all evening by yourself.'

'Yes,' I say.

My mother closes the door softly. She understands.

It is with trepidation that the following day I approach the Big House again. I walk slowly up the gravel path and admire the exterior. This is the third house to be built here. The first, a small, uncomfortable fortified manor, dated back to the days of Henry I. By the time my great-grandfather gave his ill-advised support to Essex's rebellion, only the cellars of the old house survived. A homely red-brick house well suited to a long-established but only moderately wealthy county family had been built over them. The Cliffords contemptuously pulled it down brick by brick and erected a modern stone building in a severe classical style, with much glass and many ogees. It was the cost of this rebuilding more than anything that began their ruin. The Colonel looks unlikely to repeat their mistake of overspending on construction work. Indeed, the exterior is acquiring an uncared-for appearance that my mother has already commented on. She would do things differently.

I take a deep breath and knock on the door.

'Roger Pole is well, thank you for asking,' says the Colonel. Though it is sunny outside, I must say there is a distinct chill here at the Big House.

'I trust the cellars are not too uncomfortable,' I say. I hope, in view of my promises to Aminta, that I am not smirking too much. I try to remind myself that I now wish Pole well rather than merely dead.

'He has the freedom of the house and the Park,' says the Colonel. 'And I have his word *as a gentleman* that he will not attempt to escape.'

I am led by this to understand that, were I his prisoner, I would not necessarily be entitled to the same terms.

'Obviously,' I say, 'it was not my intention to . . .'

'What *was* your intention, John? I've been wondering a lot about that. If you did not desire Roger's arrest and imprisonment, what could your intention have been? You found it necessary to strike shadily and without any warning to Roger or to myself. Surely, I deserved more from you than that, even if your understandable jealousy of Roger clouded your judgement. Surely, you might have trusted me enough to bring the charges to me – as your magistrate and your lord of the manor – rather than make a public accusation in some low inn.'

The inn is nothing like as low as some in Saffron Walden, but that is not perhaps the Colonel's point.

'At least there is a witness who will clear him,' I say.

'Who?' asks the Colonel.

This enquiry rather forestalls my own question: did Jem arrive safely at the Big House last night?

'Ben's stableboy, Jem. He was in hiding with the charcoal burners in the wood but was to come to you last night – or tonight if not – and tell you what he saw.'

'No boy came here last night. And what did he see?'

'He would tell you and only you. But I believe he knows who the murderer is.'

'Not Roger?'

'You will need to hear what he says. But no, I think not.'

'If you think not, why did you accuse him?'

'Because . . .' I say. I suppose it was because I had not then spoken to Aminta. Yes, I could have worked it out for myself before that, but for some reason I did not. Since I have not said any of this to the Colonel, he looks on, still mystified.

'Let us hope that Jem comes here safely tonight. Does anyone else know where he is hiding?' asks Colonel Payne.

'No,' I say, meaning that I can trust everyone I have told. And yet I am strangely worried that Probert may somehow have discovered the secret.

'Good,' says the Colonel. 'Well, if he comes here, I am forewarned.'

'It is important that Probert does not learn of this,' I say.

'Surely, it must be possible for you to arrest him. At least until we know that Jem is safe.'

'That might be difficult,' says the Colonel.

I think of the Colonel's face when he saw Probert. He knows who Probert is. He is at least a little afraid of him. And Probert orders people around with a confident manner.

'Are you saying he is not a Royalist spy?' I ask.

'That would seem probable,' says the Colonel. 'Probert is in any case likely to be busy today with the exhumation of Henderson's body.'

'Would he not need your authority for that?' I ask.

'Yes,' says the Colonel. 'Yes, he would.'

'And you granted it?'

'I must have done, mustn't I?'

The Colonel looks as coldly as before. However little he trusts Probert, he trusts me just a bit less.

'I must go to the charcoal burners' encampment,' I say. 'I pray to God that Jem did not leave there last night and is preserved safe and well. At least his whereabouts are concealed for the moment from those that might harm him.'

The Colonel says nothing but looks out into the Park, where the deer are cropping the short grass. There seem to be fewer of them than before, but some may be hiding in the trees. It's a good place to hide.

'He left last night, as he promised,' says Kit. 'And he knew the paths well. I had told him where to climb the wall into the Park. I should have gone with him . . . intended to go with him . . . but he left without even telling us. I think he trusted nobody.'

'He may have fled,' I say. 'Gone to Colchester or Cambridge

or London. Or Ely. He is only a boy, after all, and owes nothing to me or to the Colonel.'

Kit shakes his head. 'We must search the woods. Jem may have twisted an ankle on a tree root and be unable to go on to the manor or to return . . .'

I do not need to say that this is unlikely. Kit is already calling together the other colliers, and we are soon combing all of the most likely tracks and the bushes that flank them. An hour makes us hot and tired but no wiser; then we hear a call from a little way off. Nothing about the call makes me hope that we are about to see Jem alive.

His small body has been dragged into the undergrowth within a mass of brambles and then poorly concealed under some dead branches. His throat has been cut by somebody skilled in the use of a knife. Like Henderson, he would have died quickly. But unlike Henderson, he clearly died much where his body came to rest. The leaves close by are covered with sticky red blood, on which flies are already feasting.

'This is a bad business,' says Kit. 'Whatever sins Henderson may have committed, Jem's were few. He did not deserve this.'

'Once we catch the killer,' says one of the charcoal burners, 'he should hang from the nearest tree.'

There is a general murmur of agreement, and our eyes turn instinctively to a large oak close by. It's definitely the nearest. The problem, of course, is that we first have to catch the killer.

In the midst of this horror, my mind continues to work in small, logical steps, as if trying to break a particularly difficult cipher. I note that the body is cold but not yet fully stiff. There is no sign yet of putrefaction, though it is a hot day. The bracken is beaten down between the path and where he is now, but there is no suggestion of the undergrowth being trampled by two or more men fighting. Perhaps there was a struggle. But more likely there was none. An ambush last night, then, and a sudden death. I explain this to Kit.

'You know how a dead body should look, John Grey?'

'Yes,' I say, 'I know how a body ought to look.' I explain how it would look after a day and after two days and after three. And how that changes, depending on whether it is summer or winter. And how the body grows stiff after a few hours, then limp again after three days. Jem died more than six hours ago – but, I think, less than twelve. The cut is clean – a single wound made with a very sharp weapon, deeper on the right than the left. It bears the signature of Henderson's killer.

'Do they teach this to all lawyers?' asks Kit.

'I learned it from the dead themselves,' I say. 'They were good tutors.'

'So you know who killed Jem?'

'I know that he died during the night and not this morning. And I think the killer knows the woods well – well enough to guess by which path Jem would have to travel. I begin to fear that it may be somebody who lives in the village.'

'Since the war, half the world knows how to kill a man,' says Kit with a sigh. 'And many have grown hardened to killing babes in arms. But I do not enjoy the thought that it may have been one of us who did this.'

'Jem left without revealing who he saw at the stables?'

'I would have said.'

'So we shall never know why he would not tell me,' I say.

'On the contrary,' says Kit, 'he said he could not tell you, because you would never believe him. Not in a hundred years.'

At the Church, and Afterwards

We are a sorry party. Four men walking, three in leather jerkins and rough woollen breeches, one in a fine suit of green a little stained with mud and blood and now rent at the knee by thorns. And we carry with us a small burden in a sack – the only winding sheet that we have at our disposal. We pause at the lych gate and say a brief prayer, in which Kit leads us.

For a moment I think that the Rector must, through some strange visitation, already know our purpose. There is a pile of earth and a deep hole and two sweating men resting on their spades. But they today are removing a body, not committing one to the ground. Henderson is about to give evidence for the prosecution.

As we approach, their attention turns from the new grave to Jem's body. The Rector and Mr Probert emerge from the porch, where they have been sheltering from the sun's heat.

'It's Ben's stableboy,' I say.

'Where did you find him?' asks Probert.

'Near one of the paths in the wood,' I say.

'The fool,' says Probert, shaking his head. 'He would have been much safer if he had stayed where he was. What on earth made him leave?'

Kit looks at me but says nothing.

'Has the Colonel been informed?' asks the Rector.

'Not yet,' I say. 'Nor has Ben.'

'They must both be told,' says Probert. 'Take the lad down to the crypt, you men. In the meantime let me see Henderson one last time.'

The gravediggers both stretch their limbs in preparation for their final task. Strong cords have already been placed round the coffin. The two of them, aided by Probert and myself, pull on the ropes and watch the simple oak box rise slowly. Henderson died in the hope of resurrection but cannot in his wildest dreams have expected it so soon.

Once the coffin is firmly on the ground, Probert takes an iron bar and works his way round the lid, loosening the nails. I give him a hand to wrench the top of the coffin away. A pungent odour of rotten meat washes upwards and around us. Henderson's deathly grey face looks up with sightless eyes. In place of the black and bloodstained suit of clothes that he had been wearing, he is now wrapped in a cheap winding sheet, tied round his body and up and over his head. The women who laid him out did well, but there is still something about his neck that is not entirely pleasing. He does not have the air of a man who has died happily.

Probert takes a deep breath, almost a sob, and says, 'That is he. That is all that remains of my dear friend Henderson. My ever-loyal companion in life, whom I hope to embrace again in God's heaven. *Vitae summa brevis spem nos vetat incohare longam.* Now nail up the box again, for he stinks worse dead than he ever did alive.'

'Wait!' I say. I had wanted to compare the button that I found in the field with those on Henderson's doublet, but he now has only grave clothes. 'Where is his doublet?'

'It would have been removed, of course, when the body was washed and dressed for the grave,' says the Rector.

'And where is the doublet now?'

'You would have to ask the women. Mistress Hardy and Mistress Mansell. They deal with matters such as that. Now, if everyone's curiosity is satisfied, perhaps we can return Mr Henderson to the ground. Today is not the Day of Judgement, and I have a baptism to perform this afternoon. I do not yet know all of the superstitions of this part of the world, but I suspect that not baptising children within sight of an open coffin is one of them.'

Nails are again hammered home. The gravediggers prepare to lower a coffin once more. *Vitae summa brevis.*

'Why the interest in his doublet, Grey?' asks Probert over my shoulder as the first shovelfuls of earth rattle onto the lid.

'It is of no importance,' I say.

'Grey, though I do not understand why, I feel that our relationship has got off on the wrong foot. I feel that you do not trust me as you ought. The Rector tells me, for example, that you found the body, and yet you said nothing of that to me. You must have realised that I would be curious to know more.'

'Who exactly are you?' I ask.

He raises his eyebrows. 'I thought I had introduced myself

already. But meet me tonight at the inn. We shall have supper together, and I shall try to explain myself more clearly. In exchange you can tell me then about the doublet, for I am sure that it is an interesting tale.'

'And if I decline?'

'You won't. You'll come. You love knowledge for its own sake, Grey, just as I love withholding knowledge. One day that may be the death of both of us, though not tonight. But even if you were risking all, you would still come. You are drawn to a mystery as a bee is profitably drawn to the flower, or a foolish moth is drawn to the candle flame.'

'You will eat alone,' I say.

But Probert merely smiles.

I wonder which I am. Bee or moth? Not moth, I hope.

'I am sorry to hear of Jem's death,' says the Colonel. 'Sorrier than I can say.'

'The Coroner must be informed. And this time before the burial takes place.'

'I do not need you to remind me of my business,' says the Colonel. He wasn't so prickly a couple of days ago. Things change. A couple of days ago I wasn't an informer.

'No,' I say, 'I'm sure you don't. I think that Jem's murderer was the same man who killed Mr Henderson. In both cases their throats were cut expertly with a sharp instrument of some sort. I think the killer knows the village well. He is skilled in the use of a knife. And I think he is still here amongst us.'

'I assume you exclude Roger Pole. Or are you now suggesting that he would kill innocent children?'

He's right; I'm not planning to suggest it. Pole is vain, arrogant, annoying, cynical and beribboned – and children are murdered every day by people with no visible mark of evil on them. But it cannot be Pole.

'When the second murder occurred,' I say, 'Roger Pole was here at the Big House under arrest. Jem's death speaks for his innocence as eloquently as if he had lived to testify.'

'Almost,' says the Colonel. He has a point. In Pole's place I'd also prefer a living witness to a clever hypothesis by a lawyer without clients. 'And presumably you also exclude this rider of yours, who must, if he ever existed, be many miles away by now.'

'No, I still think the rider played a part. Perhaps he is the unlikely person referred to by Jem, or perhaps that person assisted him. Indeed, we have to accept the possibility that somebody in the village was the killer of Henderson or Jem. I think Ben still has many questions to answer.'

'You are very free with your allegations,' says the Colonel. 'You have already had to concede that you have spoken unjustly against Roger Pole. Henderson's death caused little stir. But there may be people in the village who will find this less easy to forgive, and they may decide that due legal process is a little too slow for their liking. And even if Ben might know something about Henderson's death, he would scarcely have murdered his own stableboy. Have a care, John, before you make further accusations in public.'

I nod. This is good advice. It is just the sort of advice I would give my clients if I had any.

'I saw Probert heading into the woods,' I say.

The Colonel shakes his head. 'Probert certainly didn't kill Jem. Stay out of this, John. If Jem's death hasn't shown you how dangerous this business is, then please accept my word for it.'

'Who exactly is Probert?' I ask. 'You have met him before. I saw it in your face at the inn.'

'He's somebody to keep clear of,' says the Colonel. 'Be grateful that you can do that, even if I cannot.'

'If I had made an appointment to see him this evening, what advice would you have for me?'

'Don't keep the appointment. This may be my business, as you have pointed out to me many times, but it is no business of yours. If there are things I have not told you, it is for your own good.'

'How is Roger Pole?' I ask. 'I hope that he is bearing his captivity well.'

The Colonel looks a little uncomfortable and says: 'We have a small problem there. Roger Pole has . . . left. Early this morning.'

So much for his alibi then. So much for his word as a gentleman.

'The clothes of the departed are my perky-seat,' says Mistress Mansell.

'Didn't the Colonel pay you for laying out Mr Henderson?' I ask.

'That's my business, not your'n,' says Mistress Mansell. 'Maybe he did and maybe he didn't. Maybe I told him the going rate for the job, and maybe I told him double. But the dead man's clothes belongs to me.'

'I wish only to compare the button I have with the buttons on his doublet.'

'Why's that then, boy?'

'I think a button I found in the meadow was one of his.'

'That so?'

'I'd just like to see the doublet,' I say. I take a sixpenny piece from my purse and hold it up.

'Worth something to you, is it?' she asks. I realise that I have shown my hand too soon. 'That'll be five shilling if you wants to see his clothes,' she adds.

I stand up as if to go.

'All right, sixpence it is then,' she says quickly, to avoid losing her chance of taking money from an idiot. 'But I'll have it now, like.'

I give her the coin and sit down again while she vanishes into a small back room. Her fire is smoking a great deal, and my eyes are watering. She seems used to it, as she is to the smell of damp that pervades her cottage even on a hot day. The aroma of dinner bubbling away in a pot on the fire is also far from appealing – good root vegetables from her garden ruined by a few scraps of half-rotten meat. She returns after a while with an untidy black bundle that is unwrapped into a doublet and a pair of breeches.

'You're lucky as I've still got 'em. I was going to Saffron Walden Saturday. Sell 'em there. They've cleaned up nice, they have. Nobody'd know the last owner had his throttle cut. Not unless you look careful, and hopefully I'll be back here by the time they do that. And I always tells customers I comes from Thaxted, just in case. You got that button, boy?'

I unwrap my button in its turn and hold it up against the doublet. It is the same size and pattern as those in place, and there is a button missing from the doublet at the point where Henderson's ample midriff would have exerted the greatest pressure on the fastenings. I check the small piece of thread hanging from the doublet against the small piece of thread hanging from the button.

'Happy now, ducks?' asks Mistress Mansell.

'I think it matches,' I say.

'Anything else, boy? You can see his shirt for thruppence,' she adds, keen to strike another easy bargain.

'I could buy his shirt outright for less than that,' I say.

'Not from me, you couldn't.'

'Did he have a hat?' I ask.

'No hat that I ever saw,' she says. 'Do you want to buy one?'

'I have one already.'

'Looks like you've slept on it.'

'I'm happy with it as it is.'

She feigns surprise, but not much – after all, she doesn't have a hat to sell me. But she does have one last trick in her pocket.

'And then I've got this'n,' she says. She takes a small wad of paper from her placket and holds it aloft. It is not unlike the one that I found in Henderson's boot. 'Sewn into the hem of his doublet, that was. I always checks the hem, because sometimes dead folk leaves their gold there, and it's a horrid shame to bury money in the cold dirt.'

I reach out my hand, but this proves a mistake. I have indicated that it too might have a value.

'Paper that is,' she says. 'With words on it.'

'What does it say?' I ask.

'How should I know that, boy?'

I shrug. 'Keep it,' I say. 'Sell it in Saffron Walden.'

'Half a crown,' she says. She's heard a rumour that others can read, even if she can't.

'Let me see it,' I say.

She unfolds it awkwardly and then holds it out just beyond my reach. There are blocks of letters in groups of four. I see:

'PIEX NECT FEWS RRMB SUGE'. Then she snatches it away again.

'It's not words,' I say, 'just letters.'

She's trying to work out whether letters are worth less on the open market than words. Normally, she sells badly laundered shirts and carefully checked doublets.

'One and six,' she says, marking it down as damaged goods.

I shake my head.

'Penny then. Paper's got to be worth a penny.'

I hand her a penny and stuff the sheet carelessly in my pocket.

'So the button was his? From off of his doublet?' she asks.

'Yes,' I say.

'It's mine then now, ain't it? One of my perky-seats.' She holds out her hand.

I render unto Caesar that which is due unto Caesar. Her bony little fist closes on it. Even Ifnot wouldn't be able to prise that tiny hand open again.

'You're trying to find out who killed Mr Henderson, ain't you?'

'Yes,' I say.

'And Jem?'

'Yes,' I say.

'Then good luck to you,' she says. 'I'd like to shit on who-ever killed the boy.'

'We'd all like to do that,' I say.

I wonder if she is about to tell me anything more out of the kindness of her heart. But these are not her standard terms of business. She gives me a twisted smile and trots off to the back room with her bundle newly folded. Rubbing my eyes,

I grope my way to the door and step out into the mercilessly hot afternoon.

Once I am home, I open up the crumpled sheet of paper. It reads:

NUMBER 9 PIEX NECT FEWS RRMB SUGE OBYS NMEO HEIT HOUG ATDE EDTH GKIN VHAS GERY SOOD OUPP ERTH UREB ETTH DLEA HERS FIPO KTHE INOT ISBE HNGC EALL DNGE HBYT UEYO RNGE SONE MFOR TJRE SURN EHOM NSOO UIWO ELDR DMIN OYOU UFYO ORPR EMIS 472.

I think of the cipher that I found in Henderson's boot but immediately see that it will not serve. This message has been coded in some other way, and I must start anew. But I have done this many times before.

When deciphering any coded message to which one lacks the key, it is necessary to go through a number of steps. With a simple substitution code, one counts the occurrences of each letter or number, then ranks them according to their frequency. If the message in is English, the most common should correspond to the letter *E*, the next two to *T* and *A*, the next to *O* and so on. Frequently found combinations such as *TH*, *ER* and *ON* can also be searched for. Doubled letters are likely to represent *SS*, *EE*, *TT* or *FF*. These simple patterns enable the code breaker to have a first pass at a solution, and often words will spring from the page as if by magic. If they do not, then it is a matter of trial and error. Close study and practice will still make a simple code deliver up its message within an hour or two. Henderson's code used numbers for letters. Here, it would seem, letters are substituted for other letters. Strangely, *E* is the most common letter in the coded format – and my doubled letters are *R, E, O* (three times!), *P, T* and *L*. Of course, short messages yield more slowly to this type of analysis than long ones.

I struggle for an hour and make no progress at all. Perhaps it is not a substitution code after all. Is the grouping of the letters significant or a distraction? I look at the group that reads 'GERY' – which is, as you will have noticed yourself, an anagram of my name. Such things happen coincidentally, of course, but it is a coincidence that worries me a little. And something else worries me too. Like the stranger's voice, these blocks of letters are unaccountably familiar. When I look at the page, words seem to spring at me, then fade away again. Another person's eye cast over this might see immediately how it is put together. But I shall tell nobody of this for the moment – not until I am sure what it is and what it has to do with me.

I fold the paper up again and stow it away in my pocket. A supper awaits me.

At the Inn, and Afterwards

'I thought that we would sup in my chamber,' says Probert. 'We may converse all the more discreetly.'

'You are expecting others?' I indicate the pickled pike, cold beef, lamb cutlets, pies, pease pudding and salads that are spread before us on the table.

'Others? They would go hungry if they came,' he says. 'I had intended this for myself alone but then remembered my invitation to you. However, thinking you were no great eater any more than you are a great drinker, I resigned myself to sharing it.' He takes a clasp knife from his pocket, opens it and cuts himself a large slice of pie. Since no invitation comes from him for me to follow suit, I take my knife and, on my own authority, cut myself some beef. He neither condones my action nor objects to it. This is a matter of open competition rather than hospitality. Probert looks me in the eye and seizes upon the largest cutlet. I think he will swallow it whole, but his teeth deal dexterously with the flesh in small, rapid bites, and the bone is thrown over his shoulder. Before it hits the floor, he is already cutting into the second pie. I am still on my first slice of beef. Without saying a word, I get up, take the flagon of ale from the side table and fill a tankard for myself. I offer none to Probert. The rules of this contest are already clear. Probert looks up briefly and disdainfully, then scans the table and selects the pike as his next target. Most of it is transferred to his trencher at a single sweep. I take what is left of the first pie. It proves to be rabbit and well cooked and seasoned. I add some of the salad of cucumber and eggs, dressed with oil, but then realise that Probert will scarcely see this as eating at all. He is already throwing a second bone to the floor. This is fast work. I did not see him even pick the cutlet up. I want to ask him whether he normally eats meals of this size, but there is simply no time. He has seized a hunk of rye bread and is ripping it with his teeth. He has a cutlet in his other hand. I take a piece of bread and use it to scoop up some of the pike from its serving dish. I cram it all, bread and fish, straight into my mouth and chew. We eye each other up, our mouths still masticating, and both reach for the last cutlet. I get there first. Probert sneers and scrapes all of the remaining cucumber and egg onto his trencher. A small victory for me, I think.

We eat like this for half an hour, interrupted only by Nell's arrival with a hot gooseberry pie, a trencher piled with strawberries and another with apples. Finally, I have to say: 'Mr Probert, I can eat no more. The palms of victory are yours.'

'Yes,' he says, 'that is very true, Grey. I have won. But to eat as I do, *ab ove usque ad mala*, you must accustom yourself to it. You cannot simply hope to sit down with me and outeat me at the first attempt.'

'Do you always take meals like this?' I ask.

He shakes his head. 'Not always – merely when I can,' he says. He munches thoughtfully on an apple. '*Est modus in rebus*. Now, Grey, to business. I fear that you believe me to be in the pay of Charles Stuart.'

'Are you not?'

'I was once an agent of the late, unlamented Tyrant. That is true. Later – being captured and imprisoned in the Tower of London may have influenced my thinking – I saw that the true path was to work for Parliament. I am now employed by Mr Secretary Thurloe, of whom you may have heard, and who has, as you know, heard of you. We are on the same side, Grey.'

'That's easy enough to say.'

'Exactly. And I have said it. What proof can I offer you then? Would it help if I said that I knew you had been in correspondence with a mutual friend? A good friend of mine and a fortiori a good friend of Mr Secretary Thurloe's. That is, by the way, where I discovered Dr Grahame's opinion of you.'

'You could have come across that information by foul means as well as fair.'

'You are a difficult man to please, Grey. You make what should be a simple conversation very awkward. I like that. It shows promise. But we must get down to business. These summer nights are short. Do you intend to deny that you have written to Mr Samuel Morland, formerly also of Magdalene College, seeking employment as a cryptographer in Mr Thurloe's department? Mr Morland looks favourably on your application and would look even more favourably upon it if I were to send him a good report of your abilities. So far, I can commend only your caution and admirable lack of trust. But I trust *you*, Grey. And together perhaps we can find out why

Henderson died. And Jem too. The two deaths are linked, and if you wish to find Jem's killer, then you must come with me in my search for Henderson's.'

'Was Henderson also working for Mr Thurloe?' I ask.

'Ah, Henderson! My beloved Henderson! *He* began as a Parliamentary spy, then became a Royalist one, then a Parliamentary one again. Double-dealing, you see, was his great joy and his supreme talent. *Ad unguem factus homo.* Those of us who choose espionage as a career do it because we take pleasure in deception. We enjoy knowing things that others do not know. But when that game palls, we can add a little nutmeg to our ale by turning all on its head and playing for the other side. And when that game too grows weary, as it will . . . But you see my point? So, was Henderson working for Thurloe when he died? Mr Secretary Thurloe thought so. I thought so. But only Henderson would have known for certain.'

'He had a ring with the royal coat of arms,' I say.

'Do you remember the good old days when we had theatres and plays?' asks Probert. 'The people on the stage were merely actors, but with a tin crown and an old velvet cloak lined with rabbit, they could appear to be King Henry the Fifth of glorious memory, or with a cushion shoved up the back of their doublet they could hobble round and be mad King Dick. Henderson missed his true vocation. I think he enjoyed playing a Royalist agent – but it was to be his final role. The curtain has come down.'

'Why was his final scene played out in this village?'

'Have you heard of the Sealed Knot?'

'I have heard rumours of it. It is a secret Royalist organisation.'

'Indeed. It was formed by some young men – silly boys too green to have fought in the late wars – to raise a rebellion that would restore the Stuarts to the throne. They report to Sir Edward Hyde, currently exiled in Bruges – or at least they used to. Now a faction, dissatisfied with the Knot's inefficiency and Hyde's supine inactivity, has formed itself into the Action Party, as they like to call themselves. To Lord Protector Cromwell, these squabbling little Royalists are all no more than gnats that buzz on a summer evening. But they must be swatted nonetheless, and His Highness sends the likes of me and Henderson to do the swatting.'

'Their cause is hopeless,' I say.

'Not quite,' says Probert. 'You have grown up under the Republic. To you, being ruled by Parliament and by a Lord Protector is God's natural order. And to others – those who have acquired cavalier property, for example, or who inadvertently signed the last king's death warrant – a restoration of the monarchy would be very inconvenient. In any case, why should anyone wish to be an impoverished Royalist when the Republic can offer well-paid employment? Charles and his court are in despair, while his followers sneak back to London one by one to pledge allegiance to Cromwell. In ten or even five years' time, few will remember a king as anything but a painted devil in a picture book. But should Charles Stuart return in the meantime at the head of an army, or should Cromwell die . . . We are not safe yet, Mr Grey.'

'Henderson, then, was posing as an agent of the Sealed Knot?'

'Exactly. He was to meet the secret Royalists here in this village, nominally to distribute amongst them warrants from Charles Stuart, titular King of the Scots, giving them commissions in the Royalist army and the right to wage war in his name.'

'And then?'

'They would inform Henderson of their state of readiness. We would discover who they reported to and so on. That last point is a particularly important one. Mr Thurloe is convinced that a particularly important correspondent of the Sealed Knot resides in the village. A large fish in a small pond, you might say. A fish who is passing information to Hyde on activities both in Essex and beyond. Henderson hoped you might be able to put a name to this fish. He was told to ask for you.'

Pole, I think. Of course. What else is he doing in a village like this? As the secretary to a once-influential member of Cromwell's inner circle and as a purported supplicant of the Lord Protector, he would hope to avoid suspicion. But who else can it be? And yet I find I cannot say it. I have promised Aminta that I shall help prove his innocence. And I have promised the Colonel that I shall be less free with my accusations. But I do at least now understand why Henderson should, on Mr Thurloe's instructions, have been asking after me. And if my rider was his killer, then it is surely my rider who was a Royalist agent.

'The night Henderson died,' I say, 'a stranger passed through the village. Though nobody admits to having seen him, his horse is still at the inn.'

'Ah yes, I have heard of your imaginary horseman. He provides much amusement for the vulgar crowd. You should tell the story more often. You would gain a reputation as a rare wit.'

'You also think I dreamt him?'

'On the contrary. Strangeness followed in Henderson's

wake like scavenging gulls behind a ship at sea. A ghostly rider seeking the inn where Henderson was staying? Yes, that could have happened.'

'You mock me, Mr Probert.'

'Not at all. I am in deadly earnest. Henderson survived one night in the village, surrounded by members of the Sealed Knot, but then died shortly after this horseman arrived. I am inclined to think that he was sent by Hyde.'

'And yet,' I say, 'I do not believe that he acted alone. Jem's murderer at least was no stranger to the village.'

'So, an accomplice?'

'I think so. I fear it may be Ben Bowman, though the Colonel doubts it can be true.'

'I agree with the Colonel. He is an unlikely murderer . . . Has Bowman lived here all his life?'

'He has – though his wife is from London.'

'Indeed? Tell me about Mistress Bowman. What did she do in London?'

'She earned her living from play-acting.'

Probert looks perplexed. 'A woman on the stage? I have heard of such things in France, but not here.'

'Her father was the manager of a theatre in London. She helped him with selling tickets and running the company generally. She can still quote whole acts of Shakespeare's plays if you ask her. Ben Jonson's too.'

'I thought her face was familiar. Though I do, of course, strongly disapprove of theatricals and all other entertainments banned by our enlightened government, there was a time when I gained foolish enjoyment watching one band of actors or another. I have visited most of the London playhouses. Perhaps I saw her there. How grateful she must be to the Lord Protector for saving her from such a debauched existence.'

'I fear she finds her new life rather dull.'

'Indeed? I grant that she would have few other ladies to converse with – I mean, anyone with any learning.'

'My mother reads and writes of course. So does Dickon's mother. They exchange receipts sometimes for jam or pies. Oh, and Aminta Clifford was taught by the same tutor as her brother.'

'Your village is a veritable Athens of the eastern counties. But I am racing ahead of myself. Tell me first what you know about Henderson's sad demise. Then let us return to the dramatis personae.'

I take a deep breath and tell him what I know of the murder, as far as my discovery of the missing button.

'Very clear so far, Mr Grey. I thank you. And where is the button now?'

'Goodwife Mansell claimed it as one of her perquisites for laying out the body.'

'Did she? No matter. I'm sure Henderson would wish her to have it. He was brutal, but not ungenerous. And the letter?'

'It is at home,' I say.

'But you are sure that the signature was 472.'

'Yes.'

'I have seen others from the same source – from the person we believe is the coordinator of the Sealed Knot here in Essex. If Henderson had it, it is one that had already passed through our office. Perhaps we shall look at it together later, but I am no cryptographer and it is not urgent. Please continue.'

'Then I found more blood in Ben's stable – a lot more. And

finally, Jem, who lived above the stables, was killed, as you know.'

'Yes,' says Probert. 'Jem's murder troubles me almost as much as it troubles you. I have seen many deaths – more than I can reasonably be expected to remember. I fought in England and in Ireland. I have seen the corpses of whole families killed by soldiers during the late wars; the children were not spared then any more than Jem has been spared now. But this death seems particularly unnecessary. *Was* it Henderson's killer who did this, I wonder? To kill an enemy agent is one thing . . .'

'The wounds were much the same. I would swear that it was the same hand.'

'Indeed? That rules Pole out then. He was under arrest when Jem died.'

'Pole has escaped,' I say.

'That is inconvenient when I have had no opportunity to question him myself. I thought it would have been better to have put him in the lock-up, even if it did mean that Harry Hardy's pigs had to be inconvenienced. Flight signifies guilt. So, perhaps Pole is our man after all.'

'I think not. Jem was willing to tell the Colonel who the killer was. If it had been Pole, surely he would have trusted me more than the Colonel. And Kit said Jem would not tell me, because he said that I would not believe him. If Jem had said he had seen Pole in the stables, I would have had no difficulty believing it.'

'Because you do not like him?' asks Probert.

'I do not like his haughty airs or his finery,' I say.

'Tush,' says Probert, inspecting the arm of his stained and shabby doublet. 'If it were a crime to be well dressed, then you would have to suspect me as much as anyone. Still, your defence of Mr Pole is noted. I am intrigued, however, about Jem's remark that the killer is the last person you would expect. Who in this village would you expect least? That may help us.'

Sadly, the list is a long one. It is difficult to believe that any of my fellow villagers would commit murder, though I much fear that one has. I return to my suspicions about Ben, but Probert remains unconvinced.

'He has been evasive,' Probert agrees, 'and he is certainly worried about something. But if Jem had seen Ben murder Henderson, would he have stayed with him, even as long as he did? I think not. I agree that your rider may be involved in some way. He is the only outsider to enter the picture. Or have any other strangers passed through?'

'Nobody has stayed at the inn since Henderson, other than you. But now I think of it, there was also a Mr Clarges visiting Colonel Payne at the manor.'

'Thomas Clarges? Here?'

'Yes, Thomas Clarges. Where should he be?'

'He was in Scotland when we last heard. He's General Monck's brother-in-law . . . I think, Grey, you may have stepped into deeper water than you intended. As indeed so may I. You say that you do not suspect the Colonel in all this?'

'It is true he has acted tardily in his investigations. And yet he is a good man – he lets Sir Felix live in the Steward's cottage, for example, and does not trouble him unduly concerning the rent.'

'Even though he is a Royalist?'

'If Sir Felix had fought for Parliament, his fortune would be intact.'

'You believe that? But a thought occurs to me: if Sir Felix is in the Steward's cottage, where does the steward live?'

'There's no steward now,' I say. 'Sir Felix's steward left when he did.'

'What was his name?'

'We called him Grumpy Mansell. He was forever chasing us out of the orchard or accusing us of trapping rabbits in the woods.'

'You mentioned another Mansell – a woman.'

'Goodwife Mansell? She who is a silver button better off than she was? I think she must be his aunt.'

'And Steward Mansell's first name is what?'

'I can't remember. We wouldn't have had much use for it. It began with a *C.* Charles? No, I would remember that. What was it? Much though we children disliked him, by the bye, I have to say that he was a great asset to Sir Felix. He understood the estate work better than any man. He could hedge and ditch if he had to, and he knew the woods as if he had grown up in them. What was he called? Christian? Crispian? No, it was Christopher!'

'So, would they have called him Kit Mansell by any chance?' asks Probert.

Yes, of course. I wondered why Kit was so well informed of my youthful misdemeanours. I had not recognised the formerly well dressed and closely shaved steward when meeting the bearded, weather-beaten collier. But I could see that, once dismissed by the new owner of the Big House, he might turn his hand to charcoal burning as well as anything else if he wished to stay in the village. Aminta at least knew who Kit was; hadn't she said that Jem would be safe with him?

'I wonder what Kit knows?' I say.

'I wonder what they all know,' says Probert. 'But we only need one person here to break his silence and perhaps *we* shall know. Let us apply a little pressure to the weakest part of the wall. I rather think you are right in one respect – that part is Ben Bowman. His mortar is crumbling. We shall dig a sap beneath him and watch him collapse. Then we shall storm the citadel shoulder to shoulder. But enough for tonight, Grey! We make good progress. Tomorrow morning I shall talk kindly to Ben and see if he will tell me what I want to know. Then perhaps I shall talk to him less kindly. One way or another, I shall crack him like a hazelnut. Meet me here again at noon. Is it not good to be working together?'

As I am leaving the inn, I meet with Dickon, who is also on his way home. I draw him to one side.

'Dickon,' I say. 'Good news. I have just spoken with Mr Probert. He is not the Royalist agent we suspected he was. He is the loyal servant of Mr Secretary Thurloe and is as anxious as we are to solve the riddle of the two deaths that have occurred in our village.'

Dickon nods. 'Ben said you were closeted with him. If you supped together, I hope you took a long spoon.'

'He's on our side,' I say, because Dickon does not seem to have understood this.

'Is that what he says? And you believe him?'

'He has given me good reason to trust him.'

Dickon says nothing.

'Look, Dickon, I think we are close to finding out who the murderer was. Kit gave us a clue: he said that Jem told him Henderson's killer was the last person I would suspect. Tomorrow morning Probert will talk again to Ben. One way or another, he thinks he can make him crack.'

'You seem strangely happy about that,' says Dickon.

'Ben is an amiable soul,' I say, 'and I would have no hurt come to him. But this small discomfort he will have brought upon himself.'

'If you say so, Mister Lawyer,' says Dickon.

'It is what is right, Dickon,' I say.

'He'll not talk to Ben tomorrow morning anyway,' says Dickon. 'Ben will be up before first light to ride into Saffron Walden. It's market day.'

Of course. Goodwife Mansell will be going to sell Henderson's clothes, and Ben will be going to buy whatever he needs for the coming week.

I look back at the inn, wondering whether to tell Probert now. 'I'm sure the afternoon will be an equally good time to talk,' I say.

Dickon nods and wishes me a good night.

'Will you walk with me as far as the crossroads?' I ask. I am aware that Dickon does not quite approve of what I have done, and I do not wish to part on bad terms.

'I'm riding back, not walking,' he says curtly, and sets off towards the stables.

I stroll slowly to the crossroads, but Dickon does not overtake me. He may have taken the shortcut through the Park, which the Cliffords would never have allowed, but to which the Colonel feels unable to object.

I'll seek Dickon out tomorrow. I feel some sympathy for Ben, but really I have acted for the best. Now that Probert is closing in on his quarry, how can we not have a swift and satisfactory resolution? It is impossible that it can be otherwise.

Another Letter

Letter Number 15
2 July 1657

To Sir Edward Hyde, Lord Chancellor, c/o The Abbess,
Benedictine Convent, Ghent

My movements in the village, as I explained in my last, are somewhat
restricted by circumstances, else I might have hoped to have told you
much of interest. I regret to inform you however that the boy Jem,
who witnessed Henderson's killing, has himself been killed. I do not
know where this will end, but I fear he may not be the last.

For M – P grows fretful. I am concerned as to what he might
do. Probert is inquisitive, but I think I can deal with him. He is
not as clever as he believes.

Your obedient
472

At the Stables, and Afterwards

Probert rubs his eyes. 'It would have been better if you had told me last night, but I can talk to Bowman as well this afternoon as this morning. And Bowman's absence will allow me greater latitude than usual for my investigations here. Show me some blood, Mr Grey.'

Again I enter the twilight world of Ben's stable. The grey is still there. He'll be needing exercise. He scarcely pays us any attention as we cross to the far side of the building. Again I push the straw to one side to reveal a reddy-brown patch of earth. It seems less convincing than before, just a stain, but Probert nods.

'And Jem lived where?'

I indicate the hayloft with the narrow ladder leading up to it.

'You'd better go up then. I'm not sure I'd squeeze through that trap door.'

He would in fact squeeze through quite easily, but why go himself when he can send me? The gloom in this smaller space is more all-encompassing, but I stand for a moment to let my eyes become accustomed. Jem's simple straw mattress is in one corner, with two blankets untidily dumped in the middle. There is little hay in evidence – last year's is almost all used up, and this year's will not arrive for another week or two.

'What am I looking for?' I yell down to Probert.

'How should I know that?' he says. He makes it sound as if this was my idea.

I look under Jem's mattress and then kick what is left of the hay. It's harder than expected. I kneel down and examine what I have found. Then I carry one of them carefully down the ladder, for it is very heavy, and hand it to Probert.

'How many are there?'

'Six, under the hay,' I say. 'Much the same as this one. There may be others.'

He hefts the musket in his hands. 'Any powder or shot?'

'Not that I could see.'

'This has the Sealed Knot's signature on it,' says Probert. 'Six old muskets and no ammunition. That's their idea of military action. They'd have put these in the hands of a bunch of frightened village lads and left them to face a troop of battle-hardened dragoons.'

'Was this what Ben Bowman was hiding in that chamber?'

'Probably. Too spineless to say no if the Knot asked him to do it and they were regular customers. Put that one back anyway. It will do less harm up there than anywhere else. And we may need to show the evidence to the Magistrate.'

'You'll go to see the Colonel?'

'Yes, I think it's time for that too. And then I may try to get to know the countryside a little better. Your friend Grice has a farm just off the London Road, does he not?'

'The quickest route is over the fields. But Dickon was at the inn all night and then went straight home. He says he milked the cows and slaughtered a pig.'

'An industrious young man,' says Probert. 'Slaughtered a pig? That is the sort of irrelevant detail that distinguishes the true narrative from the fanciful. I'll see you back here at dinnertime.'

'Do you want me to do anything in the meantime?'

'Yes, you might try to find out a little more about Kit Mansell. He was the last person to see Jem alive – or the second last anyway.'

'I'll ask Aminta,' I say.

I suppose I should have expected Aminta to be distressed at the news of Jem's death. She has taken it worse than I, who saw the body.

'I can't believe it,' she says eventually. Her face is grey.

'Nor can I,' I say. 'But isn't that doubly untrue? The sight of a small body amongst the brambles will never leave me, much though I wish it would. I have no cause to doubt his death. And haven't I feared for Jem since the moment he vanished from the stable?

'You have heard that Roger Pole has also now fled and is not to be found?' I ask. Under different circumstances I might smile.

'Yes,' Aminta says blankly.

'Of course,' I say, 'he wasn't to know that Jem would be killed last night, but the timing of his flight will make some suspect him. Obviously, I don't mean that *I* think he killed Jem.'

On the other hand, it is probable that Pole is the Sealed Knot's coordinator in Essex and as such may know something about Henderson's death. Perhaps I should not be surprised that Aminta and Pole, as the only Royalists in the village, should be drawn together.

'I do not doubt Roger's innocence,' says Aminta. 'My fear is not that a killer has fled but that a killer is still amongst us.'

This is my concern too.

'I had suspected Ben of being involved,' I say, 'but Probert thinks not.'

'Ben?' Aminta looks at me as though I am some sort of ninny.

'He has muskets hidden in the stables.'

'Henderson wasn't killed with a musket,' she says. 'In any case, from your description of Henderson's body, it could not have been Ben who wielded the knife.'

This is true, though I had not expected Aminta to understand why. I look at her with a new respect.

'He could still have helped the stranger on horseback . . .'

'I don't think he helped anyone. Certainly not your stranger.'

'Do you mean you know who the stranger was?'

'Of course not,' she says. 'I simply mean he's gone – long before Jem's death. It can't be him.'

'But you do suspect somebody here?'

'The whole village will be suspecting each other soon. Yes, I suspect somebody, but it is better not to blurt out one's suspicions before the evidence is there.'

Unlike me.

'And you know as well as I do,' she adds, 'that there aren't more than three or four people who could have done it.'

I nod. 'There is something else I need to ask you,' I say.

'Kit Mansell – why did he not become the Colonel's steward? The Colonel must sorely need a man of his capabilities. And Mansell's talents are wasted as a charcoal burner.'

'While my father and brother were away fighting, Kit looked after the estate for them.'

I try to think back to the war. I was too young then to wonder who looked after an estate when the owner was away. These things seemed to manage themselves. The apples were certainly guarded as well as ever.

'Of course,' I say.

'Kit resented it even more than we did when we were forced to sell. He refused the Colonel's offer of a place. He went away but has very recently returned.'

'But charcoal burning . . .'

'He finds it congenial. He says there is no need to catch charcoal poachers or chase boys who would steal his charcoal.'

'Aminta, would Kit have had any reason – any reason at all – to want Jem dead?' I ask.

She considers my question carefully before shaking her head. 'No, Kit would not kill anyone,' she says, 'except perhaps to defend me or my father. Then he might. Jem's killer may be a monster, or he may be desperate to protect somebody or something.'

'Jem was no sort of threat to you?' I ask.

'Quite the reverse,' she says. 'But you will have to excuse me; I must start preparing dinner. I have some rabbits to deal with. Kit traps them and kindly brings us a few now and then. Some might call it poaching, but he says the rabbits are still ours by rights. I have to skin them and draw them myself of course. When you've no servants, you have to be quite handy with a knife.'

'Yes,' I say. 'I suppose most women do.'

*

The charcoal burners' clearing is empty. No fire smoulders today, but the scent of ashes hangs in the air, and the logs are stacked and waiting. It is as I retrace my steps to the road that I meet one of Kit's companions.

'He had to go to the inn for the inquest,' he says.

'What inquest?'

'Jem's of course. And that man from London's.'

'But everyone is away in Saffron Walden,' I say. 'How will they be able to take evidence properly?'

I run all the way back to the inn, but by the time I get there the Coroner has come, opened the inquest, closed it and gone. Both Henderson and Jem were killed by footpads from another county. Suffolk probably. Nothing more to be done.

Jem is to buried this afternoon.

Probert is less concerned than I.

'It is irregular,' he concedes. 'One might go so far as to say that it is contrary to the Law and to all precedent, but it makes little difference. I have conducted my own inquest, you might say, and formed my own views. The Coroner is clearly a good friend of the Colonel's, and holding an unannounced inquest on market day is a stroke of genius. Payne is playing a weak hand of cards well enough.'

Probert is sitting at a table outside the inn, making do with a mutton pie, pease pudding and apples for his dinner. He offers me none, nor does he ask me to take a seat. Perhaps I was better competition than he is willing to admit.

'How did things go with the Colonel?' I ask.

'As well as they might,' he says.

I take a seat anyway. I think it is, if anything, even hotter today and would prefer that we sat inside the inn. The air is suffocating. It is like trying to breathe warm water. The sky is no longer pure blue, however. Clouds are building in the distance, and there is a sort of crackle in the air. Probert finishes chewing sheep and prepares to address me again.

'Payne prevaricated, as I expected, and tried to tell me he had good reason for not reporting Henderson's death. He does not like you, by the way. He feels that you betrayed Pole in a scurvy manner. He regrets Pole's escape but blames Cobley for not keeping the village lock-up in good order. He wriggled and squirmed. He tried to tell me he was a close friend of the Lord Protector, but that was, I think, many years ago. He worries about what I shall report back to Mr Secretary Thurloe.'

'He worries about most things,' I say.

'Perhaps this time with cause. I do not intend to report favourably on his zeal and efficiency.'

'Does he know where Pole went?' I ask.

'He says he went north. I don't know why he thinks that, still less why he expects me to believe it. I asked Payne about Clarges, by the way.'

'And?'

'He was not pleased that you had mentioned Thomas Clarges to me. He seemed to think that you had betrayed some sort of confidence, in which case I am most grateful to you. But he claims Clarges is simply an old friend who called in on his way from Scotland to London, where he had other, perfectly legitimate business.'

'I have never suggested otherwise,' I say.

'Did you not? But you thought Payne's actions suspicious. I know you said that Payne had not investigated Henderson's murder with the eagerness that might be expected in a justice of the peace.'

'Did you say all of that to Colonel Payne?'

'Of course. I think you have somehow made an enemy there, but no matter. For the most part he accepts my conclusions – that Henderson was indeed close to uncovering a Royalist plot. He seemed uncertain whether it was less blameworthy to have suspected such a plot himself or to have had no inkling of it – he danced from one position to another quite charmingly. He did agree, however, that we should leave the muskets where they are for the moment.'

'Until you have questioned Ben?'

'Yes. Payne proposed that Jem himself might have stored the muskets there, but that seems unlikely. Of course, I see the attraction of their being gathered together by one who can no longer hang for it. Your friend's story appears to be true, by the way – in some respects at least. A neighbour remembers being woken by the squealing of a pig being slaughtered at some early hour. So, it would seem that the Grices did go straight home at the time Dickon claims. But Dickon may not have been as sober as he would have you believe. One of his brothers says he made a bit of a mess of the pig. Blood everywhere.'

'And your conclusion is . . . ?'

'Your friend is telling the truth about the time of his return. Of course, that doesn't mean he was at the inn all night. But he has given me the names of his fellow drinkers, whom I shall also need to speak to. But not yet. You say the charcoal burners were at the inquest? I shall seek them out and discover what more they can tell me. Then perhaps I shall call in at the Steward's cottage before returning to the inn to question

Mr Bowman. So, Grey, meet me here this evening. I begin to think I know who the murderer is, and Jem was right that it will surprise some in the village, though not all.'

Throughout the afternoon the clouds gather into a dark billowing mass that hangs furiously above us, a giant bruise in the sky. Far off there is a rumble of thunder like an echo of a battle fought long ago. A breeze appears from nowhere and whips the branches of the trees into a brief frenzy. Then all is still again, waiting.

It is as Jem's coffin is being carried from the inn to the church that the first drops of rain fall, throwing up the dust. The fat, warm summer rain darkens the road spot by spot, until there is no more powdery, buff surface to be seen. The villagers far-sighted enough to bring cloaks wrap them close around, and most of the women pull shawls or their white scarves over their heads; but those bearing the coffin – and I am one – have to suffer the constant assault from the sky. We are soaked before we have reached the crossroads but trudge on bareheaded, stepping over small rivulets that spring somehow from the grass and weave across the road. There is a brief respite at the lych gate, where we huddle while the Rector says a prayer, then it is onwards to the awaiting grave.

Some clergymen might hurry a service like this for a recently arrived and scarcely noticeable inhabitant of the village, but Abraham Reading, much to our discomfort, accords Jem the respect that is due to him. We cluster around the grave as if for warmth. The church is just a looming grey mass beyond the swirling sheets of rain. Reading stands ramrod straight, water dripping from his lank hair, prayer book threatening to dissolve in his hands. He alone seems not to flinch when the lightning flashes and the thunder explodes above us.

Word has spread quickly. Most of the village is there. The Colonel stands apart from the rest, hunched in his cloak, his hat in his hands. Away from the manor house, he seems slight and insignificant. Sir Felix, at the very edge of the grave, has given his own cape to Aminta. I see him touch her shoulder and whisper something, but I can scarcely hear the Rector himself above the noise of the rain. Aminta nods. I catch her eye, and she smiles briefly. Sir Felix stands perfectly still, apparently not noticing that he is soaked to the skin. When you have faced a hail of Roundhead musket balls, this must seem very little. I will speak to Aminta once the service is over. With Pole fled, perhaps everything is not lost.

The lightning flashes again. My mother, beside me, frowns as if at an unnecessary interruption. She wishes to blame somebody for this downpour but cannot identify any culprit other than God. Briefly she bows her head and clasps her hands together. Prayer is my mother's way of holding God to account.

Ben and Nell are a short distance off, sharing Ben's – or more likely Nell's – wrap. Ben is clearly back from the market – as is Mistress Mansell, who is enveloped in a bundle of garments of various sizes, presumably her unsold stock in trade. Will Cobley stands looking at the ground, his hat firmly crammed onto his head. I wonder if the Colonel has reprimanded him for sleeping through another murder. It's scarcely his fault this time. Ifnot, bareheaded, looks up at the sky, then wipes the rain out of his eyes. Like Sir Felix, he disdains any cloak, and the water drips from his leather jerkin. Harry Hardy has pleaded age and rheumatism and taken shelter in the church porch. Will Warwick is creeping away to join him. I do not see the Grices, though word of the burial may not have yet reached the farm. Nor do I see Probert.

One of those assembled round the grave may well be Jem's killer. I look at each face for some sign of guilt or remorse, but I see only weariness and suspicion. They too are wondering which of them has done this thing. Then Abraham Reading holds up his hand. We are about to sing a hymn.

Sodden earth is thudding onto the coffin lid when I see Kit come striding through the gate, his eyes searching for somebody. I should have noticed his absence too, which now seems odd. I expect him to talk first to the Rector or the Colonel, but it is me whom he approaches and draws to one side. Water drips from his hat and his clothes. There is blood on his collar.

'Probert has been shot,' he says.

'Where? When?'

'In the woods. Not far from where we found Jem. As to when . . . I couldn't say. We found him as we were coming along the path to the church. He was lying almost on the path. A little way off we found a musket.'

'Probert's dead?' I ask, aghast.

'Not dead,' says Kit. 'Not yet anyway. The ball is lodged in his shoulder. He's lost more blood than is good for a man, and I don't know what damage the shot has done. He has a strong constitution, but God alone can say what the outcome will be.'

'Where is he?' asks my mother.

'He is being carried here through the woods.'

'Go back and direct them to the New House,' says my mother. 'We will take care of him. I shall go home at once and prepare. Jem will forgive me if I leave others to see him safely to his last resting place.'

My mother, as the sometime wife and unpaid assistant of a surgeon, is regularly consulted in the village on breaks and sprains and fevers and stomach ache. She and Martha prepare all manner of ointments and potions, of which I know little but which some villagers set much store by. Even in my father's time, many preferred my mother's ministrations to his. But a wound like this is surely beyond even her.

'Was he able to say who shot him?' I ask.

'He was able to say nothing at all that made sense. He kept saying "the least expected", as if that signified a great deal,' says Kit. 'Does he mean what Jem meant?'

'Perhaps,' I say. 'But a name would be more helpful.'

'He may tell us yet. And if he is capable of telling us who fired the shot, you may be better able to understand his words than others.'

'I'll go back to the road,' I say, 'and direct the men to our house.'

'Thank you,' says Kit. 'Then I have done all I can for Probert. I shall stay and pay my respects here.' He removes his hat and gives it a shake. Then, bareheaded, he walks slowly towards Jem's grave.

'He has a fever,' my mother says, 'but that is as it must be. His shoulder is now free of musket balls, and the wound is clean.'

Probert is in my bed. I have no idea where I shall sleep tonight. Perhaps none of us will sleep. We sit by the bed for an hour. Neither of us speaks. We are listening for the slightest word from Probert, but Probert sleeps soundly. That, at least, must be good. He wakes briefly, shivers and mumbles but does not look in the direction of his audience. Then he is still again.

Outside the sun is shining on the wet garden. The air is full of the freshness that you get after summer rain. I hear a horse approaching rapidly. There is an urgent banging on the door below, and Martha brings Dickon into the room.

'He lives yet?' asks Dickon anxiously.

My mother nods. 'By tomorrow we shall know God's intentions,' she says. 'Of course, I have already informed God what outcome would be best.'

'It was a musket shot,' I add. 'The weapon is downstairs. Kit found it nearby and carried it along with him.'

'Is it one of the muskets that you came across at the inn?' Dickon asks. 'I have been with the Colonel and he told me about them.'

'Does it matter?' I ask.

'It would be another piece of evidence against you,' says Dickon.

'Against *me*?'

'Listen,' says Dickon urgently, 'I have come to warn you that the Colonel plans to have you arrested.'

'Arrested? For what? When Probert was shot, I must have been carrying Jem's coffin – or at all events, at the inn beforehand.'

'Do you know when Probert was shot?'

'Not to the minute,' I say.

'Exactly,' says Dickon. 'But it is worse. The Colonel is also going to arrest you for Henderson's murder. And Jem's.'

'But . . .' I say.

'He says you were out all night when Henderson was killed.'

'True,' I say, 'but so were others.'

'You were also the First Finder but failed to raise the hue and cry.'

'Technically correct, but I did report it to the Colonel as soon as we had taken Henderson to the crypt. He was satisfied enough at the time. He said I did right.'

'Who did he say it to?'

'Me.'

'Any witnesses to that?'

'No.'

'Then you may not be able to rely on it in court. You also destroyed or lost important evidence.'

'What?'

'A silver button apparently.'

'Well, yes,' I say. 'I did that, but . . .'

'And you invented a strange horseman whom you could accuse of the murder you committed.'

'He was real.'

'John – *nobody else saw him*. Not Ben, who was at the inn, nor Ifnot, who lives just beyond the inn. How can the rider be real and nobody else see him?'

'But I saw the horse. It was in the stable. You must have seen the horse too.'

'I saw a grey horse in the stable. Ben says it was Henderson's.'

'Don't you believe me?'

'Yes, but even if they put me on the jury, I'll be just one of twelve.'

I sigh. 'What else did the Colonel say?'

'You were the only one who knew where Jem was hiding.'

'Except Kit and the charcoal burners.'

'Are you accusing them?'

'Of course not,' I say. Nor am I accusing Aminta or my mother or the Colonel.

Dickon looks at me significantly. 'Kit apparently said that Jem refused to go with you out of the wood but preferred to risk going alone. Jem was frightened of you and would tell you nothing.'

'I told the Colonel myself that Jem preferred to go alone,' I say. 'It signified nothing. Jem wasn't frightened, just cautious.'

'Just cautious? Again that is a distinction that you will need to explain very carefully to the jury. The Colonel says you then placed the ring, which you had stolen from Henderson, in Pole's hat to put the blame on an innocent man.'

'But you know that I didn't do that. You saw the note. It was hidden under my tankard when we went to search for Jem. We were both out of the room.'

'*I* was out of the room,' says Dickon. 'When I came back, you were standing by the table.'

In spite of the warmth of the day, I feel a chill in the room. So, this is what fear is like. There's more than enough to hang me there – even if my family did own the village almost from the Conquest to the time of Good Queen Bess.

'Surely you don't believe that I put the ring there myself?' I say.

'No,' says Dickon. 'No, of course not. But if I were asked in court, what could I reply? I'd have to answer the question truthfully. I would be under oath.'

He says this in such a sanctimonious way that I wonder if I am being paid back for approving Ben's being cracked like a hazelnut. If so, it is a little harsh, I think. In the end, Ben wasn't cracked at all.

'And then,' continues Dickon, 'you knew exactly where to find the muskets.'

'Probert suggested I should search there,' I say.

We both look at Probert, who is in my bed, saying nothing.

'I am innocent of all of these crimes,' I say.

There is a pause during which I hope for some agreement on this point. It is my mother who eventually breaks the silence.

'Of course he is,' she says so sharply that Dickon actually takes a pace backwards. 'What possible reason would John have for killing any of these people?'

Dickon is looking at my mother with a strange respect, as if she really was still the lady of the manor. He coughs nervously before he speaks.

'The Colonel says that John, as a Republican zealot, killed Henderson, believing him to be a Royalist spy. Jem saw John at the stables that evening and fled when John later threatened him. John then had to kill Jem to stop him testifying to the Colonel. Probert was getting close to discovering Jem's murderer, and so John crept out just before the funeral and waylaid him as he came through the wood. He then hurried back to attend the funeral as if nothing had happened.'

'Nonsense,' says my mother. 'As you know well.'

'I'm only telling you what the Colonel is saying,' says Dickon. 'I think that John may have upset the Colonel in some way. I tried to dissuade him, but I believe the Colonel will issue a warrant this afternoon.'

'If I am a Republican zealot,' I say, 'what am I doing with a cache of Royalist muskets?'

'There are others plotting revolution,' says Dickon, 'not just the Royalists: Fifth Monarchy Men, for example, like General Harrison. Or Levellers.'

'Fifth Monarchy Men? Levellers? He thinks I am one of those madmen? God save us all.'

Was Aminta right? Do I now resemble a Puritan or even an Anabaptist? Is that why there is some secret in the village that I am not to share?

'The Colonel must be made to see sense,' says my mother, as though I had not been trying to do this since the discovery of the body. 'I am sure that John has simply been maladroit in his dealings with him. It is a way he has. The question is, where is the safest place for John in the meantime?'

Probert chooses this moment to open his eyes. He looks at the little group of us clustered by the doorway. With great effort he raises himself painfully on his elbows, then lifts one hand and points straight at me. 'That is the man!' he gasps.

I look at my mother in horror. 'I swear to you . . .' I say.

'No matter,' she says. 'The fever is upon him and he knows not what he says. Tomorrow he may prove more rational.'

'Tomorrow may be too late,' says Dickon. 'If he is not alive in the morning and those chance to be his dying words, no jury can fail to convict you. It may only be for Probert's murder, not Henderson's, but a man cannot hang twice however many times he is found guilty. You are not safe here. John, as your friend I beg you to flee.'

'Where should I go?' I ask.

'To London,' says Dickon.

'But that will just make people believe I am guilty,' I say.

'Only for a while,' says my mother. 'One way or another, I think this will resolve itself in time. Indeed, I think it will resolve itself very soon. But for the moment you must take our horse and ride to London. It is easier to hide there. I shall give you money – I do have a little gold that I have put aside. Please do not tell Martha, however, or she will expect me to pay her wages; the lower orders of society are sadly mercenary.'

'Just keep clear of Thurloe,' says Dickon. 'Or any of his agents.'

'Unless you have been properly introduced,' says my mother vaguely.

I turn and look at her. I am in mortal danger and she is worried about social niceties? She smiles at me as if she has just given me good advice. I despair of her. Truly, I despair.

'That mare of yours will never reach London,' says Dickon more practically. 'You must take my gelding.'

I clasp Dickon's hand. 'You are a true friend,' I say. 'A true friend in my hour of need. But how will you explain the loss of your horse to your father?'

He gives me a crooked smile. 'I can always say somebody stole it, can't I? But you need to leave now, before they come to arrest you. I wouldn't want you spending tonight with Harry Hardy's pigs. They've been spared Pole, but I'm too fond of those pigs to want them to have to share their sty with you.'

I pat Dickon's roan gelding, which is tied up in our yard, and strap on my saddlebag. I unhitch him and lead him quietly onto the road. We have agreed that it is better that neither of our servants witnesses my departure. It will be easier for them if they are questioned. But there I run straight into Ifnot Davies.

'Thou hast taken to Dickon Grice's horse,' he observes. 'And, to judge by thy baggage, thou art not taking him for a quick canter across the fields.'

You can't lie to somebody like Ifnot. Or tell him to mind his own business.

'I'm off to London,' I say. 'I seem to have upset the Colonel, and it may be better I'm elsewhere.'

Ifnot nods. 'God be with thee, then, John Grey,' he says. He proffers his hand.

I know I'm going to need my hand to ride the horse, but I give it to Ifnot to be crushed anyway.

'You know that Probert has been shot?' I ask, wincing as I receive Ifnot's good wishes.

'Yes. Will he live?'

'I don't know,' I say.

'I spoke to him this morning,' says Ifnot. 'There was little I could tell him. He does believe in thy horseman though.'

'I think it's too late for that to matter,' I say.

'The truth always matters,' says Ifnot.

'You're a good man, Ifnot. Look out for my mother while I'm away.'

'I'll pray for her,' says Ifnot. 'And for Probert, though he blasphemes in strange tongues. And for thee – in whichever city thou are bound for. York, wasn't it?'

So he does know how to lie after all.

'Thanks, Ifnot,' I say. After all, I'm going to need all the help I can get.

I am here, at the crossroads of the village. I am here because I am no longer at my mother's house. I am no longer at my mother's house because, because . . .

Even three hours ago this would have seemed the most unlikely of outcomes. Dark forces are working against me, and I cannot say what those forces are or whether they may seek to pursue me southwards to the capital. As it is, I am being obliged to flee to London, with just a spare shirt, a few of last year's apples and, I notice, a jar of preserved cherries in my saddlebag.

It would be safer to make this a short farewell, and it would be best to use the few remaining hours of daylight as well as I can. Once in London, I must seek out Mr Samuel Morland, who it seems is inclined to offer me work. Unless his mind too has already been poisoned against me.

I rein in Dickon's gelding and pause for a moment. Was it my imagination, or did I notice a movement in the bushes ahead? A minute passes slowly, and I see nothing more than should be there. And yet if nobody waits in that bush with a dagger or an arrest warrant, there is always the next bush and the one after that and the one after that. Whatever dangers lie ahead in London, I cannot stay here.

So, for one last time let us both breathe in the cool, damp air that has followed in the wake of the storm and which speaks to us of everything that is in the village which I am about to leave – the sweet white roses over the door of this beshitten cottage, the green-leaf smell of the orchard beyond and the rich, many-coloured stink of the cowshed.

The road to noisy, friendly London stands open to me.

London

'A report from Essex, Mr Secretary,' says Morland.

'Can it wait?' asks Thurloe.

Morland gives a rhetorical sniff and looks down at his seated master.

'Yes, of course. It will still be here at ten o'clock or any hour that you wish to call for it. But you said you wanted to read anything from Probert as soon as it arrived.' He tosses a copious head of blond hair. There is perhaps just a hint of contempt in his look, but his voice is honey.

'Is it enciphered?'

'It is not in code, though it is partly in Latin.'

'Horace or Plautus?' asks Thurloe with a sigh.

'The Latin is, I think, from the liturgy of the Romish Church,' says Morland. 'But that is merely conjecture. I have never been an adherent of that false religion.'

Thurloe grunts in apparent approval – it's always prudent

to be an adherent of whichever religion currently enjoys official endorsement. He skims the letter. 'Probert is obscure and complacent,' he notes. 'He says Henderson is dead, by an unknown hand. Sic transit gloria mundi, *he adds. I think that you are right, by the way, that the phrase relates to dead Bishops of Rome. I have no idea why Probert should apply it to Henderson. He also reports that Mr Thomas Clarges, General Monck's brother-in-law, has visited the village. What do you make of that?'*

'Does he make any specific charge against Clarges?'

'I think not. Still, it is a strange coincidence. Probert believes that his own life may be in danger but that he is well able to manage things. That is, on the face of it, unlikely.'

Morland tilts his head on one side as if considering this point. 'Had you asked my advice, Mr Secretary, I would not have sent Probert . . .'

'Well, I did, and now I'm reinforcing him. I've sent him four dragoons under a good officer. There is no further need for secrecy. They can stay and guard him if needed or bring us a further report if not. I merely hope they are not too late. A lot can happen in a couple of days.'

'I'm sure the dragoons are a wise precaution. As you have observed, something odd has occurred.'

'Another odd thing,' says Thurloe, 'is that the young man who was recommended to you for a place in this department comes from the same village.'

'John Grey?' asks Morland.

'You hadn't noticed?'

'I was aware only that Grey had just completed his studies at Cambridge. But if you say he does . . .'

'There are a lot of coincidences here for one small village,' says Thurloe. 'We might question Grey a little when he arrives in

London if Probert has not already done so. I asked Probert to look him out and to examine him cautiously.'

'Cautiously? I would be interested to know what Probert made of that instruction,' says Morland.

Thurloe pauses. His directions had seemed to him to admit of only one meaning. But it is in Morland's nature to see several. That's why he is so useful to him.

'I assume that we shall see Mr Grey in person very soon,' says Thurloe. 'When can we expect him?'

'If it is a choice between Probert's cautious questioning and coming to London, then he will be with us quite soon, I would think,' says Morland.

A Traveller Requests a
Room for the Night

'Yes, we've got a bed. You mind sharing?'

'The room or the bed?' I ask.

'The bed. Already got two gentlemen in the other bed,' says the innkeeper.

'How much?'

'Fourpence for supper, fourpence for the bed, tuppence for your horse, farthing for beer.'

The price is not unreasonable, and I shall need to stay at worse places than this if I am to make my money last.

'You're lucky,' adds the landlord. 'A party of dragoons almost stopped here. There'd have been no beds left then and no room in the stables neither.'

'I saw them on the road,' I say. 'Five of them. They were travelling fast.'

'Going to Saffron Walden or some such. I told them to rest their horses. Told them they'd never be in Saffron Walden before dark.'

'They won't be. And they may break a leg if they are not careful.'

The innkeeper nods. 'With luck they may break a neck. And where might you be bound for, young man?'

'London,' I say.

'You've still a good few miles to go.'

'So they tell me.'

'And your name, my good sir?'

'Henderson,' I say.

'You'll have a pass, naturally, Mr Henderson. Just so as I know you're travelling on your proper business.'

'I don't need a pass. Do I look like a vagrant? Am I likely to become a charge on the parish? I'll be in London by noon tomorrow anyway.'

'Legally, everyone needs a pass.'

'I don't.'

'Of course not, Mr Henderson. That'll be fourpence for the room, then, and tuppence for the illegality.'

'Very well.'

'And thruppence for stabling.'

'I'll pay you two. My horse needs no pass. You may bring me some beer now and bring my supper when it's ready. I'll be sitting over there in the corner.'

'Over there? Away from the candles and the fire?'

'That's right. And tell the stableboy I'll need my horse early. At first light, tell him.'

London

So this is it. Well, it's bigger than Cambridge.

It is the slender spires and the towers that I notice first, and the smoke that rises from every chimney. From up here on breezy Highgate Hill, London has a silver haze drifting above it. Below the haze, the sun glints dully off the mass of dwellings, churches, slaughterhouses, palaces, tanneries, halls, foundries, shops, breweries and one great cathedral, all spreading like the flood tide across the broad plain of the muddy Thames. It's difficult to say precisely where this shimmering thing called London begins and ends. Countryside merges into orchards and gardens. Fingers of brick inch out along each country road. From here you can just make out the noise of the far-off city streets. Is this not, after all, where Dick Whittington and his cat paused and heard the sound of Bow Bells summoning them to return? But this morning no bells invite me on. Today London is making no promises.

I take one last breath of wholesome country air and, leading Dickon's horse by the bridle, I start to descend the hill.

Now I am in London, I wish myself back at Highgate. The press of people in each street is overwhelming, all moving ruthlessly towards some destination that has not yet been disclosed to me. I cannot say how far I have come since I trustingly left the gelding at the inn, munching hay at an unknown price. I doubt I have progressed half a mile, and even then at a pace that a snail would regard as unchallenging. The city conspires to close in on its inhabitants. The houses are above me as well as to each side. If you look up, all you see are the grime-streaked overhanging floors that jut out into the roadway, each storey encroaching a little further than the one below. How does anyone breathe here in these airless lanes? Do they not notice the constant stench of piss and rotting vegetables, or do Londoners grow to love it? Are they not deafened by their own voices? How does any child grow to manhood or womanhood without being crushed under the great wheels of one of the painted coaches that creak and rattle by? Perhaps they don't need to. As I came in from Highgate, half the countryside seemed to be flocking with me, more than making up any chance losses amongst the native Londoners.

St Paul's Churchyard, with its leafy plane trees and its bookstalls, seems to offer some sort of haven – at least of a relative kind. Not that I can afford to purchase any books. I have already established that a room in a London inn costs more than one on the road, though fortunately nobody here cares whether you have a pass signed by a magistrate or indeed by the giants Gog and Magog themselves. I have established too that food in London costs more than anywhere else and is much worse. It is fortunate that I have the offer of employment here in London and am on my way to take it up. My new employer, moreover, cannot yet have heard that I am wanted for murder in Essex. It is important that I reach Morland quickly and can tell him my own story first.

I find it difficult, however, to pass so many bookstalls without stopping briefly to examine the wares. I pick up an old, battered copy of Horace, flick through its well-thumbed pages, then reluctantly return it to the table. The bookseller, a small man with bad teeth and worse breath than he supposes, attempts to strike up a conversation with me.

'Perhaps Horace is not to your taste,' he says with a wink. 'I have some other books that I keep for discerning gentlemen who like something a bit different. Some books in French, if you'll understand me right. That is to say, the words are all French, but the pictures require little translation. And very instructive withal for a gentleman like yourself. I have one here written by a young French lady, explaining the many ways in which ladies in France may be gratified. You can examine it, good sir, if you choose.'

He places a slim volume into my hands. If he had hoped to arouse my curiosity, he has chosen a bad moment to do it. Something more interesting is happening behind his back. A man in a mulberry-coloured coat is moving across the churchyard.

'It is a most moral tale,' the bookseller continues, 'for the young ladies of France, though very wicked, are often *punished* for their vices. There are a number of plates illustrative of the punishments accorded them and, though I cannot vouch myself for their accuracy, they are detailed enough not to leave you in any uncertainty as to what is intended. Should you meet a French lady and need to correct her. Five shillings, including a discreet and careful wrapping.'

The man in mulberry has his back to me, but I still cannot mistake that hat or its ridiculous feathers.

'Or I have here the confessions of a young gentlewoman,' the bookseller is saying. 'In English, newly translated . . .'

'Pole!' I exclaim. I do not know whether he has seen me, but he has started to walk briskly towards Fleet Street.

'Sir?' enquires the bookseller. Of the many possible responses he had anticipated to this offer of fine literature, 'pole' was not one. It puzzles him. I feel I owe him some sort of explanation.

'Roger Pole,' I say. 'It could be no other.'

The bookseller understands no better than before. Sadly, it would take some time to tell him the full story, if I understood it myself. And I need to decide quickly – do I let Pole slip away, or do I follow him? I have no wish for a long conversation with him, but to know what he is doing and where he can be found may be of use to me.

'Indeed,' says the bookseller. I am clearly a madman, but madmen do sometimes buy books. 'Now, in this fine tale, the young gentlewoman is enamoured of a rough highwayman, who . . .'

'I'm sorry,' I say. 'I have to go.'

'You'll settle with me first, young sir!' he says. 'For that most instructive book. Let's call it four shillings and sixpence.'

I look down at my hands. I am still holding a book that would, apparently, assist me if I need to discipline a French lady. I doubt that I shall have need of it today.

'You'll damage the gold leaf!' exclaims the bookseller as he sees the book land back on his stall.

'Do you think anyone buys this sort of thing for the binding?' I ask.

The bookseller may be about to explain to me the many advantages of a fine binding, but he has spotted a more likely prospect – a rather bumptious young clerk, by the look of him. The bookseller brushes the leather cover with a loving hand.

'Ah, Mr Pepys,' he says. 'I think I may have something here to your taste, sir.'

But sadly I cannot stay to listen to Mr Pepys's reply.

Though Pole has a good start on me, his progress is no more rapid than mine. He is going in the opposite direction from the one in which I should be going, but if I miss this chance I may never catch sight of him again in a city this size. Perhaps he is evading me, or perhaps he is evading somebody else, but he moves with a steady purpose.

My progress, conversely, is slow and constantly checked by fools who insist on going the wrong way. While I am now pushing back in the direction from which I lately came, I still feel like a salmon swimming upstream. Perhaps the tide of Londoners has turned while I was at St Paul's. Ahead of me, halfway down Fleet Street, Pole's ridiculous hat is still bobbing above the crowd. Then the hat darts into one of the many narrow, twisting lanes on the right. It takes me a good two minutes to reach the same turning. The side street is clear, and at last I can run. Slipping on rotten cabbage leaves and straw, I skid down the stinking lane. Yes, that is Pole's hat and that is Pole beneath it. Then the sound of a coach approaching makes me step back very quickly into a doorway. When the deafening clatter of the wheels has passed on by, Pole has gone.

At first, there is only one way for the hat to have fled, then the lane splits into two, then into two again, each time halving the chances of hitting on Pole's route. Finally, passing through a low, narrow passageway that no rider let alone coach could negotiate, I come to a dead end in a foul, sunless courtyard pervaded by the greasy memory of suppers long ago. The black and grey half-timbered buildings lean out over me. Small, ragged London children stop playing and come over to menace me. 'Ma!' yells one. 'Customer!'

I raise my hands, palms out. 'I'm going,' I say.

'Don't you want to do it with my ma?'

'Not now,' I say.

'You ain't after a woman then?' asks the London child.

'No, a man,' I say.

'You'll need to go to Southwark if you want boys,' says the London child. 'Why don't you take my ma? Two shillings for half an hour, she is.'

'Thank you,' I say. 'Thank you kindly. I'll remember that.'

As I make my way by fits and starts back to where I came from, I resolve to think more carefully before I set off in pursuit of any other suspicious characters. I know no more than I did before, and whatever else I might have done with the past hour would have been more profitable than spoiling my boots in the London mire. Eventually, the broad arc of my travels brings me to the Guildhall, a great brick-and-stone building close to the city wall. By its door are posted a number of notices – missing people, lost animals, cures for the plague. Some are desperately old and ragged, and I doubt that the plague cure would work. But a bright new one catches my eye.

The description of the felon seems deliberately disparaging – was it really necessary to say that he has 'a loose tongue and a love of ale' for example? Or that he is of a dangerous and unpredictable temper? The description of the horse, on the other hand, is quite flattering. But it is the first line that really gets to the heart of the matter. I read it several times to digest it fully.

> Wanted for the murder of three men and the theft of a horse in the county of Essex: John Grey.

It would seem likely, then, that my future employer does know that I am not merely a murderer but – Dickon's inventiveness having proved less than I had hoped – also a horse thief.

I must change my plans. Perhaps Morland will rescue me from the jaws of a trap that seem to be closing even as I stand here admiring my poster. Or perhaps going to him will prove fatal. I remember my resolve. This time I shall not rush in. This time I shall think carefully before I act.

In the meantime I am alone in London with a fine horse but little money. I pull my hat down hard over my face and I proceed towards Holborn.

More Letters

Essex, Monday, 7 July 1657
To John Thurloe Esq, Whitehall Palace, London

Ave! May it please your lordship, I am returning your troopers to you with this letter. Though they have enjoyed their holiday, having them lounging around at the village inn was of no value to me.

It will gratify you to learn that I am somewhat recovered from being drilled through with a lead ball. A physician from Saffron Walden has assured me that being bled in this way has allowed the egress of many harmful humours and that I will ever be the stronger for it. I offered him the same physic as soon as my fingers are strong enough to pull a trigger, and he has not ventured inside my chamber since. So, I recover my strength bit by bit in the country air. Integer vitae scelerisque purus.

But this is not what your lordship wishes to learn from me. I am therefore pleased to report that I have completed my investigations. John Grey was helpful, as your honour suggested he might be. I commend him to you in whatever capacity you plan to use him.

Henderson is, as you already know, dead and buried. In the view of Colonel Payne, the Justice of the Peace, and of a jury convened by the Coroner, Henderson was the victim of footpads from neighbouring Suffolk, who, with the stupidity and dishonesty for which that county is apparently known, stole his hat but left behind his purse. Though my knowledge of the character of Suffolk is imperfect, I must concur. There is no evidence of any Royalist sentiment in the village. It is true that some antiquated muskets have been found in the stable at the inn, but the landlord assures me that they were left behind by Royalist deserters during the late conflict and were stored by him in the hayloft for safety. He offers them to the Lord Protector, at no more than the cost of conveying them to London, if His Highness feels that they are of any use to the Republic. The boy, Jem, would appear to have been the unfortunate victim of the same footpads, who must have remained hidden in the woods for some days after Henderson's murder. I believe my own wound to be an unlucky chance shot by one poaching in the same woods. I am told everyone poaches in the woods except Colonel Payne and the Rector. Whoever it was, I forgive him entirely, for who does not enjoy a fat little rabbit? So much, my lord, for that.

Mr Grey and I disagreed only on one point. He was convinced that he had seen a stranger on horseback the night Henderson met his end. I have spoken to many in the village, who assure me that Mr Grey slept soundly the whole night and was in no position to see anyone.

As to the conspiracy that Henderson was investigating, I am pleased to report that the county is unfailing loyal to His Highness.

Any documents that you may have that suggest otherwise are almost certainly forgeries put about by our enemies to confuse us and to waste our time. Nor, having had time to reflect on the matter, do I believe that Mr Clarges's visit is in any way suspicious. Colonel Payne assures me that Mr Clarges is simply an old friend. To the extent that they discussed General Monck, it was merely to confirm the General's continuing high regard for the Lord Protector.

I therefore trust that this letter will thus lay to rest certain doubts and fears that your lordship may have harboured. I shall write again when I am once more fit to undertake your excellency's commands. In the meantime I continue to recover slowly at the house of Mistress Grey, whither you may direct further letters and not to the inn, which is altogether less convenient.

Vale! Henricus Probert

The Steward's Lodge
7 July 1657
To Mr John Grey, London

My dearest John, I send this by the hand of a trusted friend in the hope that it will reach you.

All is well here. By dint of your mother's nursing, Probert continues to recover and has sworn that he does not believe the shot was fired by you. The Colonel has, however, already issued a warrant for your arrest. This is nailed to the door of the guildhall at Saffron Walden and, for aught I know, to the door of some great building in London too. I have told him that you are innocent, but he tells me that somebody in the village swears he saw you out on the Cambridge road shortly before Henderson was killed. John, I

*fear there are forces working against you that I do not understand.
I am trying to find out more, but in the meantime trust nobody
but me.*

*Please reply as soon as you receive this. Until then I am fearful
for your safety. I wonder constantly what you are doing.*

*Yours ever,
Aminta*

Letter Number 17

*Essex, 8 July 1657
To Sir Edward Hyde, c/o The Abbess, Benedictine Convent, Ghent*

*We understand from P that 444 is amenable to helping us when
the time is right. If he were to send his forces south and to bring the
arms we so sorely need, North Essex and other places would rise as
a man. But if he does not, things will go on as before — certainly as
concerns P, who constantly vacillates.*

*As to our affairs here, the boy Jem was buried on the same day
that Probert was shot. His death seems particularly unnecessary,
and I did what I could to prevent it. But* homo homini lupus, *as the saying is. Probert remains in the village, making a good
recovery. He too is now inclined, I think, to be helpful rather
than otherwise, though I have not seen his dispatches to 777. The
damsons are ripening and the cucumbers are plentiful.*

*For M — I have conveyed your last message as you asked. I shall
let you know when I receive a reply.*

*Yours to command
472*

A Problem

*T*hurloe *holds the letter a little further away. Nothing to do with his eyesight, he tells himself, merely that the light is not good.*

'There is something odd about Probert's letter. He has changed his views,' he says.

Morland frowns as he considers his reply. 'That is what happens when you conduct an investigation. He gives Grey a good character, I see.'

'Colonel Payne, conversely, seems convinced of Grey's guilt. He has issued a warrant for Grey's arrest.'

'Payne is a fool.'

'Colonel Payne was a close friend of the Lord Protector's.'

'The two things are not incompatible.'

Thurloe looks at Morland to see if he can detect the slightest trace of treason in that last remark, but what Morland has said is no more than the truth. Look at Lambert. Look at Fleetwood. Look at Harrison. *All generals. All once close to the Lord Protector. All imbeciles, though it would not pay a man to say so. And then there's Monck. No fool, but can he really be trusted?*

'Have Grey arrested,' says Thurloe. 'Payne is, after all, a magistrate.'

'I think Grey will come to us.'

'Have him arrested anyway. What harm can it possibly do? You must be able to find him.'

Morland says nothing. London is a spider's web, and this office is its very centre. He can find anyone.

To Southwark

This city has no uniform stink. Each part of London has its own jealously guarded odour. In certain streets there is the sickly and overpowering fragrance of malt from neighbouring breweries. Around the tanneries there is a constant reminder of the decay of all flesh. The herb market in Bucklersbury speaks of the countryside, though one that is dried and autumnal. At low tide the alleys that lead down to the Thames smell of oily mud and nameless things that float on the river. The only universal ingredient, shared indiscriminately over every neighbourhood, is sea coal; you can taste it – sometimes you can almost see it – in the air, and the resulting grime besmirches every building in the city.

The Red Lion fronts onto Holborn, just outside the city walls. It is a large inn, old-fashioned and half-timbered. Its face is caked with soot, but the sign is newly painted, and the improbably bright red beast swings gently in the breeze, snarling at nothing in particular that I can see.

I enter and take my place in the large parlour, calculating how many more meals I can order before my silver runs out. While I wait for my pie and ale, I look again at the sheet of paper I have been carrying in my pocket. The solution to the riddle has so far escaped me.

NUMBER 9 PIEX NECT FEWS RRMB SUGE OBYS NMEO HEIT HOUG ATDE EDTH GKIN VHAS GERY SOOD OUPP ERTH UREB ETTH DLEA HERS FIPO KTHE INOT ISBE HNGC EALL DNGE HBYT UEYO RNGE SONE MFOR TJRE SURN EHOM NSOO UIWO ELDR DMIN OYOU UFYO ORPR EMIS 472

I am again struck by the anagram of my name, and not out of pure vanity. I pick out the words 'hers' and 'the' and 'had'. Could 'THE INOT' really mean 'the Knot'? Or perhaps 'Ifnot'? And 'GKIN' is an anagram of 'King' . . .

'There were some troopers here while you were abroad, Mr Henderson,' says the innkeeper softly as he places food and drink on the table. He pretends not to notice me fold away a dirty scrap of paper, but I suspect little escapes his eyes.

'There are troopers all over London,' I say.

'They were looking for a John Grey from over by Saffron Walden,' says the innkeeper.

'I wish them every success in finding him.'

'Me too, Mr Henderson. We always wish the officers of the Protectorate well, don't we? I told them we had nobody *of that name* staying here. Didn't you say you'd just come from Essex though?'

'I didn't say I came from Saffron Walden.'

'No, you didn't say that. They were asking after a gelding too. Roan. White blaze. A bit like the one you have in my stable.'

'Well, I didn't buy him from . . . what did you say the gentleman's name was?'

'Grey. John Grey. They didn't call him a gentleman. He's just a lawyer or something.'

'Well, if I see John Grey, I'll let him know.'

The innkeeper looks at me, doubtless trying to work out if I can pay my bill. He makes up his mind.

'You planning on staying long, Mr Henderson?' he asks.

'I might be.'

'Then your purse is full no doubt.'

'And if it's not?'

'Well, you probably won't need a horse in London. Best sell him and save the cost of oats and hay. You'll get a good price over in Islington. And they don't ask too many questions. Not in Islington.'

I don't look up from my pie, but I nod in acknowledgment. After all, I can always buy Dickon another one.

Riding out to Islington in sunny weather was pleasant enough. Returning on foot with the clouds gathering again is less so, though the gold in my purse is some recompense. I have for once taken some of Ben's advice, but I am wondering whether London thieves might not look in my boots before they look anywhere else – particularly since I am unable to stop myself patting my lower leg from time to time to check that all is well. I can only hope that nobody took too much interest when the money changed hands and that nobody has followed me from the rather obscure stable where the transaction took place. For the moment a handful of gold coins sit there snugly enough, pressing uncomfortably against my calf. I look behind me. There are plenty of people on the same path, but that is to be expected on a well-frequented route between the city and one of its closest villages – a village that is, moreover, gaining an enviable reputation for dairy products and loose living. Somewhere in the distance there is a rumble of thunder, and a cold breeze whips across the open space. The field I am crossing feels a lot bigger, and the people somehow look smaller. Everyone quickens their pace.

I am, however, back in Holborn before the first large drops of rain start to fall. I sprint the last few hundred yards and gain the open door of the Red Lion. As I shake the water off myself, I wonder briefly whether it is raining in North Essex and whether they got the hay in yesterday while they could.

'I thought,' says the landlord, emerging from some back room, 'that you might like to pay me for your room and board – up to this evening. Now you are, I trust, richly in funds.'

'Certainly – after supper,' I say, not wishing to display a purse so full of gold in such a public place. 'Could you kindly send a grilled chicken up to my chamber later? The walk back from Islington has given me an appetite.'

'You see,' says the landlord, 'I was rather hoping that you might settle your reckoning straight away. I have many expenses, and my suppliers insist on ready money . . .'

Does he think I'm about to run off without paying? That is unlikely. Not before I've eaten anyway. 'I'll pay you when you bring supper up,' I say.

'Very well,' says the landlord to my departing back. But he says it with great regret.

I am halfway up the stairs before it occurs to me that he has not asked me what I wish to drink, though when I open my chamber door it becomes clear why this might be so and why the landlord might have preferred an early settlement of any debts. The room is not large but it already contains an officer, sitting in my only chair, and three troopers, standing in various poses round the walls. The officer rises. 'You are Mr Grey, I think?' he says.

Since he appears to know the answer to this question already, I decide that I do not need to stay and confirm it. The officer should perhaps have placed a man closer to the entry, or at least should have assumed that a lawyer might be fairly agile. And that they, in their riding boots, might be slower than they wished. I leap the last four stairs in my haste to regain the parlour. The landlord watches open-mouthed as I send chairs flying in my desire to be away from his inn. I do not look back as I run down Holborn, but I think I have left them all far behind.

The road across London Bridge is no more than a tunnel, sometimes with a line of sky above it, sometimes entirely covered over. The houses and shops that have been allowed to grow up on it have reduced the width of the road to just twelve feet, but everything on wheels that enters London from the south must come this way. Everyone fleeing London to the south must go this way too, unless they choose to pay to take one of the ferryboats and gain some precious minutes. On foot you have plenty of time as you shuffle along to look up at the dusty beams supporting the floors of the houses above. Voices and horses' hooves echo strangely, competing all the time with the rush of the water below; the Thames, ponded back by the bridge, is constantly gushing between its many arches, its force slackening briefly only at high and low tide as it switches direction. Such is the strength of the flow that it amazes me that the bridge and its many-towered superstructure still stand. Now and then I emerge into the drizzle for twenty or thirty yards, only to plunge again into another dark, humming passage. Much of the time I am pressed up against the back of the man in front or trodden on by the man behind. I am getting to know both quite well. And there are no fresh breezes to blow away the stink of humanity. Finally, and much to my relief, I pass under the Great Stone Gateway at the southern end and am in Southwark. From there I am able to look back at the bridge's most remarkable feature. On long spikes on the very top of the gateway are the boiled and tarred heads of such traitors as have been caught and dealt with. Perhaps murderers and horse stealers too. Though they are far above me, my impression is that they look wet and unhappy. It would be as well not to join them.

I pause for a moment in the shadow of this awful gateway, knowing that if the troopers decided to take a ferryboat, then they will now be ahead of me. I wait, watching, as long as I dare, for they may equally be behind me, then plunge into the heaving mass of South Londoners.

Grimy, generous Southwark opens up and swallows me whole.

A Summer's Day

Only the greenness of the trees gives any clue as to the time of year. The day is grey and unresolved, the air moist without any visible proof of rain, the breeze cold but without bite, the clouds low and ill-defined. The landlord of the Red Lion stands in his doorway, eyeing the crowd milling along Holborn. A day like this must be bad for trade – too cool for thirst; too warm for a seat by a blazing fire. Then out of nowhere a customer emerges – a farmer, by the look of him, with a ruddy face, an open smile and good appetite. What can be seen of his short blond hair is dishevelled beneath his broad-brimmed hat. He wears a new and very serviceable brown worsted suit, a garment that is perhaps not entirely ridiculous in whichever part of the country he hails from.

'What can I do for you, my fine gentleman?' the landlord enquires.

'I'm after some information,' says Dickon Grice.

'Then please to enter, good sir, where we may the better converse, *and you might perhaps wish to sample our ale. Or a gentleman of good breeding such as yourself might prefer a pint of wine. I have some excellent claret. Or Rhenish, if claret is not to your taste. Or sack or canary if you have a mind to them.'*

'No wine, thank you, nor ale. I just need to know if somebody called John Grey is staying here.'

'Who's asking?'

Dickon notices that he is no longer being addressed as 'good sir'.

'My name is Dickon Grice. I'm a friend of his.'

'A good friend?'

'Yes.'

'Might your friend have been going under the name of Henderson?'

'He might. The man I'm looking for is medium height, a little over twenty years old, dressed in a green suit of clothes — nobody would mistake him for a man who does a proper day's work in the fields. Indeed, he both looks like and is in cold hard fact a lawyer.'

'We had somebody here named Henderson very like your friend. He left without paying his bill. I suppose you wouldn't like to settle it for him, sir? Seeing how you're his friend.'

'That's right,' says Dickon. 'I wouldn't like to settle it for him. Where did he go when he left?'

'Since he left in a bit of a hurry with two soldiers in hot pursuit, I couldn't rightly say.'

'Did you at least see which road he took?'

'He ran off towards the city, if that's any help. But a man may travel some distance in a couple of days if he does but run fast enough.'

'He ran off? So he left his horse behind? A roan gelding?'

'Didn't have no horse — at least, by the time he ran off he didn't. He just left me a leather bag with a clean shirt, two pairs of

stockings and a jar of preserved cherries. You can have them if you settle the bill.'

'I'm happy that you keep all. I doubt the shirt would fit anyone with a healthy appetite. If he returns, though, could you get a message to me? I'm staying at the White Boar, near the Tower. I'll make it worth your while.'

The landlord looks doubtful that this last promise will come to anything, but he nods anyway. 'He owes you money too then?'

'It sounds as if he owes me a horse, but I'll take that up with him later. His life is in danger. Tell him, whatever he does he should not go near Roger Pole.'

'Roger Pole?'

'That's right. A thin gentleman with a pale, pockmarked face and a sneer for a mouth. If he comes here asking questions – and he may – you haven't seen John Grey or me, do you understand?'

The landlord watches Dickon depart. He'll certainly look out for Roger Pole, though what he tells him will depend very much on how deep this Pole person is prepared to dig into his pockets. Deeper hopefully than the fat yokel in a cheap country suit.

Thurloe looks out of his open window and wonders if it will rain. He takes in a lungful of the sooty Westminster air – a little fresher than that in the city, though not as fresh at that at Hampton Court, where the Lord Protector is today. Cromwell's coach set off at dawn. Not even Thurloe knows the route that it was to take, such is His Highness's fear of assassination. Probably, until the moment of departure, Cromwell had not allowed himself to consider which road they would travel by. The fate of the Protectorate hangs on a slender thread, and many citizens possess scissors.

Samuel Morland brings in a packet of letters.

'The results of last night's opening and reading,' he says. 'The *letters from the Spanish Netherlands are increasingly despairing. I think we may expect more defections.'*

'Anything more from Essex?'

'Not lately. I heard that Probert has returned.'

'Glorying in what seems to be a relatively minor wound. "Non omnis moriar", as he observed to me several times. He seemed to have made himself very comfortable in Essex.'

'It is a comfortable county. But I think that the shot might have killed him without Mistress Grey's nursing. We have much to thank her for. Did Probert have anything to say about Mr Grey?'

'He repeats that the shot could not have been fired by him. I'm not sure how he knows, because he was shot from behind and didn't see his assailant. But Grey seems to have given him good service. Probert commends him to us as an intelligent young man.'

Morland smiles. He does not need to say that he has been proved right.

'Once Probert has fully recovered,' Thurloe continues, 'I intend to send him somewhere where he will be busier. He has had too much time on his hands. Before he left Essex, he clearly commenced some quarrel with Colonel Payne. He tells me that Payne has performed his duties ill as a magistrate and recommends Payne's removal – well, that is a matter for the Lord Chancellor, not me. Any thoughts, Mr Morland?'

'As you say, it is not for us to dismiss magistrates. I thought the only difference between Probert and Payne concerned Grey's guilt. Colonel Payne has, however, now written to us. He no longer judges that Grey is the killer. He has withdrawn the warrant and begs our pardon for having troubled us.'

'Indeed? Has Probert persuaded Payne then? If so, I fail to see why they should have fallen out.'

'It does seem odd. Having finally reached an agreement with

Payne, Probert denounces him. But there does at least now seem to be some consensus that Grey is innocent.'

'Then Grey may come to us safely without any impediment.'

Morland nods. 'Yes. Sadly, following your instructions, soldiers were sent to arrest John Grey. He escaped. He was staying at the Red Lion in Holborn, by the way, under the name of Henderson.'

'That was careless. Still, we at least now know Grey is calling himself Henderson. It suggests a ready wit.'

'Or a sad lack of imagination,' says Morland.

'Or a sad lack of imagination,' Thurloe says. 'Why is it, Sam, that you always think the worst of everyone?'

'Because you have trained me so well, my lord,' he says. 'Do not worry too much about Mr Grey, however. He knows where to find us. And my informants will track him down sooner or later. I shall discover some way to reassure Mr Grey that it is safe to come to us.'

'Thank you, Sam. I think you are the only person I can trust to get things done properly.'

Samuel Morland smiles, bows and is gone. There is no sound of footsteps. Perhaps he has learned the art of walking on air.

This city, thinks Dickon, has a foulness all its own, and the only reason people drink the ale is because you'd die if you tried to drink Thames water. He is beginning to long for a tankard containing just under a pint of Ben Bowman's weak so-called beer. Outside it has begun to rain. The carriages and the carts splash through the muddy puddles, throwing up a fine spray that coats the lower storeys of the houses and shops. It is already too dark in here to read – not that Dickon is a great one for reading – but too early to expect candles to be brought out. Candles might in any case assist the customers of the inn in counting their change and would thus be a double expense for the innkeeper.

Now, if a hunted man were to go into hiding in a place such as London, where would he go? Dickon has asked himself this question several times, the lack of an answer being attributable in some large part to the fact that he still does not know London well. John Grey has vanished from the sight of his friends every bit as much as from the sight of his enemies. In the course of his enquiries Dickon has, however, established that Roger Pole is somewhere in London and frequents an inn in Clerkenwell. Perhaps Pole might, wittingly or not, lead him to John Grey. Dickon takes another swallow of beer and grimaces. The sooner he can find his friend, the sooner he can stop drinking this bilge water. He pays his bill and, cramming his hat firmly onto his blond head, sets off into the rain.

The Jerusalem Inn looks as old as London itself, which in a way it is. The blackened bricks from which it is put together are from a Roman temple, and they in their turn are made of the same earth that lies beneath the city. It is also the tenth tavern in Clerkenwell that Dickon has tried. His clothes are sodden with the rain, and his shoes are starting to leak. He is just about to cross the road and try his luck there when he sees a tall figure slip out of the door, wrapped in a cloak.

Dickon ducks back into an obscure and foul-smelling alleyway. There is at least no shortage of those in London. He turns up his collar, but rainwater seems to be dripping from everywhere. Pole pauses for a moment and looks over his shoulder; then he sets out southwards. Dickon tracks him through the narrow, muddy streets to Leather Lane, then south again to Holborn, which Pole follows briefly before plunging into Chancery Lane. He appears to be heading for the Temple, but at the Strand he strikes off westwards, towards Westminster. Dickon follows as closely as he dares. He is now very close to the untidy mass of buildings that make up the

Palace of Whitehall. Pole is heading for an obscure doorway at the rear of one of the buildings. He enters.

Dickon finds himself another doorway from which he can watch, unobtrusively he hopes, for Pole to re-emerge. After an hour there is still no sign of him. Seeing a man leaving the building, however, he approaches him.

'Whose offices are those?' he asks.

The man eyes him up and down. 'Why do you need to know?'

'I'm looking for the Lord Protector's steward. He's my cousin.'

'You won't find him in Westminster today. The Lord Protector is at Hampton Court. Anyway, that's the Secretary of State's office over there.'

'Mr Thurloe?'

'That's right. Mr Secretary Thurloe. So I wouldn't stay where you are unless you want to catch an ague. You certainly won't find your cousin.' The man looks up at the sky and pulls his cloak more tightly around him.

'I may as well be getting home then,' says Dickon, touching his hat to the rapidly departing figure.

But he makes no attempt to leave. Pole will have to appear sooner or later. Dickon wraps his cloak round him and prepares for a long wait.

More Letters

Letter Number 19
Essex
Friday, 10 July 1657

  To Sir Edward Hyde, Lord Chancellor, c/o The Abbess, Benedictine Convent, Ghent

  Probert has recovered sufficiently to leave for London, though I think he left with reluctance, not expecting to find so soft a billet wherever 777 sends him next. I believe he sees things more clearly than before, and this is shown in his latest report to 777.

  For M – P has, I think, now accepted that Henderson's death had naught to do with J, but he continues to fret as to whether he has done right. I do not know what His Majesty's thoughts are on whether, on his restoration, he will remove those like Payne from the estates they have acquired and return them to their former owners, or whether they will be allowed to remain. Since, as you will understand, this is a matter of some importance to me, I would be much obliged to you for guidance. In the meantime, this rain will help the fruit.

Yours ever,
472

PS Could I possibly have a pleasanter number than the one I have? I can never remember whether I am 472 or 742 or 274 or something else entirely. Could I be 333, if nobody yet has that cipher?

10 July 1657
To His Highness the Lord Protector, Hampton Court Palace

My Lord, I have returned to Whitehall, but no easier in mind than I was before. I would beg you, above all, to reconsider the matter of the Crown. I agree it is a mere glittering bauble, but then why tarry over picking up what is of no value to anyone but yourself? Who else can wear it except you? And if this worthless bauble would make us all the safer, then it cannot be accounted Pride or any other thing to Your Highness's detriment. If Your Highness were only to take the Crown, I do believe that that would check some of those who look even now towards Charles Stuart's court.

With regard to the rising in Northwest Essex, I think now that the danger is not so great. Our agent there confirms that all is now quiet. As to the lying report that General Monck should disobey Your Highness's orders, I think there is no colour in these

Fancies, there being not a man in all the three nations more loyal and dutiful to Your Highness than he is.

Your faithful servant,
John Thurloe

To Mr John Grey

My dear Mr Grey, I send this by the hand of one of my servants who claims to be able to find anyone in the city. I do hope this is no mere conceit on his part, because I should like to see you here soon, if you are desirous to take up the post offered to you. I understand that you may be experiencing some minor problems with the judiciary. Should any officious fellows try to detain you on your way to Westminster, please show them my signature at the bottom of this letter and assure them that I, and indeed Mr Secretary Thurloe, will vouch for you.

You may trust the bearer of this letter completely. Follow his instructions. London can be a dangerous place for those who do not know it well.

Yrs,
Sam Morland

Night in Southwark

A moonless night in a London alley is as black as any other moonless night, except where the dull red of the linkmen's torches washes fitfully against the blank walls, or the anaemic light of a candle peeps cautiously through an unshuttered window. Now things move that dared not move during the day, sniffing their way from dark corner to dark corner. Small things that cast great shadows. Now is the hour of the rat.

A door opens briefly, and light and noise flood into the street, then it closes again. I have paused here because a shadow has been following me for some time as I make my way through the streets. Either I failed to shake off my pursuers at the bridge and they followed me to where I stayed that night, or somebody has found me out anew. Before I can find another resting place, I need to ensure that I can slip through its doorway unobserved and under any name I choose.

A narrow alleyway invites me, and I follow its meandering turns as it drifts gently downhill. Finally, I am brought up before the broad, black expanse of the Thames. Far across the river, the spire of St Paul's rises darkly above the housetops. I can hear the water rushing beneath London Bridge and, round a bend in the riverbank, I can just see the flickering row of lights that marks the bridge's course. A chill wind whips across the water. I must, perforce, swim or return.

I wait and count to a hundred. Behind me nothing stirs. I think I have lost my shadowy friend. I count to a hundred again, then slowly make my way back along the lane. But it is blocked.

'And where might you be going, my good sir?' asks one of the group of men in front of me. The raggedness of his cloak and the halo of alcohol that surrounds him suggest that he is not an officer of the State. I think that may prove small comfort.

'It's none of your business,' I say.

'This is an expensive road to travel,' observes one of his companions.

'Expensive?' I ask, because it seems incumbent upon me to say it.

'There is a toll,' says the first man.

I do not need to ask to whom the toll is payable.

'There is no toll,' I say. 'Out of my way, you men.'

It is too dark to see who is laughing at this remark. I think they all may be. I hear the sound of a sword leaving its scabbard. It's not a sound that you want to hear in a place like this.

'I think you must pay the toll, young gentleman.'

'How much?' I ask.

'How much have you got?' asks the first man.

'A shilling or two.' I take out my purse.

'Hand them over.'

I hand over a shilling and some pennies. I hear them being counted.

'That won't buy us all a drink,' says the first man.

'It's all I have,' I say.

'So, you've nothing in that boot you keep patting?'

I reach inside my left boot and remove a small bag of coins. I open the bag briefly so that they will catch a glimpse of the gold, then fling it to the ground.

'There!' I say.

As five pairs of eyes hunt in a mess of horse dung and cabbage leaves, I launch myself at the chest of the smallest of the group, toppling him over. Unfortunately, I stumble as I jump over his body. I am down on the ground and scrambling for a foothold. Just as I manage to get to my feet again, I feel something strike the back of my head very hard. The last words I hear before I lose consciousness are, 'Check the right boot, George. Only an idiot would keep the rest of his money there, so that's probably where it will be.'

Somewhere in the distance I hear a clock striking the hour. Then the chime is repeated in an overlapping chorus from all the clocks in Southwark. It is midnight in a stinking lane close to the Thames. As I stagger to my feet and retrieve my hat from a puddle, a figure steps out of the shadows. Even in this light I can see that his clothes are dirty and his hair hangs in greasy rats' tails from his head.

'You're too late,' I say. 'I have no money left for tolls or anything else. You'll need to rob some other fool.'

The figure approaches slowly and smiles at me, allowing

me to admire the three or four teeth he has left. He holds out a letter.

'Mr Morland presents his compliments,' he says, 'and requests that you accompany me to his office. It looks as if I found you just in time, doesn't it?'

Westminster, July 1657

Here in these dim, narrow corridors people pass like wraiths. We address those we know well with a smile, but we do not hail strangers. In their presence we bite our tongues and offer no introductions. It is not that we are nameless. Indeed, many of us possess more names than we can remember. If the dark panelling of these passageways and these small, cramped rooms could speak, it could tell a story or two. But the panelling remains dumb – perhaps so that it can listen all the better.

Here I move quickly and silently; the only sound I make is the rustling of the bundles of paper that I carry to one place or bring back from another. Yet my footsteps are louder than I intended, because an obscure door in the panelling opens and a head emerges round it.

'You, young man – you must be Mr Morland's new clerk, John Grey.'

'Yes, Mr Thurloe,' I reply, for while he may have to ask my name, I do not have to ask his.

'A word, then, Mr Grey,' he says, beckoning me into his chamber.

I enter. It is not a large room, but that means that everything in it is no further than his fingertips away. The window is small and grimy but it casts enough light on his desk. I glance out of the window at the world beyond. The rain outside is fizzing off the cobblestones. Now and then it whips sharply across the leaded panes, rattling them and leaving them streaming. I realise that I have been too preoccupied by work to look out of my own window.

Thurloe's mouth smiles reassuringly, but the rest of his face reserves judgement.

'I understand you are from North Essex, Mr Grey,' he says.

'Yes. From Clavershall West,' I say. The name of my own village rings strangely on my ears, as if I am hearing it for the first time. It seems very far away. A distant scent of white roses over the door of some beshitten cottage. And the silence – though very different from the silence in these corridors.

'My father was Rector of Abbess Roding,' says Thurloe. He doles out facts carefully one by one. Even this he is telling me for a reason.

'Not far from us then,' I say.

'Practically neighbours. I know your village quite well. Do you enjoy your work here?'

'I have scarcely started, but yes, I enjoy it. I have always enjoyed cryptology. It was an interest of mine when I was at university.'

Morland would possibly have observed, while curling a

golden lock round his finger, that there was a little more to the job than decoding messages. Probert would have slapped me on the back and roared as if I had just said the funniest thing he had ever heard. And my tutor might have voiced the opinion that there were better uses of my time. But Thurloe simply nods. 'Mr Probert reports favourably on the help you gave him.'

'That is kind of him,' I say. Then I add: 'I wanted to find out who killed Henderson.' The words sound inadequate. Presumptuous almost. Thurloe nods again. Does he find my wish commendable? Eccentric? Treasonable? Endearing? I have no idea.

'Probert believes that Henderson was killed by footpads, who later killed a stableboy.'

'Footpads? Surely not,' I say. 'That was also the Colonel's view but not Probert's or mine . . .'

'Well, it is Probert's view now. And what is your own?'

'It would seem likely that it was a Royalist agent,' I say.

'Whenever one of our own men is killed, that is always the most probable cause. Can you be more specific?'

'The night Henderson was killed, a horseman passed through the village.'

'Probert thinks he is of no relevance.'

'That is also not what he said to me. And we both thought that the stranger must have had an accomplice in the village to help carry the body.'

'Probert thinks a gang of footpads would have needed no accomplice.'

'Then he has most certainly changed his opinion in a number of ways. Perhaps if we made enquiries in Bruges about the horseman, we might learn more . . .'

'If that is where he has gone, we may indeed learn more. We have no shortage of informants at Charles Stuart's court. But as for his accomplices – Probert is saying that there can be none in the village.'

'I don't believe it,' I say.

'Nor do I,' says Thurloe. 'You see, we have long had evidence of Royalist activity in Clavershall West. One of the tasks entrusted to this office is opening mail to obtain information that may be of use to the Republic. There have, as you know, been attempted uprisings in various parts of the country, but we have happily been able to discover them and snuff them out.'

'God be praised!' I say.

But this is the wrong response. Thurloe has no wish to share the credit with anyone, even God. He frowns and continues: 'Recently there were signs that a rising was being planned in Essex. We think – indeed the letters strongly suggest – that the organiser of the Sealed Knot for eastern England lives in Clavershall West. That's why we sent Henderson.'

'What evidence do you have?' I ask.

Thurloe hands me a letter headed 'Number 17' and addressed to Sir Edward Hyde. It is signed '472'. I read it carefully three times with growing unease. After all, I too possess a letter from 472.

'It was sent like this?' I ask. 'Not in code?'

'The original letter was in code; that is a copy in plain English.'

'What sort of code?' I ask.

'A simple substitution code,' says Thurloe. 'Numerical.'

Between my letter and this one, they have changed the cipher then.

'And now this,' says Thurloe. He passes me a second letter headed 'Number 19'.

I read it carefully three times with growing unease.

'Were the originals both in the same hand?' I ask.

'Yes. A neat but, in my opinion, an effeminate hand,' says Thurloe.

'Do you know to whom the codes refer?' I ask.

'In some cases,' says Thurloe. 'I am 777 clearly. I can make a guess that 444 is Monck, since not many people command one of His Highness's armies in the North. P is clearly Payne. M, I think, is Mary Knatchbull, the abbess to whose care the letters are addressed – though it may be John Mordaunt, who now leads the Action Party. But it is the identity of 472, the author of the letter, that really intrigues me.'

'Of course,' I say.

'It would appear to be the local leader of the Sealed Knot. It is certainly somebody in the village who is well informed. Probert felt that the letters were intended to deceive us – particularly in respect of General Monck's intentions. That corresponds very much with Mr Morland's view. I have therefore told the Lord Protector that Monck is to be trusted. And yet whether they are true or false, I should still like to know where they come from. An earlier letter reported a conversation at the inn that seemed to be of relevance. But it is not in my view a man's hand . . . Do any ladies from the village frequent the inn?'

'None that I can think of,' I say. 'Nell Bowman would, of course, as the wife of the innkeeper.'

'And she can read and write?'

'She and others.' I run through the list, as I did with Probert – Nell, my mother, Mistress Grice and Aminta. It is laughable to imagine any of them as leaders of the Sealed Knot.

'Aminta Clifford? The daughter of Sir Felix Clifford?' says Thurloe.

'Yes,' I say.

'Would the Cliffords still have any friends at Charles Stuart's court in Bruges? Or perhaps in Ghent?'

'Not that I know. Of course, many of their former friends are now in exile . . .'

'There was a son, I think – Marius?'

'Believed dead.'

'But not for certain.'

'His place of burial is unknown.'

Thurloe considers this for some time.

'Is Colonel Payne in any way disaffected?'

'I don't think so.'

'He might have reason to feel that he has been neglected by the Lord Protector . . . that his talents are not being well used. He was once part of Cromwell's inner circle.'

'I cannot believe that he would turn Royalist now. What would he gain by it?'

'Indeed. What could he possibly gain? But you think he impeded your investigations rather than otherwise?'

'Yes,' I say.

'Then later he chose to accuse you of murder.'

'Yes.'

'Thank you, Mr Grey. That is very helpful.'

Thurloe places his steepled hands to his lips, as if in prayer. His countenance is clear and untroubled. He lowers his hands and looks at me, head slightly on one side. I have not the slightest idea what he is thinking.

'Do you know Mr Morland well?' he asks.

'My connection with him is through the university. He was a Fellow of Magdalene College, where I was an undergraduate. He left in 1653 or 1654, I think, just before I went up to Cambridge. My tutor wrote me an introduction to him.'

'But there is no other connection?'

'No,' I say, genuinely puzzled.

'No other way in which you might have been recommended to us?'

'No. How could there be?'

Thurloe nods.

I wait in case he has anything further to say. He doesn't. I stand there in silence. After a while, he returns to the study of his papers. I go out. I close the door very carefully.

Should I have told him what I know? I do not need to think too hard as to the author of these letters. I have long suspected it. Somebody well connected to prominent Royalists around the country. Somebody well informed about the village. Somebody who is vain. Somebody with an effeminate hand. Somebody closely linked to the Colonel and with the Colonel's interests at heart – or at least with some concern for his own continuing employment. Who else but Pole? My promise to Aminta prevents me informing on him to Thurloe now, just as it prevented me earlier from informing on him to Probert.

I cannot betray my promise to Aminta.

Unless I have to.

More Letters

To Mistress Grey, The New House, Clavershall West
Monday 13 July 1657

My dear mother, I hope that you will be gratified to hear that I have obtained, with the help of my old tutor, a place as a clerk working for Mr Samuel Morland in Whitehall. Please forgive my not having mentioned it before, but I have for some time had such a career in mind for myself. Mr Morland values my knowledge of ciphers and has set me to work translating letters from His Highness's ambassadors and agents overseas.

Mr Morland assures me that I need no longer fear arrest for the two murders that occurred in our village. Mr Probert has spoken well of me, and in any case the arrest warrants have been withdrawn.

If Mr Probert has not yet departed, could you enquire of him why he believes Henderson's death to be the work of footpads – which I must still doubt, much though I respect Mr Probert?

And could you enquire of Ben who the lady was who visited the stables and talked to Jem?

Enough for now! Please tell Aminta that I am safe. I shall write again once I know whither I am sent. In the meantime you may write to me care of Mr Samuel Morland at his office close to Whitehall Palace, which is now happily my place of work too.

Your most affectionate son,
John

The New House
Clavershall West
Wednesday, 15 July 1657

To John Grey at the office of Mr Samuel Morland, Whitehall Palace, Westminster

Dear John,

Thank you for your letter telling me of your plan to work for Mr Morland. Whether you are wise to abandon your legal studies so abruptly only time will reveal, but I am happy that you appear to have found some work that likes you well. In that respect you are much as your father, who placed his own pleasure considerably above duty whenever the opportunity presented itself.

Mr Probert is recovered and has already departed for London. He was a demanding guest but not ungrateful for what Martha and I were able to do. I cannot say why he might have changed his mind, other than because men are shallow creatures prone to indecision. You may, of course, see him at Whitehall, and may ask him then, though I understand that Mr Thurloe's plan is to send him into Sweden. I do hope that Mr Morland has no intention of sending you anywhere that is dangerous. I should be quite cross if that were the case.

Ben says that he does not recall mentioning any lady who visited the stables. He thinks you must have misheard him.

Please remember me to Mr Morland and say that I wish you to remain in London.

Your loving mother

The Lodge, 15 July 1657
To Mr John Grey, London

My dearest John, again I entrust this to the hand of one you will know in the hope that it will reach you safely.

Though your mother assures me you are in no danger, since your work will not take you out of Westminster, I worry that she does not understand how grave a situation you find yourself in. I believe there are those who still wish you ill and will seek you out in London.

I have also spoken to Nell Bowman. She says that if Henderson was murdered at the stables, nobody at the inn knew anything of it. But why were the men there drinking so late?

And did you know that only the year before last Mr Thurloe sent Mr Morland to this very village? I cannot say what he was doing here, but it is a strange coincidence, is it not?

And finally, John, your mother has had some sort of falling-out with Mistress Grice. They were overheard arguing, and your mother openly accused her of witchcraft – to which Mistress Grice merely laughed. Of course, the mere fact that Mistress Grice can read and write is regarded in this place as perverse and unnatural. The Rector gave us a sermon last week on the dangers of educating women, a practice which is condemned by some Father of the Church or other. I hope for his sake that Mistress Grice is not a witch, or we may see a frog in a surplice preaching to us next Sunday.

Write to me as soon as you can.

Your affectionate cousin,
Aminta

A Visit

It is the following morning that the landlord bangs on my door and announces that I have a visitor.

'Dickon!' I exclaim. 'What are you doing in London? And you are abroad betimes. I am still in my nightshirt!'

'Those of us who keep proper country hours have been up and about since dawn. Only you Londoners slumber on in your feather beds.'

'Dickon,' I say, 'you have a perfectly comfortable feather bed back home, as you know well. And Mr Thurloe keeps us working late, so I may be excused not witnessing the sun rise. I shall be at my desk at eight, as is required of me.'

'You'd do well to see the sun at all in this smoky air,' says Dickon. 'But that's perhaps as well. On a dull day you notice less what a filthy hole this London is. I'm surprised they don't charge for sunshine by the hour here – these Londoners fleece you for everything else.'

'True,' I say, 'but since you clearly dislike London and Londoners so much, you must have a very good reason for being here.'

Dickon glances out of my window to confirm that the gloom of a July day in the city is as bad as he feels it should be. 'It's about that land over at Royston,' he says. 'You know – that Uncle Ruggles left my pa but my cousins claim is theirs, God rot them.'

I nod. I've heard Dickon's mother speak of that couple of acres of useless marsh. It's kept half a dozen lawyers busy for almost twenty years.

'I have to swear a deposition,' says Dickon. 'But I thought I'd look in on you while I was here. And ask after my horse.'

'I had to sell the horse,' I say. 'You know I was accused of stealing him?'

'Yes. I told the Colonel you'd done no such thing, but somebody said they'd seen you riding off on him, and he wouldn't believe me, even though I actually owned the beast.'

'But the Colonel has changed his view? He now believes me to be innocent?'

'So it would seem.'

'What convinced him?'

'Well, I told him myself that I believed your story. I hope that counted for something. Then Probert apparently told the Colonel that he had no idea who had shot him. And, of course, your mother would have put in her contribution too. I doubt that she spoke unfavourably of you.'

'And Aminta? Did she speak to the Colonel on my behalf?'

'Not that I heard. I warned you before not to trust either of those Cliffords. Courtly manners and courtly morals, you might say. I'd as soon trust Roger Pole.'

'I saw Roger Pole – briefly. He is in London. He was fleeing me or somebody else. I tried to follow but lost him south of Fleet Street.'

'I saw him too, but he couldn't shake me off as he did you. He was visiting Thurloe's office.'

'He can't have,' I say.

'I tracked him through the streets in the rain a day or two ago. It could have been no other. He headed for Westminster and vanished into that building you and Thurloe inhabit.'

'A dyed-in-the-wool Royalist like Pole could have no business with Mr Thurloe.'

'Pole wouldn't be the first Royalist to change his colours. I told you that he was full of praise for the Lord Protector these days. If he's switched sides – or more likely pretended to switch sides – it would explain his actions.'

'Pretence,' I say. 'Of that I am sure. Fortunately, Mr Thurloe is unlikely to be deceived, if that was indeed Pole you saw.'

'I know a Pole when I see one. And it's as well you didn't catch up with the rogue. Like as not, he'd have cut your throat.' Dickon nods sagely at his own wisdom. 'The sooner you come back to Essex, the better, John. I'm off home in a day or two – you could come with me. The journey would be the merrier for your good company.'

I hesitate only for a moment. London seems safe enough if you avoid narrow lanes in Southwark.

'No, Dickon, my new work likes me well. I am more useful to the Protectorate here than in Essex or in Cambridge. And I have given Mr Thurloe my word.'

Dickon looks doubtful. He doesn't think I'm safe.

'Very well,' he sighs. 'I've done my best. Now, why don't you tell me about my horse and what you plan to do about getting him back?'

My lack of funds means that my pleasures in London are for the moment limited.

To divert myself this evening, I take out the paper that I bought for a penny from Goodwife Mansell.

NUMBER 9 PIEX NECT FEWS RRMB SUGE OBYS NMEO HEIT HOUG ATDE EDTH GKIN VHAS GERY SOOD OUPP ERTH UREB ETTH DLEA HERS FIPO KTHE INOT ISBE HNGC EALL DNGE HBYT UEYO RNGE SONE MFOR TJRE SURN EHOM NSOO UIWO ELDR DMIN OYOU UFYO ORPR EMIS 472

Perhaps it is the blow to the head expertly administered by the ruffians in Southwark that has done it. For suddenly the message speaks clearly to me, though my head feels no better when I understand its full meaning.

I had been looking for something complex; I should have been looking for the obvious. This cipher was, after all, replaced with a simple substitution code. I try less hard and all is made clear.

The anagram of 'Grey' was a red herring. That part of the message, at least, was not about me. It is the anagram of 'King' that shows how it is done. When the first letter of each block is transferred to the last place in the block it gives us:

NUMBER 9 IEXP ECTN EWSF RMBR UGES BYSO MEON EITH OUGH TDEA DTHE KING HASV ERYG OODS UPPO RTHE REBU TTHE LEAD ERSH IPOF

THEK NOTI SBEI NGCH ALLE NGED BYTH EYOU
NGER ONES FORM JRET URNS HOME SOON IWOU
LDRE MIND YOUO FYOU RPRO MISE 472

Finally, rearranging the spaces:

**NUMBER 9 I EXPECT NEWS FRM BRUGES BY
SOMEONE I THOUGHT DEAD. THE KING HAS VERY
GOOD SUPPORT HERE BUT THE LEADERSHIP
OF THE KNOT IS BEING CHALLENGED BY THE
YOUNGER ONES. FOR M – J RETURNS HOME SOON.
I WOULD REMIND YOU OF YOUR PROMISE 472**

I rather think that the person from Bruges is my rider. 'Someone I thought dead.' For the rider's words have finally come back to me: he asked whether Ben Bowman *still* kept the inn. That was the phrase that had eluded me for so long. Whoever it is, he was returning to the village after a long time away from it, and those in the village had reason to believe him no longer alive.

As for J, who is about to return home, can he be anyone except me? There are other Js to be sure, but the population of the village is static. Few go anywhere from which they can return. So Pole – who else? – is writing about my return from Cambridge. But who is M, towards whom Pole is directing his asides? It is somebody for whom a simple unadorned *J* can only mean John Grey. And yet I know nobody at that corrupt and indolent court. Certainly not Mordaunt or Mary Knatchbull, as Thurloe proposed.

There were days in Cambridge when I would be sitting at my desk, absorbed in some dusty lawbook, only to find my studies interrupted by a sudden and inexplicable burst of thunder. Unnoticed by me, a storm had been brewing outside, and the wind and rain were now flinging themselves at my casement. I would stare up at the sky, unable to understand how I had been so unobservant. I stare out of my window now. The sky is blue, if a little smoky. And yet I fear that somewhere a storm is brewing.

A Discovery

Mr Morland has assigned to me the relatively easy duty of reading other people's letters. He is solicitous over the state of my head, though I tell him that the blow was not severe, and that I was unconscious for no more than half an hour at the most.

Post from all over the country passes through this office. Unknown to the senders, it is opened, read, sealed and sent on its way. Some – treasonable or potentially so – is copied out in case Mr Thurloe wishes to remind the author of its precise wording at some future date. Today's post is dull. There are letters to the Spanish Netherlands, it is true, from the families of exiled cavaliers, informing the absent head of the household of their want of credit of any sort. There are replies urging the families of the exiled cavaliers to live frugally and to be steadfast to an absent king. Unless they reveal useful information that might lead to the sequestration of Royalist funds not previously declared to the State, these are resealed and allowed on their way. There are other letters where references to a cargo of Flemish cloth to be landed at Weymouth may mean cloth or may mean something else entirely. These are copied and sent on to the relevant magistrates, who will later board newly arrived boats to burrow into bales of woollen goods, perhaps to discover weapons or perhaps merely to look foolish.

I am about to go to my dinner when the writing on one letter catches my eye. It is addressed to Sir Edward Hyde, care of a nunnery in Ghent. I open it. It is in code, but I see that it begins Number 21 and is signed by '472'.

Mr Morland has asked that I pass on any such letters to him for him to decrypt personally. But, in view of his kindness to me, I decide to undertake the drudgery of deciphering it for him. I do, after all, have a copy of the relevant tables. It does not take me long.

NUMBER 21 SINCE PROBERT'S DEPARTURE ALL HAS BEEN VERY QUIET HERE. HENDERSON IS UNLIKELY TO RISE AGAIN FROM HIS GRAVE. BOWMAN HAS MOVED THE MUSKETS TO A SAFER LOCATION.
FOR M – NOW THAT J IS IN LONDON I HOPE YOU WILL TAKE CARE OF HIM AS AGREED. 472

I put my pen down. There I am again – it says J is in London. And so I am. And now this person M is asked to take care of me. In what way? Is this an instruction to cherish me or have me lured into a cellar and pistolled to death? M will have difficulty in doing either from Bruges. Of course, if it were addressed to somebody who is also in London, that would be a different matter . . .

And suddenly I see the truth. This aside *is* addressed to somebody in London, for all the letter bears Hyde's name. All mail to Flanders will pass through this office. All mail to Flanders will be read by this office. And Morland has left very specific instructions that such mail must be delivered to him still encrypted. This is Pole writing not just to Hyde but also to 'M'. Morland! So is Pole asking Morland to protect me or – and surely this is more likely – to take some other action entirely? And Dickon was wrong that Pole was visiting Mr Thurloe's office as a supporter of the Protectorate. Pole and Morland are both plotting against the State.

Perhaps I would do well to be circumspect and hold my tongue for the moment. But Mr Thurloe has a traitor in the very heart of his office, and I fear there have been at least two murders as a consequence. This cannot wait. I seize the paper from my desk and march to where I know I shall find Morland.

'A letter from Essex,' I say, flinging it on his desk.

Morland looks up. 'Thank you, John. I shall decipher it after dinner.'

'I have done so already,' I say. I offer him my manuscript, which he reads.

'No news then,' he says. 'You should not have troubled yourself. I shall reseal it and send it on. There is no point in alerting Hyde to our scrutiny of his business.'

'Do you ever send them on?' I say. 'They are addressed to Hyde, but they seem to be for your eyes.'

'All mail is for our eyes,' says Morland. 'That is our job. But this is clearly for Sir Edward. And we always forward his mail to avoid suspicion that we have tampered with it.'

'You will see 472 wishes M to take care of me. That can scarcely be somebody in Bruges. Your name begins with *M*, does it not?'

'To take care of you? It merely refers to somebody called J. Are you saying that you are the only person who has ever borne a name beginning with *J*? I seem to remember that Charles Stuart has a brother named James. So there are at least two of you. As for M – Prince Rupert's brother is Maurice, as you know well. I should imagine that there are at least a dozen men serving the King in Bruges who might be intended by this single letter of the alphabet.'

'J is in London. I doubt that is James Stuart. I have another letter in which it says that J is about to return to my village. I am sure somebody would have told me if they had seen the late King's son drinking at the inn.'

Actually, I'm not certain that Ben wouldn't have kept that to himself as he has kept other things, but no matter. I look Morland in the eye.

Morland also looks at me, not quite with respect but with greater caution than heretofore. 'Another letter?'

'It was in the lining of Henderson's doublet.'

'From which you took it?'

'Yes.'

'I see. You had better explain yourself more clearly, Mr Grey. Are you saying that I am engaged in treasonable correspondence with Royalist sympathisers in Essex?'

'Yes,' I say. 'You've been very clever. Because the letters are addressed to Hyde, they do not implicate you, even if they were to be discovered. You are, however, kept informed of the strength of Royalist feeling in the eastern counties and General Monck's willingness to join the Royalist party. They enabled you to persuade Mr Thurloe that there was no threat from Monck.'

'That is perfectly true. General Monck remains loyal to the Republic. So, I am M, am I? And who is 472?'

I can shield him no longer. The safety of the State itself is at risk.

'Roger Pole,' I say. 'As you know well. He has been feigning allegiance to the Lord Protector but remains an obstinate Royalist. A friend of mine saw Pole coming to this office. Your office.'

'All sorts of people come to this office,' says Morland. 'Many of them are men that the Knot believe are loyal to His Majesty . . .'

I think Morland may have just betrayed himself.

'By *His Majesty*, I assume you mean the traitor Charles Stuart, titular King of the Scots?'

'I spoke ironically. I merely employed the term that the Sealed Knot would use. I am happy to give Charles Stuart his full title, if that pleases you better.'

'There is nothing about Charles Stuart that could ever please me,' I say. 'And they are fools who call him King or *His Majesty* and hope for his return.'

Morland tips his head on one side and studies me for a moment. Then, having made up his mind, he addresses me: 'Not all fools perhaps,' he says. 'How long do you think this Republic can last, John? Cromwell is a sick man. Oh, it isn't generally known, but I can assure you that it is the case. What then when he dies, as we all must? Will he name his son Richard as his successor, Cromwells following Cromwells as

Stuarts formerly followed Stuarts? Or will he name one of his generals, with England ruled for ever by the Army? Fairfax would like the post. So would Fleetwood. So would Lambert. But I doubt any of them will succeed without fighting the others off. Is that what we want, John? Another war? So, my friend, many are starting to say that perhaps – after the Lord Protector dies of course – the prudent thing may be to ask Charles Stuart back. If the Stuarts are restored – and I say "if" – those who stick longest to their Republican principles may be the first who find their heads on the block. But those who show their support before other men do will find themselves rewarded before other men are – and rewarded more richly.'

'So, is that it?' I say. 'You are ready to betray your country for a handful of gold coins or a blue ribbon?'

'A blue ribbon? Yes, it would be pleasant to be a Knight of the Garter,' says Morland. 'That is undeniable. But I have no such ambitions for myself. Still, you would do well to remember that today's treason is tomorrow's loyalty; today's danger is tomorrow's safety.'

'Treason is always treason,' I say. But it isn't of course. Treason is finding yourself on the losing side.

'What do you want, John?' asks Morland. 'You are a young man. You have, I hope, many years to live. I think you would not wish to live them in the Tower of London. You have much to gain by supporting the right party. Tell me, what do you want? Perhaps I may be in a position to grant it.'

'I want the truth,' I say.

Morland shrugs. 'What is truth?' he asks.

'Pilate may not have known,' I say, 'but I think you do.'

Before Morland can confirm or deny this, however, Mr Secretary Thurloe enters the room. He is surprised that we are discussing The Scriptures so heatedly. I need to explain myself.

'This man,' I say, pointing to Morland, 'is a traitor. He has betrayed your office through treasonable correspondence with Royalists.'

Thurloe frowns. Has he already suspected something of the sort? If so, first blow to me, I think. When he finally speaks, his words are slow and precise. 'You had better tell me more,' he says.

'Mr Morland has for some time been receiving reports from Royalists in Essex. They are nominally directed to Sir Edward Hyde, but their author knows they will be intercepted here and sends messages to Mr Morland in asides contained in the letters. There are also references to me in the letters. See – this one asks M to look after J.'

Thurloe examines my transcription. 'So, you say that you are J?'

'Yes,' I say.

'And it could refer to nobody else?'

I hear Morland laugh. 'I have already explained to Mr Grey the weakness of this argument,' he says. 'He thinks that nobody else in the three nations is called John. Anyway, if Mr Grey knows the author of the letter so well, perhaps he would tell us who it is.'

I pause, because I have already told Morland that it is Pole. But if he wishes me to tell Thurloe myself, then I will do so gladly.

'It's Roger Pole,' I say. 'His family were Royalists. He is clearly the coordinator of the Sealed Knot in Essex. He is one of the few people who would have known both that I was returning from Cambridge and that I was now in London and working for Mr Morland.'

I look at Morland, who is strangely indifferent to my having exposed his correspondent.

'And Pole has been seen visiting this office,' I add, 'to see Mr Morland.'

'You observed this yourself?' asks Thurloe.

'No, it was a friend of mine . . .'

'Who is here to give evidence?'

'Not at present,' I say.

Thurloe and Morland exchange glances. Morland smiles.

'Go on,' Thurloe tells me.

'There was also an earlier letter that I have in my possession. It refers to somebody that the author had thought dead who would bring news from Bruges. That person was the stranger who visited the village the night Henderson died. It was that person who killed Henderson and Jem. And he was able to kill Henderson because Mr Morland here had tipped him off that Henderson was coming.'

'That's impossible,' says Morland. 'I didn't know Henderson had been sent to Essex until some time after he had gone. I couldn't have tipped anyone off.'

'That's true,' says Thurloe. 'Mr Morland did not know.'

'And there is an even bigger problem with Mr Grey's theory,' says Morland. 'My informant, as Mr Grey likes to call him, cannot have been Roger Pole. We all know Roger Pole has been in London of late. But the letters have continued to arrive, have they not, my lord?'

This last remark is directed at Thurloe.

'Is that true?' I ask.

Thurloe nods. 'Yes, Mr Grey. Do you not remember the dates on the letters I showed you?'

'Which rather clears me of Mr Grey's accusation that I

have been corresponding with Roger Pole,' says Morland.

'Colonel Payne has spoken well of Roger Pole,' adds Thurloe. 'Payne has petitioned my Lord Cromwell that Pole's lands and titles should be restored, though these requests have met with little success so far. Anyway, Pole could scarcely be leading the Sealed Knot from Payne's own house.'

I beg to differ. Pole could be cozening the Colonel in any number of ways. But I do see that Pole cannot, after all, be 472.

'That simply means that the author of these letters is somebody else . . .' I say.

'That is self-evident,' says Thurloe. 'But who? Earlier, Mr Grey, you told me that you did not know who wrote them. I suggested that it was a lady, but you thought not. Now you say with great confidence that it was Mr Pole, which is simply not possible. But I agree that it may be somebody who knows you well. Somebody living in the village. Somebody certainly with a flourishing garden.'

Then suddenly I know exactly who the correspondent is. How could I have been so stupid as not to know? The question is: can I still save her and myself? While I am adding up that particular sum, Thurloe is continuing to question me.

'Let us consider. Who has damsons and cucumbers in their garden?'

'Many people would,' I say.

For a moment I see him as a hawk circling, his eyes dispassionately on some distant prey – on some small, warm creature made of flesh and fur.

'Who wants Colonel Payne out of the manor house?'

I wonder if I can still make the coming blow fall harmlessly. 'Anybody,' I say. 'It could be almost anybody. The Colonel is an outsider and not well liked. And the letter asks for clarification of future policy rather than an eviction.'

'Who is vain enough to worry about what number they are allocated in a cipher?' Thurloe continues.

'That is more difficult,' I say.

'Somebody well-connected enough to the Royalist cause to be trusted by Sir Edward Hyde. Somebody whose family fought for the late King.'

'There are certainly fewer of those . . .'

The hawk folds back its wings and falls like a dart. It sees nothing except its prey.

'The Cliffords were utterly ruined by the war, were they not? They might feel they had little to lose by plotting against His Highness the Lord Protector.'

Morland, who can see exactly where this is going, is still smiling.

I am not sure what to say next, but Morland unexpectedly fills in the gap. 'The thought occurs to me,' he says, 'that it would be very helpful to us to root out this correspondent. If Mr Grey were willing to help us identify the lady you refer to, I would be willing to overlook this strange outburst against me – caused, I think, mainly by the blow he recently received to his head.'

I don't know if you play chess. If you do, you may know of the combination of moves called Fool's Mate, by which one player can win the game in, I think, four moves. It is rarely seen in practice because it requires the losing player to actively participate in his own destruction, moving his pieces in such a way that his king is exposed but has no square to fly to when attacked by his opponent's queen. I had never been caught in Fool's Mate until now.

'And if I refuse to answer that question?' I ask. But you will probably have already guessed Morland's answer. It comes as no surprise to me.

'You would be assisting in a Royalist conspiracy,' he says. 'You are quite aware of the penalties for treason. Your head would in due course find its place on a spike on London Bridge. In any case, it would make little difference. With the assistance you have already given us, we are in a good position to say who it might be. I think your silence would not save her. And if you enabled us to arrest her before she had a chance to conduct further treasonable activity, then you could in a way be said to be saving her from a worse fate.'

'And what would her fate be now?'

'Much would depend on how much she wished to tell us about the Sealed Knot. She has merely been rather foolish. I think we could promise you that we would deal with her no more harshly than we had to.'

Morland knows my thoughts. He is offering me a way out.

'Would you like further time to consider?' asks Morland with every show of concern.

I think of Aminta's hand resting lightly on my arm as we walk through the garden. I think of the kiss she laid lightly on my cheek. I think of the duty I owe to a woman who is almost a sister to me and might have been my wife. But perhaps all is not lost.

'Have you considered,' I say, 'that the writer might still be a man deliberately disguising their hand as a woman's?'

'Who?' asks Thurloe.

Good point. It needs to be somebody who can write and who might really have the sort of contacts 472 seems to have. And not Roger Pole this time. 'Colonel Payne,' I hear myself say. 'Mr Thurloe believes him to be disaffected. He knew well that I was in London. He might have asked that care should have been taken of me.'

Even I find this hard to credit, but Morland is, surprisingly, nodding his head. Payne is apparently a piece that he is happy to sacrifice to protect his agent, if it can be done. He looks at Thurloe, one eyebrow raised.

'Why,' asks Thurloe, 'would Payne enquire about his own removal from the manor house?'

'Well . . .' says Morland. Then he looks at me and shrugs. He's done his best for me. It's scarcely his fault that I have played so badly. And now it's Thurloe's move.

'So, it's Aminta Clifford,' says Thurloe. 'It would have helped us greatly if you had said that before, but at least you have told us now.'

I sigh, but what can I do? What else can I do?

I expect a long and tedious interrogation. It is in fact mercifully brief. I am shown the letters again. I cannot confirm that the writing is Aminta's. But the Cliffords do indeed have cucumbers in their garden. Quite a few actually. And damsons. Yes, Aminta is well-educated enough to write letters like that. Yes, perhaps she is vain enough to want a nicer number than 472. Morland nods amiably.

Thurloe switches the conversation to the stranger on horseback that I saw on my first evening back in the village. Up until now I have met few who believed in my rider. For the first time I have two people together in one room who believe in him wholeheartedly. For the first time I wish it were otherwise.

Could it indeed be that the rider was Aminta's brother

Marius, believed to have died at the Battle of Worcester but in fact still alive and carrying messages backwards and forwards for the Sealed Knot? Someone everybody would have assumed was dead? Somebody who would be – to paraphrase Jem's words – the least likely suspect of anyone in the village? Is it not probable he was Henderson's killer? Is it not likely that he is also the M at the Stuart court, addressed directly in Aminta's letters? Would he not know me well enough to explain the references to me in the letters, even if the nature of his promises was unclear? So, did the Cliffords ever say anything – perhaps a brief slip of the tongue – to suggest that Marius was still living? I think about Aminta's occasional lapses into French and her father's comment at dinner about her brother. I shake my head and say nothing. And Sir Felix? Had he ever expressed treasonable sentiments? I concede that he had said it was wrong to close the theatres and to chop down the maypoles. He had said life was dull under the Commonwealth. Thurloe looks surprised that dullness might disappoint. He looks disappointed that I have offered no surprises.

Strangely, it is Morland who again comes to my rescue. 'Mr Thurloe has, as ever, seen through these feeble attempts at treason. I congratulate you, my lord, on your insight, which far exceeds mine, and I am grateful that you have shown in the process that this has naught to do with me. I believe that Mr Grey always knew that Aminta Clifford was the correspondent in Essex. His not disclosing this was foolish – but his reasons may have been more chivalrous than treasonable. After all, he has known her since they were children together. In the end, he has put personal considerations to one side and has been helpful to us – more helpful than I had dared hope. I fear, however, that the blow he has received to his head has harmed him more than he thinks. How else can we explain the strange outburst that is so much to his discredit and disadvantage? Some of his accusations earlier – particularly those concerning me – have proved to be both wild and inaccurate. Isn't that so, Mr Grey?'

'Yes,' I say.

'Inaccurate and unjustified?'

'Yes,' I say.

'Unjustified and foolish?'

'Yes,' I say.

'And you retract them all?'

'Yes,' I say.

'I think,' says Morland, 'that it would be better if Mr Grey returned to Essex to recover his wits. Then we need say no more about any of this, need we? His word will carry more weight with the court if he has willingly informed us of a treason that he has detected rather than if he appears to be a man who has simply informed on his friends to save his own neck. None of us would wish to accuse him of that.'

'Indeed,' says Thurloe. He scatters sand across the sheet of paper on which he has been taking notes, then blows it off. 'That would seem conclusive then. 472 is Aminta Clifford. And her father cannot have been unaware of what she was doing. If you would be so kind as to sign this statement, we shall then proceed against both of them. We shall also issue a warrant for the arrest of the malignant Royalist and murderer Marius Clifford, should he dare to show his face in England again.'

'What will happen to Aminta and Sir Felix now?' I ask.

'We shall get this indictment drawn up in a fair hand,'

says Thurloe, 'then they will be arrested and brought to London.'

'Perhaps,' says Morland, 'it would be better if Mr Grey delayed his departure until tomorrow. It might be more convenient for all concerned if he arrived in Essex after the Cliffords' arrest . . .'

Thurloe nods. 'Much better,' he says.

I nod. It would be much better.

'Thank you, Mr Grey,' says Morland. He is leaning against the doorframe, curling a golden lock of hair with his finger. 'That was very kind of you. I am much obliged. More obliged than I can really say.'

And Morland winks at me.

It is a fine evening in midsummer. Dickon and I sit in the garden of an inn, enjoying the last of the sunshine and a cold pie.

'You are wise to return with me,' says Dickon. 'The message you left at my lodgings caught me just in time. We can leave tomorrow at first light.'

'Or perhaps a little later,' I say.

'You're in no hurry, then, to get back to the village and continue your enquiries into Henderson's murder?'

'Dickon, I know who killed Henderson,' I say.

Dickon leans forward.

'Who?' he asks.

Do I say that I now know the horseman's identity? A stranger indeed, but one who knew the village well in the past. Do I add that in the process of discovery I have had to betray Aminta, and that she and her father were almost certainly arrested last night? Arrested and now on their way to London. That is bad enough, but naming the rider would be yet another betrayal.

'It was somebody who was once very close to me,' I say. 'As Jem said, the last person I would have suspected.'

'Not Pole then?'

'No – for all the reasons we discussed before. There was one reason I continued to suspect him for some time, but no, it cannot be Pole.'

'So what was the reason for thinking him guilty?'

Then I tell Dickon something that I have kept to myself, knowing how quickly it would spread if I voiced it, though the evidence was there all along for anyone to see who wished to see it. 'Both Henderson and Jem were killed with a single knife stroke by somebody standing behind them cutting from right to left.'

'So?' says Dickon.

'The killer was left-handed,' I say.

Dickon puts his knife down suddenly and looks at the hand in which he had been holding it.

'Don't worry,' I say. 'I don't mean that *you* killed either of them. But after Henderson was killed, I started to notice who else in the village other than you was left-handed.'

'Why didn't you say so before?'

'I'm sorry, Dickon. It was so difficult to know who to trust. It was the one piece of information that I didn't want the killer to know I had.'

'You might at least have trusted *me*. But if you're saying you are not accusing your oldest friend . . . and I hope you're not . . . who else is left-handed?'

'Pole,' I say. 'And Kit Mansell. Ifnot uses either hand equally well.'

'It could hardly be Ifnot,' says Dickon.

'Nor Kit. Nor Pole. But I know who it was. You were right, Dickon, when you said that I should stay out of this. The knowledge of who the killer is has helped me not at all. It has merely brought me sadness.'

'You won't tell me who it is?'

'There's no need, is there?'

Dickon looks at me strangely, as well he might, then suddenly slaps me on the shoulder. 'Well, old friend, you'd best away to bed. I shall be knocking at your door at first light with two horses tied up in the street outside.'

'I shall be waiting – and not in my nightshirt . . .' I stop abruptly because, leaving the garden, I spot somebody I think I recognise. And I am not sure whether we have been overheard. 'Kit Mansell,' I say. 'I'm sure that was Kit Mansell.'

'You are starting to imagine things,' says Dickon. 'But if I'd been knocked over the head by a gang of robbers, maybe I would too. You need some country air.'

'Thank you, Dickon,' I say. 'Do you know? Throughout all this you've been the only one I could rely on.'

'In which case . . .' says Dickon.

Again he looks at me oddly. I fear that, having supported me for so long, he does not like my keeping this final secret. But I cannot tell him. How can I tell anyone that the rider was not Marius Clifford but Matthew Grey, my own father?

We are on the road again but this time travelling north into Essex, Dickon riding his own horse, a new purchase, and I trotting alongside on a hired mare. His horse is fresh, but my mare knows she is billed by the day and not by the mile.

Each step takes her further from her own stable, and she goes reluctantly.

Dinner is some bread and cheese purchased from a farm. We drink from the stream nearby. The water is warm. I splash it on my face, but the day still feels too hot for travel.

'It's this mare you've put me on,' I say. 'You must have seen she wouldn't get beyond Harlow today. Not in this heat anyway.'

Dickon nods. 'You shouldn't have sold the last horse I gave you. Perhaps I should have made you walk to teach you to value good horseflesh. We'll do what we can, but I fear we'll be sleeping in the woods tonight if you can't get her to go faster.'

'It's dry enough,' I say. 'There will be bracken we can lie on.'

'No doubt you've slept out before on a summer night,' says Dickon.

'No doubt I have,' I say.

'We'd best get moving again anyway,' says Dickon. 'The closer we can get to Clavershall West, the better. I won't feel wholly safe until we are there. You may think this business is all over, but I thought I was being followed through the streets this morning. And it wouldn't surprise me if it was Pole on our tail.'

I do not share Dickon's fears about Pole, though I have fears of my own – that we shall encounter Aminta and her father travelling the other way under close arrest. That would be awkward. But we do not encounter them. The only soldiers who pass us on their way to London have no prisoner of any sort with them. They too look hot.

We ride through the afternoon, with no respite for horse or man. Sitting at a desk does not harden a person to a long day in the saddle. I am beginning to share the opinion of my mare that we have travelled far enough.

'If we are to spend a night in the woods,' I say, 'we should seek a spot now while there is good light rather than wait until we have to stumble over tree roots in the dark.'

But Dickon is looking behind him. 'Do you see that dust rising yonder?' he asks.

'Somebody else is trying to get somewhere before nightfall,' I say, looking back down the road.

'Let us hope they are not pursuing us,' says Dickon.

'Pole?' I ask.

I look at the dust storm approaching. Somebody has a fresh horse certainly. Dickon's eyes too are narrowed against the glare. 'Two riders, I'd say, with all that dust. Two riders well mounted.'

'They'll be on us in a few minutes,' I say.

'There are woods over there to the right,' says Dickon, pointing to a spot half a mile or so ahead. 'If we ride swiftly, we can gain them perhaps before they catch up with us.'

'But why . . . ?' I begin. But perhaps I should be asking, why not? That Pole was not Henderson's murderer does not stop his becoming mine. As Probert predicted long ago, I have waded into a stream that is deeper than I could have ever imagined. And Morland may already have told Pole how helpful I was in identifying 472. That may be incitement enough to kill me.

Dickon and I both urge our horses on. As we enter the woods, I look back. The man on the leading horse does look very much like Pole. Even from here, he looks sharp and unpleasant. The man on the second horse looks familiar too. Not unlike the man in the garden last night. There can be no avoiding their seeing where we have gone, but hopefully we will lose them amongst the trees, just as Jem hoped to lose his pursuers.

We dismount and take the narrowest paths. I lead, and Dickon brings up the rear. He has a pistol and is ready to fire it at anyone who follows us and to enquire about their business later. I have nothing but my pocketknife. I have no idea how big this wood is or where this path will take us. Judging by the sun, we have already swung round through ninety degrees, but we must go where it takes us or crash noisily into the undergrowth. Pole and his friend could be anywhere. Ahead. Behind. To the left. To the right. I am reasonably sure they are not up above us. The bushes on either side of the path grow denser. Dickon seems to have stopped – I no longer hear his footsteps behind me.

'Dickon,' I say as I scan the path ahead. 'I'm not sure where we are.'

Then there is a deafening roar, and my shoulder seems to explode. There is blood running down the face of my doublet and, for all I know, down the back as well.

Pole appears on the path in front of us, his pistol pointing directly at me. Just behind him stands Kit Mansell, his knife in his left hand. So much for Aminta's theory that Kit could be trusted then. Or perhaps, like Pole, he is doing this on Aminta's behalf. I can't say I'd entirely blame him if that's the case.

So far I'm only wounded, I think, *but this time he can't possibly miss.*

There is a flash from the barrel of Pole's gun, and my already-ringing ears are assaulted again. I look down at my doublet expecting to see evidence of a hole in my chest, but all is as it was before. Then behind me I hear Dickon crash to the ground.

'Good thinking, Mr Pole,' I mutter to myself. 'Aim for the man with the loaded gun first.' That was something else I learned from survivors on those battlefields many years ago. Strangely, until now it was not a piece of advice that I had had much use for. Why didn't Dickon shoot Pole first though? I turn and see that Dickon's face is a bloody mess. He won't be getting up again.

The world sways alarmingly, and I notice I too am now on the ground. Not a bad place to be when your legs won't support you any more. The bracken is as soft as I had expected it to be, and the birdsong is growing more distant. Kit is running towards me. I look from him to Pole.

Pole is smiling. And he is reloading his pistol.

Endgame, Late Summer 1657

The rain is falling gently outside my window. I hear the soft taps on the sill as water drips from the roof. The casement is a little open, and a cool breeze blows onto my cheek. I am not entirely comfortable, however, and try to roll over onto my left side. A stab of pain reminds me that this is not a good idea. I think I already know this, because I have tried to roll that way before, but my memories of the recent past are not good.

'What is the matter with you men?' asks my mother. 'First I have Mr Probert in this bed with a ball lodged in his right shoulder. Now I have you with a ball through your left shoulder.'

She implies that we had a choice in the matter. Perhaps we did.

I try to raise myself up, but the room reacts by spinning violently, and so I fall back again onto the down pillows.

'How long . . . ?' I say.

'Three weeks,' says my mother to save me the effort of completing the question. 'Three weeks and one day to be exact. Mr Probert was up and doing after two days. But he is a very robust and active man. For his size.'

'How did I get here?' I ask.

'Lord Pole brought you,' says my mother. 'He and Kit Mansell slung you over the back of your horse and brought you straight here by moonlight, whereupon I cleaned the wound, bandaged you and put you to bed. Roger says he kept a loaded pistol in his hand the whole way back – he didn't know whether there were others out to kill you too. You would have died had they not acted so swiftly. You lost a lot of blood that evening.'

'Pole?' I say. '*Lord* Pole?'

'Oh, Mr Pole, if you insist,' says my mother. 'For the moment at least.'

'But he shot me.'

'When you get those bandages off,' says my mother, 'you will observe – because, as you always tell me, you have studied these things – you will observe that the large wound you are looking at was made by a ball *leaving* your body. The smaller wound, by which it entered, is in your back. Dickon Grice shot you. Roger Pole shot him dead before he could reload and finish the job.'

'I don't understand,' I say.

'Why don't I explain it all to you tomorrow, when you are a bit stronger?' says my mother.

'Do you know everything?' I ask.

'More or less,' says my mother. 'I'll draw the curtains now so that you can sleep again.'

'No,' I say. I haul myself up again. The room lurches to the right, but I stay sitting, and after a while the spinning slows down to a speed that I can tolerate. 'I want to know everything and I want to know now.'

'Very well,' says my mother, sitting down on the edge of the bed. 'I think you'll find you *don't* want to know everything, but I'll tell you as much as you wish. You must say if I am tiring you.'

'You won't tire me.'

'But just in case I do.'

'You won't.'

'But just in case . . .'

'Start,' I say, 'with Henderson's murder. I have at least worked out that was my father, wasn't it?'

'Your *father*? Lord! Are you still feverish? Of course it wasn't him,' says my mother. 'Haven't you listened to anything I've said? Oh dear, I suppose I'd better begin from the very beginning, hadn't I? I assume Mr Morland will have explained that Henderson was sent to this village by Mr Secretary Thurloe to impersonate the Sealed Knot's courier and gain what information he could. A scurvy trick, if I may say so. Henderson's job was made easier by the fact that we were actually expecting somebody from Bruges to bring us news. So we assumed Henderson was he. You might say therefore that Henderson benefited from a lucky coincidence. But of course it probably wasn't anything of the sort. Thurloe has his agents in Bruges and no doubt knew that a visit was intended. Anyway, Henderson had been told to lie low in one of Ben's chambers. All of the Sealed Knot adherents were to meet him that night at the inn, but there was one small problem.'

'Which was?'

'You, dear. You insisted on drinking at the inn, and everyone knew you were no friend of the King's. So you were bought drinks until you were too drunk to stand, and then you were packed off home.'

'That must have cost them a bit,' I say.

'Not really,' says my mother. 'Then there was Ifnot Davies. Not a friend of His Majesty's either. But he was sent away with some story about horses needing to be shod in the morning. Anyhow, once you had both gone the others were about to summon Henderson down when the real Sealed Knot courier arrived – the one I had been expecting all along. He'd ridden all day, and his horse was quite lame, poor thing.'

'Exactly!' I say. 'My rider! Henderson's killer!'

'Don't get so excited, dear. You will break open that wound again, and it was difficult enough to dress the first time. Yes, *your* rider, if that's how you like to think of him, but no killer now or at any other time. Well, that put the cat amongst the pigeons, as they say. There we all were, with the real courier down in Ben's parlour and the false courier up in the best chamber.'

'*We?* So, you were party to it?'

'Since you had spent the whole evening at the inn, you can scarcely chide me for a brief visit myself. Yes, I was sent for too once the coast was clear. Martha was to tell you that I had been called out to visit a patient in the village – but that subterfuge proved entirely unnecessary. So, to return to the story, we all discussed what to do, and Dickon favoured prompt action. When some of us protested, he said that he wasn't afraid to carry out his proposals in person. One or two walked out at that point, but most stayed.'

'And Dickon killed him. Is that what you're saying?'

'Only after a lot of tedious discussion. The leader of the Sealed Knot tried quite rightly to persuade everyone that we should let Henderson try his worst and then allow him to leave the village quietly and harmlessly. After all, nobody here would talk to Henderson once we'd let it be known he came from Thurloe. Some of the younger members of the Knot, however, are growing impatient with Hyde's leadership – they want to side with this so-called Action Party. They favoured a shorter way.'

'And then?'

'Nell went up to Henderson's chamber and told him that the meeting was now in the stables. When Henderson duly went to the stables, Dickon was waiting for him. I shouldn't think it took long. I mean, I doubt if Mr Henderson suffered much or the poor horses were disturbed.'

'Ben can't have been too happy – about a murder in his stables, I mean.'

'He was *very* unhappy,' says my mother. 'So was Nell. There was quite a tension between her and Dickon that you must have noticed. Dickon's brothers had to carry Henderson across the meadow – fortunately, he was not a large man – and leave him by the roadside. They were supposed to leave the ring and take the purse so that it appeared he had been killed by footpads.'

'And they got it wrong?'

'Of course. You can't leave anything to those Grices. Left the purse, took the ring. They took his knife too. It should have stayed with the body, but they liked the look of it. And they left his hat behind at the inn. But what can you expect? Only Dickon and his mother can read and write out of all of them. It was no surprise that they should make a mess of it. Oh, and his mother says that she never received those preserved cherries I sent – you really are as scatterbrained as they. Anyway, Ben went out early the following morning to check that all was well, but you'd got there first, so there wasn't much he could do.'

'Dickon in the meantime went home . . .' I say.

'Covered in blood. He decided the best thing to do was to slaughter a pig and blame the mess on that. Completely the wrong time of year for pork, of course; but, being a man and no cook, you probably wouldn't have realised that. He woke everyone up with the noise. And the suit was ruined. He had to wear his old one, which was much too small for him, until he could get a new one made in Saffron Walden.'

'I just thought he was getting fat,' I say.

'So he was,' my mother says.

'But Jem saw the murder,' I say.

'Yes, silly boy. Ben told him that all he had to do was keep quiet and say, if anyone noticed it, that the blood was from a horse. That's what I told him too . . .'

'You went and saw Jem?'

'Yes, I think I reassured him. But then you blundered in – he must have seen you and Dickon together and panicked. Fortunately, I'd already told him that he could trust Kit Mansell – a good Royalist but too level-headed for the Knot's little games. I'm sure Jem wanted to tell you who it was but knew you'd never believe it was Dickon. He still trusted you enough to go to the Colonel by night, but we think Dickon had discovered where he was hiding.'

'So Dickon killed Jem too?' I ask.

'I suppose so,' says my mother with a sigh. 'If so, it was

entirely on his own initiative. I was there when Ben accused him to his face and Dickon denied it. The village might have excused Henderson's throat being cut as youthful high spirits, but Jem's throat was another matter entirely. The charcoal burners would have lynched the killer if nobody else did. But who else could it have been but Dickon? Dickon knew the woods as well as anyone in the village. He knew which way Jem would have to go, and he knew all of the points where the wall into the Park could be climbed. And I think Dickon's mother knew. She persisted in saying that it must be you. We exchanged some harsh words over it. I may have called her a witch.'

'I told Dickon all he needed to know,' I say. 'I told him Probert was close to revealing the murderer, and I told him where to find Jem. I told Dickon all he needed to know to kill me as well. I said that I knew exactly who the murderer was and that it was somebody very close to me. I thought it was my father – somebody returning after a long absence and skilled in the use of a knife. Somebody that you knew well. Dickon thought I meant him . . .'

My mother looks at me despairingly. 'I feel sorry for Dickon in some ways,' says my mother. 'I mean, the murder of Henderson was actually quite well-intentioned. As for Jem . . . Well, he wasn't from these parts. Dickon had no idea whether he could have been trusted. And Dickon wouldn't have been the only one to hang for Henderson's murder if Jem had informed on them. There were plenty of others at the inn that night, including all of Dickon's brothers. The whole family might have gone to the gallows together. I think, you know, that it is sometimes possible to do the most evil things for the very best of reasons.'

'But Jem's death didn't make him safe either,' I say. 'He realised Probert or I might still discover him.'

'Fortunately, Dickon wasn't a very good shot,' says my mother. 'He'd have been better using a knife, but perhaps after Jem he'd had enough of knives. You can understand that, can't you? Anyway, two attempts at a clean kill with a gun, and both end up in the shoulder. And in your case he must have been only feet away. Well, that's what Lord – Roger – Pole says anyway.'

'Did the Colonel know what had happened?'

'Roger told him what he knew, but Colonel Payne didn't have a really good first-hand account until I told him.'

'At least the Colonel wasn't at the inn with the rest of you. Most of the village seems to have been involved in this conspiracy.'

'Well, about half the village perhaps – though having only six muskets would have restricted us a little had there actually been a rebellion. The Colonel, as a magistrate, really couldn't be a member of the Sealed Knot. It might have amused Sir Felix to get involved in a rebellion, but Aminta absolutely forbade it and tried to prevent him finding out more about the murder than was good for him. Ifnot would have had religious scruples even if he had approved in principle. It was different for me . . . I mean, none of us quite knows how all of this will turn out, do we? We all have to try to ensure that whoever rules *in the end*, we come out of it reasonably well. So, the Colonel, as you know, was in correspondence with General Monck in Scotland, though the General himself is not yet certain for which side he has been devoted all his life. He seems favourable to a return of the King when the time is right. The Colonel will declare himself for King Charles when Monck does.'

'So Clarges *was* carrying messages?'

'Of course. What else would he be doing here? That's why the Colonel was not too pleased to have a dead Parliamentary spy on his hands. Clarges wanted to come and go without being noticed, which was difficult in a village swarming with Thurloe's agents. The Colonel was cross with Will Cobley for not keeping him better informed – he felt that, as Constable, he might have at least told him where the body had been dumped. And he certainly did not appreciate your accusing Roger Pole of the murder. He was *very* angry about that for a long time. Of course, I was quite cross myself when Colonel Payne issued the warrant for your arrest. So *unnecessary*.'

Unnecessary? My mother just for once understates her case.

'It was very sudden,' I say. 'As if he had stumbled on new evidence.'

'Dickon had informed on you the afternoon that you fled. Then he told you that you were to be arrested, so your hurried departure simply convinced the Colonel he was right.'

'And the note? And the ring?' I ask despairingly. 'Was that Dickon too?'

'Of course,' says my mother. 'Poorly written. Clumsily planted. It wouldn't have taken most people in. I think Dickon concealed the ring round that feather the evening when you were ransacking Ben's chambers – when Dickon was all alone downstairs with Roger's hat. Later he sent you out of the room to look for Jem, then slipped the note under your tankard. Roger says that even then you failed to find the ring and Dickon had to do it for you. You should hear how he tells the story! Roger really can be quite amusing about you sometimes. I think Dickon should have decided to inform on either on you *or* Roger though. Trying to make you *both* culpable was never going to work. But Dickon never liked Roger.'

'Because Dickon and Roger Pole had fallen out over leadership of the Sealed Knot?' I ask.

Again my mother shakes her head. 'Roger Pole was asleep in his bed when we killed Henderson. He was never a member of the Sealed Knot, let alone leader. He was far too concerned about getting Parliament to restore his estates. Writing all those letters to Cromwell . . . It was more that Dickon had always been in love with Aminta, and then Roger came along . . . That's another reason why *you* were in danger from him. I think that if the opportunity had arisen, Dickon would have killed you in London. But Pole was watching your back in a way that Dickon never did.'

'But why?'

'Aminta asked him to,' says my mother. 'She was quite active on your behalf. She got Ifnot to write to his Quaker friends in the City. She also sent Kit to London regularly to seek news and he obviously met up with Roger there, which meant that you had two people watching over you. They both rode after you as fast as they could when they discovered you'd fallen into Dickon's hands. When he shot you, Dickon had no idea how close Roger and Kit were – Dickon probably thought he could leave your body there in the woods and later blame it on Roger. The two of them arrived none too late, did they? So you have Aminta to thank for your life as well. Did I tell you she was always very fond of you?'

'You know I betrayed her to Thurloe?' I say. 'At least, I allowed him to believe she was in correspondence with Hyde.'

'Yes, thank you for that,' says my mother. 'That was very kind of you. Please don't think I am ungrateful.'

'I could hardly have Thurloe learn that my own mother was writing treasonable letters and signing herself "472".'

'Is that my number? I can never remember whether I am 472 or 274 or 742. I have asked Sir Edward for a better number, but he hasn't given me one yet.'

'So, if it isn't Roger Pole, who is the leader of the Sealed Knot in Essex?' I ask.

'Me, of course. Don't look so surprised. I've known Sir Edward for years. A very dear friend. And rebellion is, as I may have observed to you before, a perfectly respectable family tradition.'

'You should be grateful that it was not one I wished to see continued.'

'Yes, we have dabbled a little too much in treason over the years. As I say, I am not ungrateful for what you did. I'm sure Aminta would have done the same.'

'Would she?'

'Didn't you notice that she was providing you with information that would have cleared Roger and convicted Dickon Grice? With good reason, I might add – but she was less than honest. I wonder what you would have achieved if you had worked together and trusted each other a little more. Of course, from my point of view it was as well that you didn't.'

I think back. Had it not been for Aminta, I might not have taken the path across the meadow. Had it not been for Aminta, I would not have searched the stable. She too had understood the significance of the deep puncture on the right-hand side of the wound. She too would have been looking for left-handed killers and must have worked out it was Dickon well before I did. That business of passing him her basket at the stables; I was supposed to notice which hand he returned it with. I suspect she might have deciphered Letter Number 9 before I did too if I had shown it to her. Above all, she knew not to go into the woods and then turn her back on Dickon. Yes, working together would have been a good plan.

'Cruel necessity,' I say.

'What?' asks my mother.

'It is what Cromwell said when he viewed the body of the late King after his execution.'

'And you would apply that to Aminta's fate as well?'

'Yes,' I say. 'Confinement in the Tower seems cruel enough.'

'Denouncing her to the government was certainly an unfortunate thing for you to have done if you had hoped to marry her,' says my mother severely. 'Women can be quite unreasonable and unforgiving in some ways. As for the Tower, I doubt she'll make that mistake. No, she and Sir Felix fled to Bruges shortly before the soldiers arrived to arrest them.'

'They were forewarned?'

'It would have been inconvenient for a lot of people if they had actually been arrested.'

'Inconvenient for Morland, you mean?'

'Mr Morland. Me. And others perhaps. For you most certainly. The Cliffords would have been well on their way to Dover before the soldiers even reached the village. And once at Dover, controls there are shockingly lax.'

'But even so . . .'

'Oh tush. Aminta will come to no harm at the King's court.'

'I fear she will not forgive the choice I made, nor perhaps will Roger Pole when he discovers what has happened . . .'

'Lord! There is no reason why Roger should ever know that. Or that you accused him of being the writer of the letters – yes, Mr Morland did tell me. He can be quite amusing . . .

And Aminta herself believed that it was Dickon Grice who had denounced her to Thurloe; I obviously did nothing to discourage that view, and I doubt if Dickon will deny it now he's dead. Roger said anyway that he had seen Dickon hiding in a doorway near Thurloe's office, so it all fitted together rather nicely. Your secret is quite safe with your mother, dear. And with Mr Morland. It is perhaps as well to remember that too, in case you were thinking of writing a long, tedious letter to Mr Thurloe. In any case, Mr Morland may be a good Republican by next week – his principles seem somewhat changeable. As for Aminta, I think she is rather enjoying Bruges . . . particularly now that Roger has joined her. There is more to entertain her there than ever there was in a small village in Essex.'

'Roger Pole has fled to Bruges?'

'Not exactly. He simply decided that his chances of regaining his estates were better if he threw his lot in with the King. Cromwell proved slow to appreciate Roger's arguments so I advised Roger to visit Mr Morland. I think he may have provided him with useful contacts in Bruges. Roger left for the Spanish Netherlands the day after he brought you home.'

'So, all is well with the Cliffords?'

'Yes, all is well, and when they return they shall move into the New House.'

'That is most generous. But where shall *we* go then? Oh no, don't tell me . . . you are going to marry Sir Felix!'

'Of course not,' says my mother. 'I'm to marry Colonel Payne. We shall live in the Big House again, you and I, not in this pitiful cottage with its overgrown walks. Let the Cliffords have it – house, garden, damsons and all. And Sir Felix won't have use of the Colonel's gardener once I am running the Big

House again. Or access to the wine cellar. No servant of mine shall be allowed to stoop to such knavish tricks. My first act as Mistress Payne will be to sack that butler. I've waited a long time for this, but the Wests are finally back in the Big House.'

There is one minor detail concerning this arrangement that worries me.

'Is this wise?' I ask.

'Oh yes,' says my mother. 'Mr Morland assures me that the Colonel will most certainly keep the manor after the King is restored. You were quite right about the Law. The sale was perfectly legal. Have no fear that we shall be ejected again.'

'I don't mean that,' I say. 'Mother, consider: my father is still alive. You are proposing to marry the Colonel. Bigamy is a capital offence.'

'We don't *know* your father is alive,' she says.

'Yes, we do. He may not have been the murderer as I feared, but I certainly saw him, as you know well. He came from Bruges with a message for the Sealed Knot in Essex. He was riding a grey horse. He was wearing a cloak. His voice was very familiar. He threw me a shilling. I always knew the rider was far too old to be Marius. Once I realised that you were 472, his identity was plain.'

'A shilling? Well, it was time your father sent us some money, I must say.'

'You saw him too. You saw him at the inn, and for all I know here at the house. You actually let slip to me that you had had news of him. He came to see you as well as the Sealed Knot. Then the following day he rode off on Henderson's horse, leaving his own in the stable.'

'Possibly,' says my mother. 'My memory isn't what it was.' Again I think of Probert's rules for lying. She would do well to have a properly rehearsed story for the Rector when she comes to be wed to the Colonel. 'Anyway, your father will hardly object when he has married again himself.'

'To Bess Clifford?'

'No, to some young strumpet he met in Bruges. I think that was what he really came to tell me. Perhaps we might denounce him as the murderer after all. As you say, it was the sort of wound a surgeon might have inflicted. A left-handed surgeon.'

We both consider this from all points of view while the rain drips onto the windowsill.

'Or we could just tell the Rector that we have a sincere and reasonable belief that my father is dead,' I say. 'That would be simpler.'

'Well, I can't see him living long anyway,' says my mother. 'Can you? Not at his age. Not married to a young Flemish strumpet.'

Of course, there are plenty in the village who would be able to say at my mother's forthcoming wedding why this man and this woman might not lawfully be joined together in holy matrimony. But it will be difficult for them to explain themselves clearly without admitting to being an accessory to murder.

Then I ask: 'How long have you known Mr Morland?'

'Some years,' says my mother. 'He came here first when you were at Cambridge. I think he must have only just been appointed by Mr Thurloe then. He was asking questions about the Sealed Knot. We got on quite well – well enough that I suggested to him that perhaps he might overlook my occasional letters to Bruges, and that in return I would mention him favourably to Hyde when the time came. He saw very quickly that he had almost nothing to lose and a great deal to gain. I do hope that his allegiance to the King is not as temporary as I fear it may be.'

'Is that also how I was invited to join his department?'

'You never seemed entirely happy with the Law. So, I might have suggested something to Dr Grahame, and he might have suggested something to Mr Morland. Or perhaps I wrote to Mr Morland and he wrote to Dr Grahame. Sam Morland promised to look after you anyway. And I think he kept his promise too. I mean, you are not in chains in the Tower of London, are you?'

Sir Felix. Roger Pole. Colonel Payne. And Samuel Morland. Yes, truly, I am beginning to see my mother in a new light. Then I ask: 'Do you know why Probert changed his mind about the murder?'

'Oh, I made him see sense,' says my mother. 'Footpads from Suffolk are something everyone can believe in. A bit like hobgoblins or chastity. Of course, I would not have minded seeing Dickon arrested, especially after Jem's death, but it is unlikely that he would have gone to the scaffold without implicating everyone else in the village.'

'How did you make Probert see sense?' I ask.

'The usual way,' she says. 'He is a prudent man who understands that the restoration is inevitable. He became unreasonable when he heard I was to marry the Colonel and wrote quite unpleasantly to Mr Thurloe, but I smoothed things over.'

Just for a moment I have a vision of a small grubby boy asking me: 'Don't you want to do it with my ma?'

'Are you cold, dear?' my mother asks.

'No,' I say.

'I thought I saw you shudder.'

I decide that perhaps my mother spoke the truth when she said I might not wish to know everything.

'The weather is improving,' she adds. 'I think the sun may actually break through soon. And very soon we shall have the King back with us. Those of us who have been loyal to him will be rewarded when he returns. The Colonel is happy that he has been able to help with the negotiations between General Monck and His Majesty. And Mr Morland will certainly have Thurloe's job when the King is back. If he does nothing stupid in the meantime. And, as I say, Roger is now in Bruges too. That seems sensible. His family has done the King good service here, but it is better to be close to the court to remind the King, who can sometimes be a little forgetful, I am told. Viscount Pole sounds so well, does it not? And Viscountess Pole, of course. Yes, I think that this may work out handsomely for us all. Except perhaps for you. What a *shame* you threw away your career with Mr Morland and your chance to marry Aminta. All you had to do was keep quiet about one silly little letter.'

'Twenty-one,' I say.

'Did I send as many as that? ... But look! The sun is shining again on the garden. We shall have a splendid evening.'

'You are right, Mother,' I say. 'The air is chill, and my shoulder still troubles me. I'll sleep now, if you don't mind.'

'That is very wise,' says my mother, pulling the sheet back over me and fussing with my pillow. 'Then, tomorrow or when you are stronger, you should go and lay flowers on Dickon Grice's grave. We buried him next to Jem. Dickon was, after all, a good friend of yours. You mustn't hold it against him that he informed on you and then shot you in the back. These things happen, my dear John. Cruel necessity.'

Acknowledgements

When I was very much younger, I was able to declare at the end of a composition that it was 'all my own work'. I cannot make any such claim for *A Cruel Necessity*. Many people have helped me along the way, and I need to acknowledge at least some of them here.

I received a lot of helpful advice on various drafts of this book. Will Atkins, once my editor but now sadly reduced to writing books for a living like the rest of us, gave me some invaluable comments early on. Eliza Graham, whose own writing I much admire, persuaded me with some difficulty that one prologue was more than enough for any book. My agent, David Headley, revived my interest in this project and much else in my writing career. My editor at Constable & Robinson, Krystyna Green, and my copy editor, Marcus Trower, finally knocked it into shape and made John Grey a nicer person. My thanks are due to all of them – and, of course, as ever to my family, who have, during this book's production, had to live far more in the seventeenth century than any normal person would wish to do.

Many writers like at this point to list a few reference books to show that they haven't made it all up. Since *A Cruel Necessity* is a work of fiction, I have in fact made most of it up, but readers who wish to check whether some of my more outrageous statements are correct may like to refer to some of the following. First, though both deal with the period that begins a year or two after my narrative, I drew heavily on Lisa Picard's excellent book *Restoration London* and also on the diaries of Samuel Pepys in various editions. For information on the Sealed Knot and the politics of the 1650s, Geoffrey Smith's *The Cavaliers in Exile* is a very thorough and readable account, as is his *Royalist Agents, Conspirators and Spies* and David Underdown's *Royalist Conspiracy in England, 1649–60*. In creating individual characters in my novel, I owe a debt in particular to H. W. Dickinson's *Sir Samuel Morland: Diplomat and Inventor, 1625–1695*, D. L. Hobman's *Cromwell's Master Spy: A study of John Thurloe* and Philip Aubrey's *Mr Secretary Thurloe*. Jeffrey Forgeng's *Daily Life in Stuart England* and Miriam Slater's *Family Life in the Seventeenth Century* provided a lot of the detail about what my characters did and thought and ate. For what they said, Charles Barber's *Early Modern English* is a detailed study of the evolution of the English language in the sixteenth and seventeenth centuries. For Essex dialect words, I drew not so much on my own childhood in Southend as on Edward Gepp's *A Contribution to an Essex Dialect Dictionary*, which contains an interesting definition for the word 'wanked'. J. A. Sharpe's *Crime in Early Modern England, 1550–1750* provided an excellent account of the roles of the various officials and the process of investigation of murders at that time, as did Malcolm Gaskill's *Crime and Mentalities in Early Modern England* and Eleanor Trotter's *Seventeenth Century Life in the Country Parish with Special Reference to Local Government*. Two websites also need to be mentioned – in addition to that essential writers' resource Wikipedia: www.englishcivilwar.org is fascinating and contains a great deal of information that it is not easy to find elsewhere; www.pepysdiary.com provides not only the text of the famous diary but also helpful comment and clarification.

Finally, my thanks to the staff of the British Library for locating many of the above books and delivering them to me so efficiently, and to the Weald and Downland Open Air Museum for helping me understand some of the practicalities of living in a seventeenth-century house.

Other than that, it's all my own work.